Ek Safar

Khwabon Se Haquikat Tak

Flairs and Glairs
Publication House

"Ek Safar Khwabon Se Haquikat Tak"

ISBN No: " 978-93-90416-68-4"
1st Edition
Language – English and Hindi

Flairs and Glairs
Publication House
Regd. Under MSME Act.

Disclaimer

Cover Designing
Shubham Shah

Acknowledgement

Dear Almighty, thank you for blessing me with the power and zeal to be able to complete this Anthology. Also, Thank You dear parents, for trusting in me, and letting me work whenever I wanted. My family is the one who supported me for what I am today.
When it comes to this Anthology, I would like to start with Thanking the Co-authors, without your help and support, I would have never been able to complete it.

Thank You all of you, for being there. Much Love to all of You. I am glad to see you all standing by me.

Co-Authors

1. Shubham Shah (Flairs and Glairs)
2. Ishani Agarwal (Co Founder Flairs and Glairs)
3. Bisakha Seksaria (Compiler)
4. Jaydaev Satpathy (Compiler)
5. Shivangi Jaiswal (Project Head)
6. Sanjay Kumar Seksaria
7. Ishika Agarwal
8. Rahul Pratap Singh
9. Shubham Panda
10. Subhalaxmi Behera
11. Kritika Seksaria
12. Karan B Rathod
13. Tanishka Yadav
14. Ashok Surya Narayan Thakur
15. Zahwa
16. Anisha Panda
17. Sasmita Singh
18. Sushree Archana Swain
19. Udita Das
20. Zikra Rashid
21. Chandan Kumar Nayak
22. Naman Rele
23. Reeta
24. Shweta Srivastava
25. Ashish Keshri
26. Mehere Darakshan
27. Pragyashree Choudhury
28. Swati Priya
29. Nand Kashyap

30. Pen_The_Creative
31. Sohini Ghoshal
32. Pranjalika Sabat
33. Maitri Lal
34. Barnali Priyadarshni
35. Priyanka Kumari
36. Sourabh Jalan
37. Bidyaswini Sahu
38. Rabeya Sarbar
39. Nitish Kumar Sahoo
40. Ritesh Behera
41. Rakesh Behera
42. Riya Kumari
43. Palak Das
44. Kaushal Sao
45. Srushti Prajana Mohanty
46. Ritu Roumya Samal
47. Bhavika Asmi Verma
48. Ratan Prasad
49. Avinash Muduli
50. Avisek Rout
51. Sucharita Sahoo
52. Sourav Ketan Sahu
53. Najmus Shaheda
54. Rajeswari Ojha
55. Subhashree Mishra
56. Rishi Vinayak
57. Arpita Priyadarshini
58. Sristi Raj
59. Deepak Pani
60. Ankita Sahoo
61. Maheswari Tarai
62. Rakesh Kumar Nag

63. Awadh
64. Anupum Devjyoti Jena
65. Tuhina Choudhury
66. Anwesha Bahinipati
67. Sangeeta Prasad
68. Pradeep Kumar Shill
69. Kratisha Singh
70. Pratyush Jena
71. Rishikesh Sahoo
72. Tanisha Nanda
73. Sriya Sudeshna Behera
74. Kaushal Budhadev
75. Pallavee Das
76. Pratikshya Dhal Samanta
77. Abhishek Sahoo
78. Manisha Nanda
79. Tanmaya Mallick
80. Disha Sankhyashree
81. Biswasmruti Mangaraj
82. Jagannath Prasad
83. Snehasrita Swain
84. Sarvagya Prasad
85. Ankita Jethy
86. Sonit Patanaik
87. Ankit Mishra
88. Vickey David
89. Azad Kumar
90. Vivekanand Sahoo
91. Anil Kumar Behera
92. Madhusmita Padhi
93. Yuvraj Singh
94. Swapna Tamnaya Jena
95. Jhilik Pathak

96. Kushal Ganeriwal
97. Mohit Chaturvedi
98. Anubha Minz
99. Pritam Marandi
100. Kaibalya Panda
101. Abhishek Kumhar
102. Parwana Bibi
103. Ananya Nayak
104. Subhasmita Mahapatra
105. Ashish Mohapatra
106. Swati Upadhyay
107. Swati Barik
108. Aayushi Agarwal

Shubham Shah

(Founder- Flairs and Glairs)

Shubham Shah, entrepreneur at "Flairs & Glairs" a brand with dynamics in events organizing and cultural educational pan INDIA, He is a 26yr. old guy who recently has entered, the digital platform of imprinting emotions. He has initiated with his own open mic platform to help budding poets and aspiring writers under his brand named as "Teekhe Zasbaaat" He is a commerce graduate from Bhagalpur City of Bihar.
He says Writing has impersonated him since childhood and he has now been writing for over a decade!
Cooking, on the other hand, is his passion! He also mentions, trying out new things just tickles him!
When asked sir, Why SPICY EMOTIONS?

He smiled and added, “agar jasbaat teekhe na ho toh wo jasbaat kaha” Spices are all that blends! So do his words!
As a chef, he presents to you his dish! Hot and freshly served! Taste it! Feel it! Enjoy it! You can also find his writing in the Solo book “Teekhe Zasbaaat” and 70+ anthologies. With his passion to explore opportunities across Platforms he is working with keen devotion and We wish him all the very best for his future ventures
Share your reviews on his

INSTAGRAM

@spicy_emotions
@shubham4shah

Or via email on

shubham2shah@gmail.com

To stay tuned to his work and opportunities follow his business Handles

INSTAGRAM FACEBOOK YOUTUBE

@flairsandglairs
@teekhezasbaaat

WEBSITE:

https://flairsandglairs.in/
https://flairsandglairs.com/

Ghar se nikle the ek naya ghar banane ko...
Ki ghar bhar banane ki hooodh me ghar jana hi bhul gae...

Mila waqt jab khud me...toh khudse milna bhul gae...
Zindgi ko behtar banane ki jald baji me hum zindagi jeena bhul gae...

Bachpan me hui tension ki bade hokar kya kya kar lenge...
Jawani me aae toh socha bachpan ka waqt pote potiyon ke sath jee lenge...

Jab aaya budhapa toh ghar walon ne paraya kar diya...
Jinke liye gawa kar jawani banaya tha ghar unhone hi beghar kar diya...

Jyada kama Lenge ye soch kar hum khana khana bhul gae...
Jab aai bimari...hum hospital ke bill me rul gae...

Waqt ko waqt pe waqt na de pae...
Hum sab kuch pane ke chakkar me khud ko dao par laga aae...

Ishani Agarwal

(Co Founder- Flairs and Glairs)

Ishani Agarwal
Born and brought up in Kolkata, she has done her schooling and college from here itself. She is doing her post-graduation at the moment. Ishani loves talking to people around, and is excited for this new beginning of hers! Been a Compiler for 35+ Anthologies, and in the process for more, also, co-authored in 100+ Anthologies, Ishani is very Happy with how her life is turning out now!
Insta handle: Ishani_agarwal_quotes

The Journey Worthwhile

From Strangers,
To friends,
To counterparts,
To family,
To growing old together.
They did things, they had never planned of.
When they met, they had no intention of being together.
They were just friends.
But as time went by,
So did their Journey.
They kept flourishing in each other's love,
And they kept growing, together.
With promises of living together and dying together,
Their journey did end together.

BISAKHA SEKSARIA

Bisakha seksaria a care free girl born in early beautiful autumn in Jamshedpur currently pursuing B.Pharma and has a passion for writing. Everyone can easily connect to what she writes. she is a hard core foodie and believes there is no love pure then the love of food. she is a self motivated and enthusiastic girl with positive thinking and the unique personality.She is the one who is always ready to help everyone irrespective of her on situations. Her presence is the best gift she could offer anyone.She is gifted with power of words and ocean of thoughts.

she has a beautiful potence to describe every moment what she feels in such words that makes everyone dignified for her cogitative art.

She has a very special affection for rain ,which makes her a rain lover. she says that drops of water through rain is the love for land from sky.

INSTA HANDLE:

@vishakha_seksaria , @i_pen_down_your_feelings

Life Is All About The Choices We Make:

"You are the creature who has to decide
In case you wanna do it , or fling a side
you are the being who has to make up your mind
in case you wanna Steer or loiter behind.
In case you "ll try for the ambition that's far away
or will you strive to live this way."

Everything that we do is based on the choices. we make its not our parents, our past or present relationships, our job, the economy, the weather, and argument for the age that is to to be blamed. we and only we are soulfully responsible for the choices we make.

life is like a road. sometimes it's small and sometimes it's may be too long. sometimes it may be smooth and straight but there will be times as we as well when it will be Rocky and crooked.

when we are travelling through the road of the life, we have no idea about where the road we are walking will lead us to. life is all about risk, choices and chances and no guarantees. Nobody can ever tell that it's the most correct thing to do or that choosing to do the safe thing all the time will lead you the you to happiness. loving someone with all your heart does not guarantee that it will be returned. Gaining fame and fortune does not guarantee happiness. Starting a business does not guarantee financial success these are so many possible outcomes with just about any decision you make most of which can't be controlled.

whenever you choose a path in life don't think of why you choose it? once you are on it trust your choices as they will they make you learn about the right one of perfect you in your choices.

People say that our destinies are already chosen from birth, but I believe that our destiny is defined by our own choices in life. Life is not fair and there always obstacles being thrown at us. We cannot stop the hardles from coming in aur hue but can face them and find a way out.

Everyone makes choices sometimes its good and sometimes they are devastating some impact choosing our lives in a very good way and some leaving us with regrets.

Life present us with so many decisions. A lot of them are present right in front of face and they are really difficult but we must make them. we should not be worried about the consequence, there are only two possibilities, either, you will succeed or else you will learn, and until you keep on learning you keep growing.

Just like the road, there are corners, detours and cross roads in life. There is not guarantee that we will choose the right one. Now, it's totally on us whether to take risk and explore to or to stay on the same place where we are.

The 3 'c' of life

Chance

Change

Choice

"We must take a chance

To make a choice

Or else our life will never change"

JAYADEV SATPATHY

Jayadev Satpathy is a Odia lad belonging from Cuttack,Odisha. He has a keen observation towards society . He writes mostly about the peculiar and typical things,persons and happenings which are very much integral in our day-to-day life. Not only through his writings,but also by singing he brings colours to his life... let's check it out what he writes as a writer and a compiler as well..

INSTA HANDLE: jds_its_my_time

पिता-ए-खास

ए जी!!!खाना लगाओ आते है...
बस यूंही वो निकल जाते है,
रोज नई बेदनाओं से वो...
दिल से दिलचस्पी निभाते है।
बातों ही बातों,आखों ही आखों में..
उम्र की ताउम्र वो साखों पे,
बताते गए,सीखाते गए..
खुद रो कर वो हसाते गए।
कभी फीस भरे तो कभी जख्म...
खिलाए कभी आयिस्क्रीम तो दिखाए कभी फिल्म, पर कभी ना हुआ इल्म...
न जाने कैसे सेह लेते थे हमारे सारे जुल्म।
उनके भी कुछ किस्से थे..
जो कठिनाइयों से पीस ते थे,
वो सख्श भी बहोत बोलते थे..
जो अर्सा हो गया चुप से थे।
आखिर हम जवान हो गए..
बाल उनके भी सफेद होने को थे..
मगर वो तजुर्बों ने बोल दिया..
कई और दिन अभी जीने को थे।
अभी तक जिक्र जिन का किया...
वो मेरे धड़कन और सांस है,
बंजर में रेंगते मेरे दिल के लिए..
वो खुद दरिया का आगाज है,
मेरे ज़िन्दगी के संरचक व निर्देशक..
मेरे पिता-ए-खास है।

वोह.

वोह..वोह कुछ अनजान सा थी..
जब मैं नादान सी थी,
जब किसी ने हमें सिकस्त दी.. हमने उनसे मोहबत ली,
सर्दियों भी थी और गर्मियां भी थी..
पर जिंदगी जीने की वोह दर्मियां भी थी,
जब हम रोए और धीरे से गम खोए..
पर नजाने कैसे वो भुके पेट सोए,
कभी जरूरत तो कभी इजाजत चाहिए..
पर सबसे पहले उसकी मोहोबत चाहिए
हम हस्ते गए वो रोती रही..
फिर भी लाड़ प्यार से डुबोती गई,
बचपन गए मुस्कान भी..
फिर भी जीने की ताकत दी,
जब भी ज़िन्दगी ने मात दी..
दिल वेहला कर वोह बात की,
पराठे भी थे और सब्जी भी थे..
खाने की कई और अर्जी भी थे,
मगर कभी उसके मर्ज़ी ना थे..
वोह..वोह मा है..
वोह अकेले कई किरदार निभाया है,
जब कोई बोला प्यार एक धोखा है..
तो हमने पलट कर सिर्फ उसे ही देखा है,
क्यों की.. क्यों की प्यार तो हमने सिर्फ मा से ही सीखा है..
अगर वो धोखा है तो उछला हुआ नदी भी सूखा है,
क्यों की प्यार तो हमने सिर्फ मा से ही सीखा है..

Guess Who...!!!

Guess who....guess who's truly admiring you?
Guess who's pretending you?
Guess who is looking after you all the time?
Guess who is the culprit behind all your sins?
Guess who's motivating you everyday?
Guess who is watching you very closely by all your actions?
After all guess who is loving you when nobody is with you....
I guess you are guessing completely right...
it's you man... it's you...be the person you want to be...
you will be happy without having specific reason...
because happiness will come from your soul unconditionally....
unbelievably!!!

One Is Incomplete Without The Other...

When we talk about pure true love,we always want a relationship with our sweetheart as if we are Mahabharat and Srimad Bhagavad Geeta for each other...Because one is pathetic and drastic without the other...Without Srimad Bhagavad Geeta,Mahabharat is just a story to listen and forget..where as without Mahabharat,Geeta is just a poem written by a prolific poetwhich is interesting to listen and boring to follow...but when they are alongside,they create a beautiful content to listen,learn and follow who are attached to it...But as we know this world,except some rare personalities,nobody is really caring anyone for a lifelong time...till the end of their time in this life..so i pray all the relationships to follow the lessons of "The Holy Geeta"whenever they pass through the storm of the "Mahabharat" in their life...

SHIVANGI JAISWAL

Shivangi Jaiswal is a Content Writer from Kolkata. She is a B.Com Honours graduate.
Certified in Stocks & Short Selling as well as Certified in Digital Marketing. Been a keen student, she has recently been Certified for learning Spanish Language.She is a writer by day and a reader by night. Been a Complier of 20+ Anthologies, and in process for more, also Co-authored 70+ anthologies. Shivangi is an old soul with young eyes, a vintage heart, and a beautiful mind."

You can follow her work:
Instagram
@the_knockingvibe
@house_of_compilations

A secret lie..

We say changes are good,
But no one knows the reason behind the change.
We are torn between past & future
We don't how to change & when to change..

No one knows how many times,
We are broken, torn apart
Cried begging for love..
Sometimes it's hard to think about it.

Some things don't change in life,
It remains constant and pulls us back..
We try to move forward everytime,
But some energy draws us back to the start.

We lie everyday and hide behind our smile,
No one could even understand..
Thousand reasons, hundred of pains
We say time is a greatest healer..

Let's again paint the canvas,
with beautiful colours..
Hoping that new colour, new life
would come and I would change myself
And it will be for me not for anyone else.

SANJAY KUMAR SEKSARIA

Sanjay kumar seksaria a middleaged man hailing from a beautiful city called Jamshedpur. He is a jolly and simple person. His life revolves around his family and friends. He believes in learning from all possible ways. He is a very optimistic and strong person. He is state co-ordinator of UBHRCC (United bereau of human rights and crime control) also and always stands for the truth...

जीवन संगिनी

युवा वास्था के बाद जब हम गृहस्थ आश्रम में प्रवेश करते हैं तो हमें एक नया जन्म मिलता है। हम नए नए रिश्ते में बंध जाते हैं नई खुशी नई उमंग हमारे साथ होती है। फिल्मों की तरह हम अपने जीवन को जीने का सपना मन में लिए आगे बढ़ते जाते हैं, लेकिन फिल्में काल्पनिक होती है और जिंदगी कुछ और होती है।

नई नई दुल्हन जब घर पर आती है तो प्यार दुलार से वह खूब आनंदित होती है। लगता है उसे दुनिया जहान की खुशियां मिल गई लेकिन यह खुशी उसके जीवन में क्षणिक होती है। क्योंकि हम आने वाली लड़की को संभलने और संभालने का वक्त दिए बिना ही उससे सब कुछ पा लेना चाहते हैं। मानो वह लड़की नहीं कंप्यूटर है उसके अंदर सारे डेटा सव्ड है । और हम कंप्यूटर चालू करते ही हमें वह सब मिल जाएगा जो जो हम चाहते हैं।

जो लड़की एक परिवार में जन्म लेकर युवा होने तक बिताती है वह वहां के सारे कायदे रस्मों रिवाजों को जानती है बचपन से युवा तक जो देखी वही सीखी है अब शादी के बाद एक नया परिवार मिला नए विचार मिले नए संस्कार मिले तो उसे समझने में कुछ वक्त तो लगेगा पर हम तो लड़के वाले हैं हम क्यों इस बात को समझें यह तो लड़की वाले की गलती है वह अपनी बेटी को कंप्यूटर बनाकर भेजना चाहिए था अब विचारा लड़का भी परिवार वालों के विचार का शिकार हो जाता है यदि वह लड़की की तरफ बोले तो परिवार विरोधी परिवार के तरफ बोले तो लड़की का जीना मुश्किल जीवनसाथी होने के नाते लड़का लड़की का साथ देना चाहिए।

अब लड़की बिचारी सुबह उठते ही अपने काम में लग जाए सब काम करते-करते भी घरवालों के ताने सुन ना उसका नसीब मैं होता समय किसी तरह बीता जाता है लड़की अपने हर अरमानों का गला घोट कर परिवार की खुशियां पूरी करने में मगन रहती है कभी सास के लिए तो कभी पति के लिए तो कभी परिवार के अन्य सदस्यों की खुशी के लिए वह दिन-रात लगी रहती है परंतु वह खाई कि नहीं बस सोए कि नहीं वह कैसी है वह क्या चाहती है इसकी तरफ किसी का ध्यान नहीं होता है परंतु ताने देने का काम निरंतर जारी रहता है तुम दिन भर करती ही क्या हो तुम्हें काम ही क्या है यही सब सुनते सुनते कब उसके शरीर में एक नन्हा जी पल्ले लगता है और अब उसे उसकी भी चिंता एक लड़की कितना कुछ करती है सबके लिए जब से वह इस घर में आती है तब से वह हर रिश्तो को जोड़ने मैं लगी रहती है समाज में भी अच्छे संबंध बनाना परिवार की देखरेख करना अपने मायके में भी सबको प्रसन्न रखना अब एक नन्हा जान भी जिंदगी का हिस्सा बनने जा रहा है।

जिम्मेदारी बढ़ती जाती रही पर आज भी वह ताने हंसकर सुनती थी तुम करती ही क्या हो सच पूछो तो हम कितने स्वार्थी हैं बेटे के लिए इतनी ममता इतना दर्द भी उसके घर आते ही 100 100 स्वागत चाहे बेटा कमा कर लाया हो या नहीं।

यदि हम सही मायने में देखें तुम मर्दों का काम ही क्या है अपने व्यापार में या ऑफिस में जाना है वहां कर्मचारी है उन से काम करवाना है फिर भी हम कहते हैं हम आज बहुत थक गए परंतु जो पत्नी घर पर सारा काम अपने हाथों से करती है सुबह होते ही बच्चों को स्कूल भेजना सबके लिए नाश्ता बनाना बूढ़े सास ससुर

को समय से नाश्ता देना दवाई देना फिर पति को ऑफिस भेजना टिफिन देना पति के जाते ही घर की सफाई करना कपड़े धोना पूजा करना 12:00 खुद नाश्ता करना और तुरंत बाद दोपहर का भोजन तैयार करना बच्चे स्कूल से आते ही उन्हें भोजन करवाना उनके स्कूल ड्रेस धोकर सुखा ना होमवर्क चेक करना फिर 4:00 बजे बचा हुआ खाना खाना और तुरंत बाद सास ससुर को चाय बना कर देना फिर कपड़े उतार कर लाना आयरन करना और फिर उसे उचित स्थान पर रखना शाम होते ही घर में दीया बाती चलाना आरती करना और फिर रात का खाना बनाना और सब को खिलाना इस बीच पर पति को भी फोन पर उनका हालचाल पता करना रिश्तेदारों से भी मधुर संबंध बनाए रखना इस बीच यदि कोई काम छूट जाए तो पति के आते ही उसके मुंह से यह सुनना कि तुम से कुछ नहीं होता एक काम बोल कर गया था वह भी तुमसे नहीं हुआ तुम दिन भर करती ही क्या हो ? शायद भगवान ने नारी की पीड़ा को सुना और इस लॉकडाउन में पतियों को समझ आया की पत्नियां घर में करती ही क्या है प्यारे साथियों जीवनसंगिनी को समझो और उसे मान सम्मान दो।

ISHIKA AGARWAL

Ishika is a 16 years old girl.
Writing for her is nothing else but a passion. She hails from the city of Joy and Art. She has been a Co-author in 30+ anthologies in the recent past, all adding on experiences to her.
Been a part of India book of Record projects like Black and World Record projects like 15 wonders of Poetry, Ishika is paving her way to success.

Looking at the rain pouring through the window, me and my boyfriend sat with hot chocolate in our hands.

While watching the rain pour we were talking about how we met.

It was a typical evening it was raining, I didn't have an umbrella and he out of the blue offered me his umbrella as he was just about to sit in his car and he didn't require it.

He asked me if he can drop me somewhere but i gently refused as why would I tell a stranger where I live.

I asked for his address so later onn I could return the umbrella.

He hurriedly gave me his address. We exchanged names and I took his umbrella home.

The next day I thought of returning the umbrella to Rehan but I was too lazy for that. So I thought tomorrow is the day to return.

The next day I was determined to return and I went to his home and ringed his bell.

For his defence, he didn't know I was at the door, so he opened the door half naked, I mean he did not wear a shirt and was wearing a short.

He was looking so good and handsome. I fell for him, I fell for him hard.

On that day not just I returned his umbrella, we exchanged numbers and from that day onwards a special bond created between us.

We are like soul mates and I believe I was destiny to meet him.

RAHUL PRATAP SINGH

Hardwork, integrity, perseverance and love are just a few of these attributes. He loves to scribble his random thoughts and emotions on paper. Holding a very keen interest towards reading, he is a very down to earth person and has a very special affection towards tea. Bringing smiles on everyone's face is what his ultimate aim is and he can go to any extent to fulfill that. He is a very optimistic and self-motivated guy whose words of encouragement can brighten anyone's day.

" Life is a journey, full of lessons. One grows until he does not stop learning" is what he loves to depict and his write ups.

INSTA HANDLE: @pratapsingh77177

सपनों का काफिला

देख अमन उस और देख गांव का एक लड़का सूरज ने अमन को सड़क की और दिखाते हुए कहा, आज लगता है जैसे अपने गांव में कोई मेहमान आया है। बालक मन यह देख इतना उत्सुक हो गया कि चले भागे आए उन गाड़ियों के पीछे यह सारी गाड़ियां गांव के प्रधान जी के घर के बाहर एक पंक्ति में लाइन से खड़ी थी I जैसे ही अमन और सूरज उस और जाता उतने देर तक में गांव वालों की भीड़ जुट गई सूरज और अमन के मन में उत्सुकता जाग रही थी कि आखिर इनका फिल्मों में किस महानुभाव ने अपने गांव बिजरुक पधारे हैं। जिसकी इतनी खातिरदारी हो रही है I

इसी जिज्ञासा से अमन गांव के चाचा से पूछ लिया I चाचा ने बताया बेटा यह डीएम साहब है यानी "डिस्टिक मजिस्ट्रेट "I इन्हें जिलाधिकारी कहा जाता, है मतलब कि यह इस पूरे जिले में सबसे बड़े प्रशासनिक अधिकारी हैं और यह हमारे गांव आज जिला अस्पताल के उद्घाटन समारोह में उपस्थित होने आए हैं I चाचा का इतना बताना ही अमन और सूरज दोनों डीएम साहब की एक झलक पाने के लिए दौड़ पड़े शाम होते-होते समारोह के समापन के पूर्व ही डीएम साहब अपने साथ आए ढेर सारे पुलिस वालों के साथ समाहरणालय लौट गए I

लेकिन अमन और सूरज इन दोनों में से अमन के मन में यह सारी घटनाएं प्रभावित कर गई I वह दिन रात डीएम बनने का ख्वाब देखने लगा I

अमन इस वक्त अपने नानी के घर पटना के एक छोटे गांव में रहकर पढ़ाई करता था। पढ़ाई में अच्छा होने के कारण उसे अपने मामा जी का साथ मिला और उसने अपनी प्राथमिक शिक्षा गांव में ही विद्यालय से पूरी कर अपने घर जमशेदपुर वापस आ गया I इसी शहर में रहकर अमन ने अपने दसवीं बारहवीं तथा स्नातक भूगोल से पूरा किया I भूगोल की परीक्षा प्रथम श्रेणी से उत्तीर्ण कर ही अमन के सपनों को पंख लग गए थे, क्योंकि "यूपीएससी" की

परीक्षा में शामिल होने के बाद व्यक्ति की न्यूनतम योग्यता स्नातक ही होती हैं I

अभी तो अमन ने बस सोचा ही था कि, अब वह यूपीएससी की तैयारी करेगा, डीएम बनेगा ,देश की सेवा करेगा , जो मानव सपनों की दुनिया प्रवेश ही किया था कि उसके आंखों तले अंधेरा छा गया I जब, उसे यह पता चला कि उसी की तैयारी के लिए दिल्ली जैसे बड़े शहर जाना पड़ता हैI उसे दिल्ली की कोचिंग संस्थानों में लाखों की फीस लगती है यह सब अमन को धीरे-धीरे कमजोर कर रही थी I पर वह कहते हैं ना:

"जिस के इरादे मजबूत हो उनके सामने मुश्किलों का पहाड़ भी कम होता है I"

एक भैया जो कि खुद भी UPSC की तैयारी कर रहे थे , उन्होंने उसे इंटरनेट कोर्स के बारे में बताया और कहा कि जो पढ़ाई दिल्ली जैसे बड़े शहरों के संस्थानों में उपलब्ध है वैसी ही इंटरनेट के कोर्स में भी उपलब्ध हैI व्यक्तिगत शिक्षक उपस्थित नहीं रहते हैं पर उनके द्वारा कक्षा में पढ़ाई गई सामग्री का रिकॉर्ड उपलब्ध रहता हैI

एक और अमन और उसकी परेशानियां दोनों साथ-साथ चल रही थीI कहते हैं ना कि:

"सपने अगर बड़े हो तो उनको पूरा करने के लिए इंसान को सपनों के बराबर कीमत चुकानी पड़ती है I"

इसी बीच अमन के घर की आर्थिक तंगी उससे यह मांग कर रही थी कि वह कहीं छोटे-मोटे काम कर पैसे की व्यवस्था करें और दूसरी और "डीएम साहब" I पर अमन ने हिम्मत नहीं हारी वह कुछ छोटे बच्चों को ट्यूशन पढ़ाने लगा और साथ ही एक दफ्तर में काम करने लगा I धीरे-धीरे ही सही पर अमन अपनी तैयारी में लग रहा लगा रहा I एक समय आया जब अमन का चयन एक सरकारी संस्थान में एसएससी के माध्यम से हो गया I अब अमन को उसके सपने साकार होते दिख रहे थे I

अपने चयन के पहले साल से ही वह यूपीएससी की तैयारी शुरू कर दिया और पूरी जीत और मेहनत करने लगा और अपने प्रथम

प्रयास में ही वह अपनी साक्षात्कार तक की यात्रा तय कर लेता है। परंतु किसी कारण वहां मेरिट में नहीं आ पाता I वह दूसरे वर्ष फिर उसी उत्साह या यूं कहो उससे कहीं ज्यादा परिश्रम कर अपनी दूसरी प्रयास में यूपीएससी की कठिन परीक्षा पास कर लेता है I और वह अपने बचपन में देखा सपना जो उन गाड़ियों के काफिले से शुरू होता है और एक आईएएस बनकर दूसरों किस दूसरे सपने की शुरुआत में खत्म होता है I अब अमन उन सब बच्चों को उनकी तैयारी में ,समाज के मुख्यधारा में, लाने में उनकी स्थिति सुधारने में मदद करता है ,जो वास्तव में किसी कारणवश अपने आप को अभागा महसूस करते हैं। वास्तव में आज अमन कई घरों की रोशनी बनकर उनके परिवार को रोशन कर रहा है I वह अपने कोशिश से कम से कम हजारों बच्चों को उनकी मंजिल तक पहुंचाना चाहता है। एक व्यक्ति की पहचान तब बड़ी और खास हो जाती है जब वह लोगों को साथ लेकर उनके दुखों को दूर करते हुए खुद भी आगे बढ़े. जीवन का अर्थ केवल संघर्ष में है। जीत या हार भगवान के हाथ में है इसलिए चलते- चले और जीत का अपने संघर्ष का जश्न मनाते चले क्योंकि, मेरा ऐसा मानना है :

"एक जिंदगी जो आपको मिली है और एक जिंदगी जो आपको बनानी है।"

SHUBHUM PANDA

Shubham panda is student of degree College who write short poem/quotes in his free time . He from a middle class family from Rourkela, Odisha Who want to be make his name in popular.

वक्त तो लगेगा

तुम जो जा चुके
तुम्हें भुलाने में वक्त तो लगेगा, माना था तुम्हें खुशियों की वजह,
अब दिल को समझाने में वक्त तो लगेगा
खाकर कसमे कहा था तुमने,
मुझे कभी नहीं भूलोगे,
अब वो झूठे वादे भुलाने में वक्त तो लगेगा
न जाने कबसे कैद हूँ तुम्हारी यादों के पिंजरे में,
खुद को आजाद करने में वक्त तो लगेगा
तुम्हें जिंदगी समझ लिया था मैंने,
तुम तो हो जा चुके,
तुम्हें भुलाने में वक्त तो लगेगा II

SUBHALAXMI BEHERA

I am a student. Writing is my passion. I just want to express my feelings through my poems .

अच्छा लगता है

अच्छा लगता है जब आपसे बात होती है,
अच्छा लगता है जब आपसे मिलने की गुस्ताखी होति है।
अच्छा लगता है हर वो सुबह जब आपसे ,
सबसे पहले बात होती है,
अच्छा लगता है जब रात को आपसे बात करके सोने के अनमोल
मौका मिलता है।
अच्छा लगता है हर वो एक लम्हे को सोचने में जो आपसे जुडी है,
उन लम्हो के साथ अपना सारा जीवन बिताने के पता नहीं क्यों
हमेसा मन करता है।
चाहे कितने भी रूठे क्यों ना है आप्से हम, लेकिन कभी आपको
भुला नहीं पाते है,
इन्ही रुठना मनाना में यकीं मानो बहत खुसी मिलती है ।

कोन हूं में

कोन हूं में,
किस मकसद से जन्मी हूं,
किसीके लिए आयी हूं,
या खुद के लिए जिंदा हूं।
कभी कभी पूछती हूं आइना से,
क्या हूं में,
नहीं पहचान पाती हूं में खुदको,
निराश होकर बैठती हूं,
खो जाती हूं अपने आप में।
मेरा याहां कोन है, माता पिता के बिना,
वो भी एक दिन छोड़ जाएंगे मुझे,
अकेली बन जाऊंगी,
तब सिर्फ आयेगा रोना।
क्या धरती में मेरा कुछ होगा,
कोई मेरा होगा तब,
दुख में आंसू बहा रही होगी,
मेरे आंखे जब जब ।
अभी तक समझ ना पाई,
किस लिए हुआ है मेरा जनम,
सोचते सोचते,
कब बुढ़ापे में चली आयि,
अभी तक न मिटा पाई ये भरम ।

आशा की किरण

हम सब हैं बहन भाई,
करेंगे ना कभी आपस में लड़ाई।
मिलकर सब हम करेंगे पढ़ाई,
खेलंगे हम फिर छुपंछुपाई।
किसिके बारे में कभी ना कहेंगे बुराई
सबको प्यार करेंगे किसी से कभी ना होंगे जुदाई।
आशा की किरण का करेंगे खुदाई,
मिलकर रहेंगे सब ना होगा कोई पराई। अपने आपमें से क्रोध को त्याग देंगे,
तभी जा कर हम दुनिया में श्रेष्ठ कहलाएंगे।
बातचीत हमेशा सही ढंग से करेंगे, इसिसे हम अपनी भद्रता की परिचय देंगे।
कभी हम कहेंगे ना किसको कम, यही तो जिंदेगी है,
हमेशा रहेंगे साथ साथ हम।

KRITIKA SEKSARIA

Kritika seksaria 15 year old girl hails from Jamshedpur. Jolly nature foody her love for noodles and travelling is immense and these two things are enough to make her happy. She is the most kind hearted girl who is very soft spoken child presented to this earth with chants of maa Durga bhajan all over India A person who care for other more than herself and is ready to sacrifice anything and everything for her loved ones.

संघर्ष स्वाभिमान का

"सफलता तो मुस्कुराती है अकेले भी
सर ए महफिल रुला देती है नाकामी
कोई सीख ले कर छू लेता है चांद को
तो कितनों को सुला देती है नाकामी II"

यह कहानी है एक लड़की की जिसकी जिंदगी बचपन से ही चुनौतियों से भरी थी यह कहानी है उस लड़की की जिसने अपने जीवन में इतनी चुनौतियों और असफलताओं के बाद भी अपने सपनों का साथ नहीं छोड़ा और कड़ी कोशिश के बाद आखिर में अपने मुकाम तक पहुंच कर यह साबित कर ही दिया कि अगर हम दृढ़ इच्छाशक्ति और धैर्य के साथ कड़ी मेहनत करें तो हमें अपने लक्ष्य तक पहुंचने से कोई नहीं रोक सकता I

जमशेदपुर नामक शहर में जन्म हुई यह लड़की, **आकांक्षा** बचपन से ही दृढ़ इच्छाशक्ति वाली और मेहनती थी I बचपन से उसका एक ही सपना था कि उसे बड़े होकर डॉक्टर बनना है और एक अस्पताल खोलना है जिसमें वह गरीबों का इलाज कर सके I उसके परिवार वाले भी काफी सपोर्टिव थे और वह भी अपनी बेटी को डॉक्टर बनते देखना चाहते थेI दसवीं की पढ़ाई के बाद उसने आगे की पढ़ाई के लिए विज्ञान लेने का निश्चय किया I पर घर की आर्थिक स्थिति अच्छी न होने के कारण पिताजी ने उसे समझाया कि प्राइवेट कॉलेज में एडमिशन करवाना संभव नहीं हैI अगर वह डॉक्टर बनना चाहती है तो उसे खूब अच्छे अंक लाने होंगे, ताकि उसका एडमिशन सरकारी कॉलेज में हो सके I उसने उस दिन ठान लिया कि वह कड़ी मेहनत करेगी और अच्छे अंक लाएगी जिससे उसका एडमिशन सरकारी कॉलेज में हो सके I

उसने खूब मेहनत करना शुरू कर दिया I वह रात दिन कड़ी मेहनत करती थी और कहते हैं ना सफलता इतनी आसानी से नहीं मिलती I मंजिल बड़ी जिद्दी होती हैं हासिल कहां नसीब से होती हैI ऐसे ही कुछ आकांक्षा के साथ भी हुआ I नीट की परीक्षा से अनजान उसने बार्बी की तैयारी शुरू की I 12वीं कक्षा के आखिर

में उसे पता चला कि डॉक्टर की पढ़ाई के लिए उसे नीट नाम की एक परीक्षा देनी पड़ेगी I नीट की परीक्षा बहुत कठिन होती है I तो उस साल उसके लिए वह परीक्षा पास करना असंभव था I परंतु फिर भी उसने हार ना मानी और उसने जो भी 12वीं तक पढ़ा था उन सब के साथ ही वह की नीट परीक्षा देने चली गई I परंतु उससे पता था की इस साल उसे सफलता नहीं मिलने वाली I

उसने फिर 1 साल का ड्रॉप लेने का निश्चय किया उसने एक कोचिंग क्लास में एडमिशन लिया I जहां से वह नीट की तैयारी शुरू कर सके मगर जिस कोचिंग क्लास से वह तैयारी कर रही थी वह कोचिंग क्लास फ्रॉड निकली और परीक्षा के 4 महीने पहले ही वह बंद हो गईI अब उसने अपनी मेहनत से जितना हो सके उतना पढ़ाई किया और नीट की परीक्षा देने गई पर अच्छी तैयारी ना होने के कारण व परीक्षा क्लियर नहीं कर पाई I उसे पता था कि सफलता हासिल करने से पहले हमें बहुत से प्रयास करने होते हैं और उसने एक और प्रयास करने का निश्चय किया I इस बार उसने ऑनलाइन क्लासेस की मदद से तैयारी शुरू की I उसकी तैयारी बहुत ही अच्छी चल रही थी I पर यह चुनौतियां कहां सफलताओं का पीछा छोड़ने वाली I उसकी तैयारी के दौरान उसे बैक बोन सिस्ट नामक बीमारी से गुजरना पड़ा I जिससे डॉक्टरों की भाषा में पिलियनोडल साइनस के नाम से जाना जाता हैI काफी इलाज के बाद भी ठीक नहीं हुई तो डॉक्टरों ने ऑपरेशन करने की सलाह दीI

ऑपरेशन के बाद उसे बैठकर पढ़ने में बहुत ज्यादा परेशानी होने लगी I उसे कंप्लीट बेड रेस्ट के लिए कहा गया Iइससे उसकी तैयारी पर भी काफी बुरा असर पड़ा I मगर फिर भी उसने हार नहीं मानी उसी हालत में उसने इस परीक्षा की तैयारी की और परीक्षा देने भी गई मगरI इस बार भी वह असफल रही और उसने ठान लिया था कि उसे डॉक्टर बनना है वह अपनी असफलताओं से नहीं घबराएगी और उसने एक और साल तैयारी करने का निर्णय कर लिया I मगर परिस्थितियां अभी कहां उसके अनुकूल थी I वह पहली सर्जरी अनसक्सेसफुल रही, और डॉक्टरों ने उसे

दोबारा ऑपरेशन की सलाह दी I अब उसे दूसरे ऑपरेशन के लिए जमशेदपुर से बाहर जाना पड़ा और वहां उसे एक महीने तक अस्पताल में रहना पड़ा I फिर ऑपरेशन के बाद डॉक्टर ने उसे 6 महीने की कंप्लीट बेड रेस्ट की सलाह दी I इन सब चीजों में उसके साथ से 8 महीने बर्बाद हो गए आखिर के 4 महीने में जी-जान लगाकर मेहनत की नीट का फॉर्म भर दिया इस बार परिवार वालों ने जिद करके उसे एक और एग्जाम का फॉर्म भरवा दिया था I जो कि उसे फार्मेसी फील्ड में ले जाता I

अब आखिरकार वो दिन आ गया जब उसके नीट की एग्जाम थी एग्जाम देने गई और एग्जाम देने के बाद उसे समझ आ गया था कि इस बार भी उसके हाथ कुछ नहीं लगने वाला I बहुत ही मायूस हो गई इस बार भी उसके अंक इतने नहीं थे कि उससे सरकारी कॉलेज में एडमिशन मिल सके I लगातार तीन साल के ड्रॉप के बाद भी जब वह सफल नहीं हो पाए, वह अब काफी हताश हो चुकी थी I उसकी हिम्मत टूट रही थी उससे ऐसा लग रहा था मानो वह इस दुनिया की सबसे असफल लड़की है I वह जिंदगी में कुछ भी नहीं कर सकती I उसके लिए तो मानो जिंदगी ही खत्म हो गई थी I ना वह किसी से बोलती, ना किसी के साथ बैठी ,और एकदम अकेली सी रहने लगी थी I अपने मन से ही मानो उसकी लड़ाई चल रही थी I

जब सब उसके खिलाफ हो गए थे तो वह अकेली अपने सपनों को पूरा करने के लिए खड़ी हुई I उसने कहा मुझे चाहे कुछ भी हो जाए मैं हिम्मत नहीं हरूंगी I चाहे पूरा जमाना मेरे खिलाफ हो जाए ,मगर मैं एक डॉक्टर बनकर ही मानूंगी I उसने फिर से अपनी तैयारी चालू कर दी I मगर माता पिता ने उसे एक और साल ड्रॉप लेने की अनुमति नहीं दी और सब ने उसे बहुत समझाया कि वह अब अपनी स्ट्रीम चेंज कर ले I इसी बीच उसकी फार्मेसी की एग्जाम का रिजल्ट आ गई थी, और रिजल्ट काफी ही अच्छी थीI जिससे कि उसे एक टॉप की कॉलेज में एडमिशन मिल जाता I

माता-पिता के बहुत समझाने के बाद आकांक्षा ने भी निर्णय लिया कि वह अपना स्ट्रीम बदल देगी और वह भी फार्मेसी में चली जाएगी I उसने बी फार्मा ज्वाइन कर लिया और वह कॉलेज तो जाने लगी I मगर कहते हैं ना अगर सर पर किसी चीज का जुनून सर जाए तो उसे हासिल करने के लिए हमें कोई भी नहीं रोक सकता I**आकांक्षा** ने बी फार्मेसी के साथ-साथ वापस उसी जुनून से नीट की तैयारी शुरू कर दी और उसने नीट की परीक्षा भी दी और इस बार उसने बहुत ही अच्छे अंक से वह परीक्षा पास कर ली I अब तक उसके परिवार वालों को यह बात पता नहीं थी कि वह नीट की तैयारी कर रही है जब उसके परिवार वालों को पता चला तो उनकी तो खुशी का ठिकाना ही नहीं रहा I आखिरकार आकांक्षा को एमबीबीएस में एडमिशन मिल गया I

उसने अपने 5 साल की एमबीबीएस की पढ़ाई पूरी की और उसके बाद स्पेशलाइजेशन कंप्लीट कर वह एक कार्डियोलॉजिस्ट बन गई I आज आकांशा एक बहुत ही अच्छी डॉक्टर है और भारत के सभी प्रसिद्ध डॉक्टरों में उसका भी नाम आता है I उतनी असफलताओं के बाद भी उसने हिम्मत नहीं हारी और आखिरकार यह साबित कर दिया कि "अगर मन में दृढ़ इच्छाशक्ति हो और हम धैर्य से काम ले तो कोई भी काम मुश्किल नहीं है I किसी ने सही ही कहा है I

जिस राह पर तेरी उम्मीद तेरे साथ खड़ी होगी
उस रहा के अंतिम छोर पर
मंजिल भी तेरा सब्र से इंतजार कर रही होगी II

KARAN B. RATHOD

Karan Rathod is a boy born with full of talent in each and every field. He is the boy who can easily express his feelings at any kind of platform. He is person having plenty of words in his soul to express in the form poems and stories. He is soulmate for his wellwishers. His hobby is to help person in any condition and any suituation. best thing of this boy is loyality in any work and dedication towords each and every thing. another way to describe this boy is " god of cleanliness ". he is more interesting and full of happiness in his behaviour. he fits easily in any persons heart.

।।मायने मोहब्बत के।।

मोहब्बत के मायने समझ ने की,
कोशिश जो हो रही है, जनाब एहा तो खेल जारी है,
मोहब्बत कहा हो रही है।

।।जहर-ए-मोहब्बत।।

जहर-ए-मोहब्बत पि के लौटा हुँ,
थोडा नहीं पुरा टुटा हुँ ।
आपको तो कब का माँफ कर दिया मोहतरमा ,
फिलहाल तो मै खुद से रुठा हुँ।

।।बेडीया।।

तोड के जमाने कि बेड़िया ,
क्या मैं आसमान मे उड पाउँगा?
या अपने सपनो को दिल में छुपाए,
कैद हो कर रह जाउँगा?

।। सजदा ।।

खुदा-खुदा ना कर बंदे ,
तेरा खुदा तेरे पास है ,
थोडा सजदा उनका भी कर जिनके लिय तु खास है ।

।।मुकद्दर।।

बदले मुकद्दर ऐसे कई लोगो के इस मोहब्बत ने।।
किसीको प्यार में सवारा इस मोहब्बत ने,
तो किसीको जड़ से उखाडा इस मोहब्बत ने।

।।मदहोशी।।

उसे क्या एहसास होगा मेरी मदहोशी का,
जिसे मेरा होश भी रास नहीं।

।। गाँव की याद आई।।

कभी गाँव में रहने से जिनकी ईज्जत पे आँच आई,
आज उन्हे गाँव की याद आई।
कभी गाँव वालो को अपनी हैसियत की देते थे दुहाई,
आज उन्हे गाँव की याद आई।
शहर की अकड़ मे गाँव वालो की जो करते थे रूसवाई,
आज उन्हे गाँव की याद आई।
शहरो की झगमगाहट और चकाचौंद में जिन्होने गाँव पे लानत लाई,
आज उन्हे गाँव की याद आई।
जब शहरो में "कोरोना" की हवा छाई ,
तब ईन अमिर शहरवालो को गरिब गाँव वालो की याद आई,
गाँव की याद आई।

।।ख्वाईशे ।।

ख्वाईशो का समंदर आँखो मे लिए फिरते हो,
अरे दो पल को जरा ठहरो तो सहि।।
अरे जो तुम्हारे पास है उसे जियो तो सहि,
तुम्हे मुकम्मल है जो जाम उसे पिओ तो सहि।
ए दोस्त जो नहीं है उसकी चाह है,
लेकिन जो है उसे अपणाओ तो सहि।
ख्वाईशो का समंदर आँखो मे लिए फिरते हो,
अरे दो पल को जरा ठहरो तो सहि।

TANISHKA YADAV

Tanishka is a 20 year old writer, blogger and a book geek. Currently in her 2nd year of graduation, she defines herself as someone who doesn't shy away from penning her observations and perspectives of the world around her. She is sanguine, creative, headstrong and a wallflower who weaves simplest of words into relevant, meaningful and effective sentences.

Shedding Some Light On Perspective.

Being on the same page doesn't always mean you think just like someone, it sometimes mean you at a particular point of time share the same opinion with someone because it serves the purpose at that specific moment. Sharing an opinion or idea does not alter the fact that people can have different perspectives. They can have their own way of Viewing, Reflecting and Concluding various other situations. Individuals differ in many ways and so does their viewpoint. Arguing about "not understanding" when an individual does not share your notion or is not "on the same page" is bollocks. Understand and respect that humans have different ways of thinking and they can express it whenever they like, whether in scene's favor or not.

Treat Your Mind.

As humans we're prone to the monotony and dullness of life. The same thing over and over again everyday seems tiring at one point, even more so with each passing day and consequently our mind starts rejecting the same things that excited us initially. You see, to keep the excitement intact and to keep enjoying those activities you need to refresh your mind every now and then. Even if It means taking an elongated break from your typical productive life. My point is, one should keep the dosage of newness high in one's pattern of living. Consistency is great however, straying a little from regular habits and treating oneself with new found ones never hurt. In addition, it's always easy to come back to one's adapted lifestyle. Anyhow, now as a result of finding and cultivating novel habits, one gets to bring back something cool from the routine adopted for a short period of time. It could be a new pattern of starting the day, a new point of view or a new knowledge. You see, you get to keep it as a souvenir now and that'd remind you to go back at adopting and enjoying little, inexperienced quirks. There are a lot of productive habits, activities and manners of living flowing all around us. Several ideas that attract us but our dubiousness restrains us from adopting them and letting them influence change in our daily routine and life, eventually. Although you're habituated to your old routine, it never hurts to look for something new. Something that'd stir your senses all over again and push you to living the same life in a new found way. All you've to do is , Keep your curiosity alive. Keep your Keen eye in search of exercises that energise you. And, prohibit fear of adopting change take over you. Instead of treating newness and diversity as a distant and unfriendly concept, acknowledge them, adopt them and let them assist you in rejuvenating your life, habits and productivity.

ASHOK SURYA NARAYAN THAKUR

He is a boy, whose name means " one without sorrow". As his name suggest he is a boy full of joy. A struggling NEET aspirant who is still dedicated towards his goals. He is kind hearted and is helpful. He is a foodie and loves to explore new things. He loves to write and pen down his emmotions into words.

बीते कल और खुद से वादे

कितना वक़्त लगेगा मुझे
अपने पैरों पर खड़ा होने में
सफलता के बाद कि चैन की एक रात
चैन की नींद सोने में

आप सबो से मिलने के बाद
कितना बदल गया हूँ मैं
ढेरो गलतियों के बाद भी
शायद संभल गया हु मैं

शुक्रगुज़ार हूँ आप सबो का जिन्हों ने
मेरी हर गलती को माफ़ है किया
अब कहीं जा कर खुदा ने
मेरे साथ भी है इंसाफ किया

बुराईयो के जिस दलदल मे
मै था फसता जा रहा
बचपन की सारी गलतियां
एक एक करके है याद आ रहा

गलतियां जो मैंने है किया
उसको कैसे सुधार पाऊँगा मैं
अपनी जिम्मेदारियों से भाग कर
"खुद"को क्या बतला पाऊँगा मैं

बर्बस् ही पलके भीग जाती है
इतना कुछ हो जाने के बाद
कैसे कोई जी पता है
अपना सर्वस्व खो जाने के बाद
अभी उन पलो को सोच कर

अचानक सा घबरा जाता हूँ मैं
अपने दिलों की बात
किसी से ना कह पाता हूँ मैं

आज कुछ लिखने को बैठा
तो जज़्बात मन से निकल गया
वर्षो से दबाये रखा था जो
वो हर बात जुबां से निकल गया

निकल रहा हुँ उन यादो से
जिसका कोई अस्तित्व नहीं
पुरानी यादो को ढोने वालों की
होता कुछ भी अस्तित्व नहीं I

लोगों के नज़र में मैं एक
बत्मिज़् आवारा हूँ
लेकिन माँ की आखों का
मैं भी एक जग्मगता हुआ तारा हूँ I

अब आप सबको दुःख पहुंचे
ऐसा कोई काम नहीं करूँगा मैं
जिस चक्रव्यूह से निकल गया हूँ मैं
फिर से उसमें नहीं फसुंगा मैं I

ZAHWA

Zahwa, a native of Cuttack, more popular as the silver city of Odisha, is one of the budding writers of the time. Blessed with absolute wit, she lives for her love of plants, and writing, of course! So much so that she's currently pursuing graduation in plant science in Ravenshaw University, one of the oldest universities of the country. Besides that, she enjoys cooking and napping. An ambivert by nature, she is the carrier of a silent yet impressionable personality. She believes words are tonic to the outer toxic world. Her writings reflect the ordeals of the man built society in the most raw form, leaving profound effect on her readers. True to her name, she is a ray of brightness in the darkness looming on the horizon.

Husbands Don't Rape!

Post dinner it's a ritual now
Doing the dishes
And waiting for his anticipated gesture
Days when I am lucky enough
He dozes off early,
Probably consumed by the day's weariness
Putting me to relief
But not all days accompany peaceful nights
One and a half year now
Time never lessened the pain
Rather has taught me endurance
And pumped me with patience
Instances where I revolted had left me badly bruised and in unbearable agony
Slaps, punches and spanks are the least to mention
Yet when I complained "Husbands don't rape!"
Everyone exclaimed
So I submit to his virile supremacy now,
Everytime
Perceiving it to be a monoact
Lying still on the same bed I make every morning
Gazing at the dimly lit pecan painted frame hanging right above the bed
Drawing and re-drawing the eleven enormous motifs carved on its bottom edge in my head
Until he slips off me
So at the age of 23 I know
that a wife is someone
Whose consent is perpetual
It's taken in the affirmative
Along with the seven vows of the nuiptal knot
Abuse by your man is perfectly normal
Far, far from something one would call 'criminal'!

I Will Blame You Not O' My Heart!

I will blame you not O' my heart!
Not this time, not again.
For all those failures All those times
You rebelled and ended up bringing trouble.
For that early teen love blunder
Or late night regrets.
I will blame you not O' my heart!
Not now, not ever again.
But you must promise me to Search for that silver lining everytime
Even for the darkest and heaviest of clouds!
Promise me not to Let me find myself dangling from a rope end from the ceiling someday
Or jumping off the tallest building in the locality
Or gulping down poison
Or sliting my left hand's vein and slowly die.
O my heart, Promise me to keep the suicidal thoughts at bay
And I promise you not to blame again

My Dreamland

Find me a land
Where our identities
Are not sealed by
What religion we profess
Or which political party we support

A land where our skin colour
Is only skin-deep
And where our bank balances
Can't help us climb the social ladder

Find me a land
Where we are just individuals
Judged by the qualities we harbor

Where each one of us is cherished
Neither stereotyped nor segregated
Just because we are we, and not them!

ANISHA PANDA

Thodi pagli si, thodi diwani si , Apni he duniya mein rehti hai khoyi si ; Jo rakhti hai apno ko apne dil mein , Duniya se alag chalti hai apni dhun mein. This is Anisha for you. Let's see what she writes for us.

Maa

Chupa le mujhe apni anchal mein
maa is bedardi duniya se;
Tham ke mera hath le ja mujhe khich ke is andhere se.
Jane kyon sab ojhal hona chahte hain maa ki ankho se;
Maa toh wo chhat hai Jo bachati hai hame har khatre se.

Ek Yad

Ek yad hai purani, Hai magar wo ruhani.
Us yaad mein hai tera basera,
Tu hai meri zindagi ka sawera.
Aaj sham ko teri yad Jo ayi,
Guzre hue kal ko sath hai layi.
Un lamho mein ansu the ankho mein
aur hotho pe thi meri hasi,
Wo pal bhi the kitne khas
Jo meri ruh mein ja basi.
Ruh ko chu leti thi ek muskan,
Kho gaya waqt k sath q,
hun mein is bat se anjan.
Teri har ahat ki parakh thi mujhe,
Teri har ek ehsas ki samajh thi mujhe,
Phir waqt k sath ye ehsas kyon kho gaya,
Tu mujhse yun juda kyon ho gaya.

Dosti Ya Pyar

Apne khwabon mein sajaya hai hame kisi ne,
Hamari tarif mein kuch likha hai aaj kisi ne.
Un ke dil se Jo ye baat samne ayi hai,
Koi gehre raaz hai Jo yeh chupa rahi hai.
Khul Jane do is raaz ko aab Na chupao humse,
Jo dil mein hai kehdo usse apne alfazon

Dosti

Doston mein sabse Jo khas ho,
Ap ke dil ke sabse wo pas ho.
Jo Na ho kar bhi har jagah ho,
Meri zindagi mein wo bas aap ho.

Dil Dard Ka

Jo kehna tha wo keh na sake
Dard Dil Ka bayan kar na sake
Dawa karte the jo mere dil ki har dhadkan ko pehchanne ki
wo bhi dard mere dil ka kyon dekh Na sake.

SASMITA SINGH

Sasmita Singh is a simple, sweet , caring,girl whose strongness is her beautiful smile and has a impressive personality .She has earned silence from the talkative, toleration from the intolerant, and kindness from the unkind. Her talents are like rainbow. She is not only a singer but also a artist and has power to involve and motivate you positively in her words. So let's have a look to her dreamland of writing.

Kya Sach Me Tum Pyar Nibha Paoge Kya

Kya sach me tum pyar nibha paoge kya Kya
meri har dard ki marham tum ban paoge kya
Kya meri khilkhilata hua mushkan lauta paoge kya
Kya meri ashuon ke bundo ko pochhne kliye apna kameez
bhiga paoge kya
Bolona , kya sach me tum pyar nibha paoge kya
Mujhe chand sitare nehi chaiye
Tere har waqt ka waqt v nhi chaiye
Bas ek pal ki sukun ki ghadi tumhare baho me bitani hai
Kya tum ye de paoge kya..
Bolona , kya sach me tum pyar nibha paoge kya
Jism ke pyase to yahan bahut hai
Mere jism se lekar mere ruh tak rubaroo ho paoge kya
Wada karne kliye yahan hazaro ka Mela laga hua hai
Kya un hazaro se ake wada karke wada nibha paoge kya
Bolona , kya sach me tum pyar nibha paoge kya...

Chal Na Kuchh Nayi Shuruwat Karte Hai

Chal Na kuchh nayi shuruwat karte hai
Ye duriya ko thodi kam karke Nazdigiya badhate hai ..
Hamare har sapne ko dono milke apna banate hai ..
Chl na kuchh nayi shuruwat karte hai..
Raat mai chhat par baith kar kuchh sabdo ki moti samet te hai ..
Har alfazo ko kahani banate hai ...
Apas ki ankho ko padh kar kuchh apna sunate hai ..
Chl na kuchh nayi shuruwat karte hai...
Dono milkar ek dusre ki khusi ko asman me sajate hai ..
Har ek ke gam ko wo peheli barish me bhigate hai .
Chal Na kuchh nayi shuruwat karte hai...
Chandni raat me ek duje kliye chand aur noor bante hai..
Uss samandar ke geherai me thodi aur dub jate hai ..
Chal Na kuchh nayi shuruwat karte hai...
Dosti ko thodi age lete hai ..
Pyar ke khusbuon ko ehesas kartate hai..
Uss khoosbu ko mehsus karte hue ek dusre ko thodi aur pehchan te hai ...
Chl na kuchh nayi shuruwat karte hai..

Aye Zindegi Abb Tu Hi Bata

Aye zindegi abb tu hi
bata Kaise use me bhula dun..
Wo to mere khwab nehi .
. Abb raha dikha mujhe ,
Kaise me uss hakikat ko mita dun..
Aye zindegi abb tu hi bata ,
kaise use me bhula dun..
Meri peheli suraj ki wo Satata hua dhoop hai ..
Har subha uth kar mai suraj se kaise muh mod du ..
Aye zindegi abb tu hi bata kaise use me bhula dun...
Meri nashili raat me chand ka noor wo hai ..
Bina noor ke mai chandni kaise manalu ..
Aye zindegi abb tu hi bata kaise use me bhula dun..
. Khidkion ke paas khade hote waqt guzarta hua hawa ka
ehesas wo hai...
Uss ehesaso se kaise vaqif hone se mana kar dun..
Aye zindegi abb tu hi bata
kaise use me bhula dun...

SUSHREE ARCHANA SWAIN

Archana born in odisha is highly ambitious with easy going personality... She is a philanthropist and philocalist.. She enjoys music ,sharing ideas and forging friendships... She has an innate ability of expressing her emotions and thoughts through her powerful words. She is an excellent communicator against listener and good at forging...She is very optimistic with a generous heart....

Mujhe Dar Lagta Hai..

Han mujhe bhi dar lagta hai,
Ye Soch ke ki Kahi sunane wala mere darr ko ek mauka na samajh le....

Kabhi Kabhi sochti hun ki mai akeli toh Nahi Jo ye sab sehti hu! Ya phir sabke sath yehi hota hai bas koi zikr nahi karta ! Ladki hui to kya kisiki nijee sampatti nahi ke koi pass se chuu ke gujar jaaye aur mai aavaaj tak na karu? Insaan Hun koi pathar nahi ...Jee karta hai sabko cheek cheek kar sab Kuch Bayaan kardun., Jo dil ke kisi kone mai dafan hai. "PAR BATAUN TO KISE"

Sab puchte hai "KYUN TUM CHUP BETHI HO? KYUN KISI SE KUCH KEHTI NEHI?"

Dil sochta hai,yehi Sahi mauka hai,sab bol deti hun..par 'DAR LAGTA HAI'...ye sochke ki jisse kahungi ,wo mujhe doshi na samjh le, na kahe ki "Dosh tumhara hai."kya hai mera kasur?Mai ek ladki hu ya phir apni sapno ko udaan dene ke liye char deewari se bahar nikalna chaha ye meri galti hai? Kyun mujhe itna bojh samjha jata hai ki mujhe garv se hi mar diya jata hai? Kyun mere padhai karna , Apni zindegi apni marzi se jina samaj ko phuti ankh nahi bhati..

Bachpan se sunti aa rahi hu, ladki ho tum ,thoda lihaj Karo , log kya kahenge , agle ghar Jana hai tujhe thoda bardast karna sikho ,ladki hai padh likh kar kya karegi ,ladki hai usse zyada mat chadhao, warna samaj par ungli karegi ,Raat ke waqt bahar mat nikal warna log kya kahenge ! Mai puchna chahti hu ye samaj hai koun? Jo sirf mere liye hi itna kanun banaya hai . Meri ruh mujhe cheekh cheekh kar puchti hai kyun tu lihaj karegi ,kyun tu bardast karna sikhegi,kyun Tu padhai nahi kar Sakti !! Kya jabab hai iska koi bata Sakta hai kya?

Ladki ho tum thoda sambhal kar rehna ! Kya koi mujhe ye bata Sakta hai ladki hona mere takat hai ya kamjori? Mere kapde pehne ke dhang se le kar mai kiske Saath baat kar rahi hun ye sab pe kyun sawal uthate ho , meri marzi pe Apni adhikar jamane bale tum hote koun ho ?

Mere har baat ko ,har kam ko kyun galat bataya jata hai ?' HAN MUJHE DAR LAGTA HAI' ye sawal puchne se ...kahin koi mujhe doshi na samajh le ...

Log kehte hai " hum ladka ladki mai bhedbhav Nahi karte "bus......ladki ko humesha chaukanna rehna Chahiye Kuch unch nich hogayi toh !.....bus ladki ko Ghar se akele bahar Nahi Jana chahiye ,........ bus ladki ko ladko ke samne jhuki hui rehana Chahiye, ...bus ladki saree hi pehni Chahiye,...... bus ladki ko ghar ka Sara kaam aane Chahiye .....abb Kitna bus lagakar sab Kuch toh itna inequality dikhate ho...par samaj pe garv se kehte ho hum koi bhedbhav nahi karte... Kyun Nahi kehte ladka aur ladki dono ko sab Kuch ana Chahiye ,kyun nahi dete ho dono ko barbar ka haq ....koun puchega inse ???mujhe acha Khana banana na ane se ,Mera saree na pehne se ,Mera naukari Karne se sab ko farak padega ;par mai sab kuch Karne ke baad bhi mujhe farak Nahi padna Chahiye...Issilye toh economy mai mujhe asset bolte hai ...

Koi kyun nahi samjhta ki meri bhi sapne hai , meri bhi udaan hai , mai jina chahti hu jese mujhe jina hai . Bacha sambhalna sirf mujhe kyun ani Chahiye pati ko kyun nahi , agar husband Achi khasi kama raha hai mujhe kyun Naukri chodna Chahiye...unhe kyun Nahi.??..koun jabab dega iss sawal ka????

Haan' DAR LAGTA HAI' mujhe rape aur acid attack ke naam se ,par kabtak mai chup baithungi aisi hee jahil sansaar mai...!!!??

Jab Dosh mere tha to saza ki hakdar bhi to mai thi,ye sab sochkar "MUJHE DAR LAGTA HAI"

Jo puche ye mujhe ,

Jo sunane chaye ye sach, kya seh paayenge ye isse?kya koi denge mere Saath ? Ya kahange " Kuch bhi dosh toh ladki ka hai ! Pura sansaar ka izzat ussike kandhe par jo hota hai...

UDITA DAS

Udita Das is a budding writer amongst the crowd born in Hindus' "Dharma Masa" of Kartik. Although she is a science graduate but takes great interest in philosophy and literature. She is a travel freak, a voracious orator, an artist by passion and a Numismatic. Besides being a foodie she can cook all the authentic dishes. She loves to read novels which sometimes helps her to escape the reality . Being an ambivert she has a well-balanced character. Summarizing it all she is multi-talented,melomanic,fun-loving, empathetic and a friendly person.

Verse Of Chameleon

I was on my way to the school,
Having a thousand dreams to become the next Abdul.
Someone shouted, "Hey you,Fool !"
I looked around to see a chameleon drool.
Aghast ! "I'll leave my work in the foreseen future,
As it is being copied by you creatures. 'No' morals and 'No' culture. "
He gave me a full lecture. "Ahem,what do you mean?
" I asked as he changed his skin from yellow to green.
"Am gonna tell you everything my child that I've seen ."
I was so keen hence I didn't intervene
. " Oh! The humans change their colors too
, Consuming artist's butterfly like mind ,
With their flattery lingua that will blow your mind.
And It's funny how self-seekers pretend to be kind.
"They change their attributes,
Depending on the prey's route.
Engulfing them in their darkness being a shrewd.
And all their strength ebbing away absolute. "
"Like my body their personality stench.
Their fawning sycophancy is nauseating as wench.
" As he went on I thought and thought sitting on a bench,
Digested by the deep thoughts like trench.
Upper sigma of all, Gives me a wakeup call,
To keep our eyes on the ball. Who knows ,might a tragedy befall.
As everything turned Greek to me,
I rolled and fell onto the floor to break free and explore.
Still those words echo in my core,
Which I can never ignore.
O lord ! I implore mercy for men like us,

Who only gave you disgust. We bow down ,
accept our fuss;
And pledge to reconstruct.

We Indians And Year 2020

Corruption, Exploitation, molestation;
India is still struggling with basic sanitation.
From communal roits to agricultural distress,
Poverty ,unemployment and water stress.
And here comes the Corona pandemic ,
the world war 3 knocking at the door,
That shakes me to the core.
Tehran and Washington are ready to go.
Who once were friends are now foe
. But we Indians are busy finding "Jugaads"
to every problems that we have.
Playing blame games being
dependable on government to do everything on our behalf
. Heart so cold,
Wet in gore from children to old.
I can't stop those flashy images,
Crossing my mind since ages,
Where tears adorn the path,
And everyone has bloody wrath.
I pray o'lord have mercy on us,
settle down Everybody who're in rush
. Because life isn't burning and breaking,
It's about rising to the occassion bonding and making.

ZIKRA RASHID

Zikra is an Arabic word meaning the one who preaches,(does zikr). This girl's character goes no different than her name's meaning. She has spark in her eyes, efficacy in her words and allure in her voice. She has great love for poetry.she herself is an amateur poetess trying to change her passion and love into her career.The choice of her topics and words is sharp and beautiful. You can easily relate to her words and they will leave your heart touched. Other than poetry, she is good at studies too.She is an intermediate who opted for PCB. She has also been Head girl of her esteem Sunway Sr. Sec. School, Rampur. She is a cheerful, Happy go lucky girl,who will never fail to impress you by her words.

Just Have Faith....Everything Will Be Fine

Though this night is longer,
But believe me the sun will rise
Though it is darker,
But believe me the coming light will be brighter and nice
Though this time is not easy,
But believe me it will become.
Though everything seems crushed and creasy ,
But believe me it will get good and wholesome.
And who am I to be believed?
Believe the king of the kings ,
The master of the Masters,
who causes the sun to rise
Who gushes the water when it dries.
Who knows you better than you ,
So who will not believe him?
I said who?
Believe him he will bring the dawn ,
Believe him and you will move on & on
Just have faith everything will be fine,
Just have faith and one day the sun will again shine.

I AM NOT A DOLL.. I AM A WARRIOR

I am not a doll,
I will not let me fall.
I am the fighter ,
Dauntless and bright.
Don't get me wrong,
I am not a soft song.
I am the warrior,
Which can fight the wars,

Without the horse.
I am the thunderstorm,
Loud and sparky,
Dark and marky.
I am the fire,
With a burning desire.
I have the grace,
Which no one can erase

The Heart And The Mind

The heart and the mind,
One with Vision other the blind.
The heart says do what you love,
And you will be very above.
The mind says don't be foolish,
Don't listen to the heart's rubbish.
The heart find positivity in everything,
And to everyone it clings.
The mind says all are illude ,
No one is trustable dude.
The heart says be loyal to everyone,
And you will be cheated by none.
Listen to me both says,
To which I should go ,my confusion stays.

Thunders Of Clouds

Thunders of clouds, roaring loud.
It seems as today ,
That the sky want to scream and shout and say.
It seems as today ,
All its patience has come to an end,
And then it burst out on the land
It seems as today
It want everyone to listen to it.
To it's patience, it's strength and all its grit .
And then it falls and Falls and Falls ,
To the earth,in the houses on the walls .
Gracefully shattering everywhere,
Beautifully releasing all its pain here.
And then with time it stops,
Departing from the land leaving it's shimmering drops .
And now it's silence,
A heartwarming peace away from the voilence.
It seems as today,
The sky has released all its grey ,
It seems as today that now it's all okay.

CHANDAN KUMAR NAYAK

Chandan Kumar Nayak, a highly enthusiastic, energetic guy responsible and reliable friend to hang around. Multi talented and creative personality with strong will power to pursue his dream. He always keeps smile on his face. A MTech graduate who believe in Fact than rumors. He is a warm kind and jolly fellow. A software engineer who holds love for technology on one hand and love for literature on another.

Waiting For You...

Not everyone in this world has the fate to cherish the fullest form of love, some are born just to experience the abbreviation of it

Love is a hell of a sinful fruit and yet this fruit I slightly tasted

Pooja,

I can't think by what name I would call you. Love, dreamgirl, angle, sweety, all these adjectives are just losing their meanings when they are prefixed to your name. You have occupied such a place in my heart that all the beautiful things however pretty they may be, they just can't reach there.You have showered my life with your golden rays, as you are the sun in my life's horizon. The sun which gives me courage and love to live my life. Sun is known as the source of all energy so you are to me. As this whole world is dark without the sun, so you are in my life. I am like an aimless contestant without you running my life's race. I am alone in life's battlefield without you, fighting, just to catch my breath and be happy but all in a vain.Today I am just a disguised man wearing a mask of happiness. Neither I have happiness nor any joy. I am only living by your sweet memory.

I don't know the relationship with you yet. I don't fell any fearness while writing letter to you. I write to you every day as this gives me divine pleasure. This is the panacea to my living. The medicine which keeps me fresh and active all throughout the day. The moment when I write this letter your picture comes living in the canvas of my mind. I just get arrested by your immense beauty. Your those black hair just hypnotize me, and your blue eyes just leave me dumb founded. I feel like I am alone floating in that blue sea and experiencing your love. Your those rosy pink lips just poison me, and your smile which bring flowering even in deserts. The almighty has made you with so much care that I can't compare anyone or anything with you.

Pani se pyash na bujha to
Mehfil ki tarha chal nikla,
Socha sikayatt karu teri khudako,
Aur khuda bhi teri aashique nikla

You must be thinking about that I have gone mad, but don't worry u will never get this letter, neither u can hear the pain of my heart. I write to you every day but don't post it. I just tear it and throw in my heart's dustbin. I write and tear it every day but didn't dare to post it to you. I write with much hope and eagerness as you will get this letter and come to me. I always dream about you and dreams are seen to be fulfilled, but I know this dream of mine will never be fulfilled. As I awake I find all the things and everything beside me but I miss you. I pray near god that, he may permit to see you every day in my dream. Pooja I fell as almighty has bestowed all the beauty upon you. My life without you is like a beautiful tree without flowers. As u know the flowers are the real beauty of nature so you are in my life. You are the girl who gives me natural and heartily happiness.

I have heard many people say that love is divine and eternal .There is no physical attraction in true love. Love –this one word is the solution to many problems. A true lover loves her lover's heart not her physical appearance. Love does not mean only to achieve his lover, loosing the love for her happiness has some other joy. A lover of heart can walk in path of thorns only to let his love walk on path full of roses. Many of my friends have advised me to forget you and begin a new life but you say Pooja, can a person live without his heartbeat? You are my heartbeat how can I live without you? In the genesis I have loved you and will do till my last breath.

Love happens only once and the rest is just life

You are the first star twinkle in my mind's love atmosphere. You have acquired such a large place in my heart that there is no place anyone else to reside. I was, am, and will love you till the end.

Life is also very unpredictable .it doesn't give what we want but compels has satisfy with that which we don't want.I get embarrassed when I see couple walk by my side hand in hand and when they enjoy each other's presence and when the boy softly kisses the give on her forehead, check and then on lips .Seeing this I fell very humiliated and run from there because I just feel suffocated. I don't exactly remember when I would have smiled really but without you I am just like a peacock without rain.

You may not be aware of one thing that when you were with me I was loving reality more than imagination. But now when you are not with me I have chosen to live in imagination as this is the only place where I can meet and share my feelings. Pooja you are my dream. You are just like a lamp lighting my life. You are always present with me in my imagination.

You and myself get admitted in one college.The place which changed the route of my life. You were very talkative and I was little silent. I couldn't talk freely with girls. You used to tease me saying coward. And I remained coward throughout my life. I couldn't express my feeling for you. You were a good friend of mine. You used to start gossiping with me when there was time and I had to be very happy just to hear your sweet words. The pleasure I used to get from that in only known to me. I used to notice your eyes and the movement of your lips while you were talking just like a fluttering colourful butterfly.

Your style of talking, your sweet words filled with plenty of romance had just moved me .you were like a night angle in my imagination. After all this how could I control myheart? Then I started loving you. By the passage of time I had started loving you from the bottom of my heart. But this truth was only known to me and my heart. No one could ever see through my love, not even you and I also did not dare to propose you, being afraid to lose you as a friend. I had thought that we two are made for each other. I loved you very much but could not express it to you.

O janeja ,ye sachhai ki main apne dil ki bat kabhi khulkar kar nahi saka,
Magar meri ankhein hamesa mere dil ka halat batata raha
Aur tu hai ki bekhabr aaj bhi, mere dil ki har dhadkan sirf teri naam leti hai,
Sirf Teri……..

After long days of our friendship, finally I decided to break the silence of my heart. Decided to tell you my feelings for you. The day I was to tell my feelings, you told me yours. Your love for one boy, who was some other than me. Your words reached my ears as a big thunder storm. It came to me as bold from blue. All my dreams were shattered.

What did you do this Pooja and what task did you gave to me? The task whose completion could drain my eyes. You told me to tie up your relation with Sanket , whom you were loving. I could not think of what to do at that time. My dream TAJMAHAL broken into pieces. I was loving you and in love there is not always a gain. In love some lose are also made to remain happy. Just to make you lead a life of life of bed of roses.

You must have remembered your first meeting with Sanket .You proposed Sanket in my presence. That day's incident is giving pain to my heart. My love was becoming some one's else how could I see it. Having heart full of emotions I decided to bind you together in bonds of love. But truth is that I could not hold my tears when I see you two together. I had just buried mine heart when I tried to tie you together. As soon as I see you, my heart question me , why did you do like this , Chandan??????? But unfortunately I had no answer nor now. But one thing I know I love your smile more than my love. Therefore, after college was over I came very far from you, where you can't see my feelings.

Pooja, please tell me, don't you really love me?????? Is there not any love for me??????

I know this letter will not reach you. But I am hoping that one day you will understand the pain and the felling of my heart, may be in next birth. You will surely be mine,surely.

I LOVE U……

Time to say good bye, a warm farewell, enjoy your life, truly without any fail. Someday somewhere we will cross again perhaps on a sunny day or a night when it will rain…

NAMAN RELE

Naman Rele was born in Panna district of M.P. & done his schooling from JNV Panna. Afterwards He went to Sagar for his further studies where he earned his Master's of Arts degree in Geography from Dr. Hari Singh Gour University, Sagar (M.P.) in 2018. He considered himself as lifetime learner. He loves to read and write & has interest in sports too. He is a social and grounded person as his writings also focused to social causes.

'क्लास और कास्ट'

रोहित अपने दोस्तों के साथ खेल रहा है I तभी उसका भाई सम्राट उसे बुलाता है और डाँटते हुए कहता है:
" तुमसे कितने बार कहा कि इन नीची जाति वालों के साथ मत खेला करो लेकिन तुम तो बिल्कुल वहीं घुसे रहते हो!"
रोहित नीचे सर किये हुए सब सुनता है फिर धीमी आवाज में कहता है:
"लेकिन भैया मुझे क्या पता कि वो नीची जाति का है या नहीं"
यह सुनते ही सम्राट का पारा और चढ़ जाता है वो गुस्से से रोहित को घूरते हुए बोला:
"नाम से! नाम से ही पता चल जाता है। ये तुम्हारा बेस्ट फ्रेंड हरि sc है, और तुम्हे संगत करना है GENERAL वालों की, समझे की नहीं?"
रोहित और उलझन में पड़ गया उसे सम्राट की पिछली समझाइश याद आ गई जिसमें उसने रोहित को चिराग के साथ पढ़ने को कहा था।सम्राट को पिछली बात याद दिलाते हुए रोहित बोला:
"लेकिन भैया चिराग भी तो SC है!"
सम्राट को रोहित की इस मूर्खता पर तरस आया हताशा के भाव से उसने अपने सर पर हाथ फेरा और रोहित को समझाते हुए बोला:
"हाँ, लेकिन चिराग के पापा कलेक्टर है और वो......"
रोहित इतना सुनते ही उत्सुक हो उठा और सम्राट की बात खत्म होने से पहले ही बोल पड़ा
"मतलब कलेक्टर बनने के बाद SC, GENERAL हो जाता है।"
सम्राट के ओछे जातिवाद को ये शब्द मानो खुली चुनौती थे। उसने रोहित को गुस्से से देखते हुए कहा:
"उनके साथ रहेगा तो उन्ही की भाषा तो बोलेगा" और वहाँ से चला गया।

'मैं'

किसी समझाइश का तलबगार नहीं हूँ
मैं बीमार हूँ, लाचार नहीं हूँ।
रंगीन पेजों का अखबार नहीं हूँ
मैं खबर हूँ, प्रचार नहीं हूँ।
हर किसी को भाए वो विचार नहीं हूँ
मैं मुफ़लिस हूँ, बेकार नहीं हूँ।
राजनैतिक दासता का शिकार नहीं हूँ
मैं खुद्दार हूँ, चाटुकार नहीं हूँ।
तुम्हारी कहानियों का किरदार नहीं हूँ
मैं कलाकार हूँ, अदाकार नहीं हूँ
बाज़ारों में बिकता सरोकार नहीं हूँ
मैं दोस्त हूँ, रिश्तेदार नहीं हूँ।
स्वार्थ लक्षित परोपकार नहीं हूँ
मैं अवाम हूँ, सरकार नहीं हूँ।

Who Is She?

She is not your sister, She is not your wife,
Stop discussing her, Do something in your life.
She is not your authority, She is not your claim,
Stop materialising her It's a matter of shame.
She is not a servant She is not a slave,
Stop ordering her Learn how to behave.
She is not your cloths She is not your tucker
Stop discriminating her On the basis of her color.
She is not your wealth She is not your property
Stop watching her Like a craving thirsty
She is not in coffin She is not bare
Stop telling her What to wear.
She is not a victim She is not an accuse
Stop judging her And try to muse.
She is not a drum She is not an instrument
Stop beating her It's a sign of impotent.

REETA

ग़र भूल जाऊ कोई पंक्ति मैं,
मैं खुद का ही स्मरण कर लिया करती हूँ..
खामोशियों को शब्द बना,
मैं अपनी ही कहानी कविता में पिरो दिया करती हूँ..
कविताएँ भाँति भाँति की, हर अहसास का बखान करती हूँ,
अजी मैं कोई प्रख्यात कवयित्री नहीं,
मैं खुद को ही अपनी कृत्यों का स्रोत बना लिया करती हूँ..।।

ज़िन्दगी है आपसे

यूँ तो कुछ ख़ास इल्म नहीं हमे मोहब्बत का,
ग़र सोचूँ क्या है मोहब्बत ?
तो आपके ख़्यालों से रूबरू हो जाते हैं।
यूँ तो ख़ुशगवार नहीं हमे काटे,
ग़र चाहूँ साथ आपका,
तो छालों को नकार ये पग आपकी ओर बढ़े चले जाते हैं।
यूँ तो कुछ ख़ास नाता नहीं हमारा सब्र से,
ग़र करना चाहूँ दीदार आपका,
तो ये निग़ाहें मिलन आस को अश्रुओं में बटोरे चले जाते है।
यूँ तो हर कोई शख़्स गवारा नहीं हमे,
ग़र मग़रूर हैं आपके इश्क़ में,
तो समझिये "जाना"- ज़िंदगी है आपसे,
वरना ये रूह से रूह के रिश्ते सिर्फ़ बातों से नहीं निभाए जाते हैं।

बाबा (पिता)

अपने ही वज़ूद से हार रही है, ज़िन्दगी की धूप में जल रही है,
बाबा तेरी बिटिया तेरी छाँव को तरस रही है..
ये नज़रे तुझे ढूंढते हुए हताश हो रही है,
इन आँखों में जैसे तेरी यादें अब सिसकियाँ ले रही हैं
बाबा ये निग़ाहें तेरी एक झलक को तरस रही है..
लफ़्ज़ों को ख़ामोशियों में बहा रही है,
मुस्कान भी जैसे, तेरे न होने की लाचारी दिखा रही है,
बाबा मेरी नन्ही सी दुनिया तेरे दुलार को तरस रही है..
गैरों में अपनों को तलाश रही है,
स्वार्थी दुनिया में, नन्हें क़दमों से लड़खड़ा रही है,
बाबा तेरी बिटिया, आज तेरी ऊँगली पकड़ चलने को तरस रही
है..।।

तू हौंसला रख

तू हौंसला रख, रात ग़र सामने है,
तोह सूरज भी सुबह दिखलाएगा.
माना कि जल रही मशाल सी ये ज़िन्दगी,
यही मशाल तेरा पथ प्रदर्शक बन जाएगा,
यूँ तो राह में कई ख़ार तेरे,
मग़र तू खुद में यूँही निखऱ आएगा,
अभी कई इम्तेहां है बाकी,
तू उम्मीदों का दामन पकड़,
एक दिन यही तेरी जीत का डंका बजाएगा,
तू हौंसला रख,
ये वक़्त भी तेरा कदरदान बन जाएगा..।।

SHWETA SRIVASTAVA

श्वेता श्रीवास्तव का जन्म झारखंड स्थित जमशेदपुर में हुआ। वह बहुत आत्मनिर्भर, उत्साही लड़की है। कहने को तो ये (b.com) 2 वर्ष की विद्यार्थी है। परन्तु इन्होंने इस छोटी उम्र में अपनी शायरियों और कविताओ से लोगो को चौकाया है। श्वेता ने हर विषयों पर कलम चलायी है। सकारात्मक सोच और एक अद्वितीय व्यक्तित्व के साथ। भगवान ने उन्हें शब्दों की शक्ति का उपहार दिया और आप इनके साथ आसानी से जुड़ सकते हो। वह अपने शब्दों और कल्पना की शक्ति को एक साथ रखकर भावनाओं और विचारों को व्यक्त करती है। आपकी जीवन तथा आपके जीवन में होने वाली परिस्थितियों का उसके शब्दों मेंआनंद लें।

"फ़ौज़ी"

धुप में उसने अपना पसीना बहाया है।।
और चोट लग जाये तोह मिट्टी का मरहम लगाया है।।
तब जा कर वो एक फ़ौज़ी कहलाया है।।
माँ की ममता को वो आँखो में भर कर उनकी गोद म एक सुकून की नींद सो कर आया है।।
अरे वो फौलादी तोह अपनी राखी तक खोल कर आया है।।
तब जा कर वो एक फ़ौज़ी कहलाया है।।
अपनी मोहब्बत को गले लगा कर अपनी उंगलियो से उसके चहरे पे मुस्कान बनाया हैं।।
तुम एक फ़ौज़ी की बीवी हो ये कह कर उसकी हिम्मत बढ़ाया है।।
तब जा कर वो एक फ़ौज़ी कहलाया है।।
माथे पे कफ़न बांध कर वो जंग के मैदान तक आया है।।
अपनी मौत को सामने देख कर भी वो मुस्कुराया है।।
तब जा कर वो एक फ़ौज़ी कहलाया है ।।
छाती चौड़ी कर कर वो सीने पे गोली खाया है।।
लहू-लुहान हो कर भी वो गर्व् के साथ "जय हिन्द" चिल्लाया है।।
तब जा कर वो एक फ़ौज़ी कहलाया हैं।।

"अधूरा प्यार"

अगर मिलना ही नही होता तोह प्यार होता ही क्यू है?
कुछ दिनों के सुकून के लिए उम्र भर का चैन खोता ही क्यू है?
हस्ती हुयी आँखो से अश्को को नाचाहत्ते हुए भी बहना ही क्यू है?
बाहर से खामोश होने के बाद भी अंदर एक तूफान सा उठता ही क्यू है?
सब कुछ जानते हुए भी लाचार मेहसूस होता ही क्यू है?
पता नही हर true love story में प्यार अधूरा ही क्यू है?

"हवाओ की शरारत"

ये हवाएँ अक्सर मुझे छु जाती हैं
और मेरी आँखे बन्द हो जाती है
नशा-सा छा जाता है
मेरा मन भी मदहोस हो जाता है
हवाओं का क्या है
ये तो छु के गुजर जाती है
गलती तो नज़रो की है
खुली आँखो से दिन के उजाले में भी सपने सजाती है
हर रोज खुद से खुद के मन में लिखती एक कहानी हैं
झूठ ही सही पर मिलने की आस हर रोज दिल में जगानी है
अजीब बात है जिंदिगी मेरी है
पर लिखी किसी और ने कहानी है
मेरी हो कर भी ये जिंदिगी लगती मुझे बेगानी है
कभी तो फुर्सतो का दिया जलेगा
इंतज़ार भी पूरा होगा कभी मौका मिले
तो उससे भी जरूर कह दूंगी
ये राधा आज भी अपने कृष्ण की ही दीवानी है

"भाई-भाई"

मेरी और मेरे भाई की *ज़िन्दिगी एक किताब है
जिसमे किस्से बेहिसाब है।।
इसमें पतंग उड़ाने से लेकर,
बीट बॉक्सिंग तक वाला प्यार है।।
एक दूसरे को समझाने से लेकर ,
किसी और के अकल ठिकाने लगाने तक को तैयार है।।
हम लड़े एक दूसरे से वो अगल बात है
पर कोई और अगर तुझे छू दे तोह एम्बुलेंस को उसका इंतज़ार है।।
और जब जब तुझे जरूरत होगी ,तेरा भाई हमेशा तेरे साथ हैं।।

ASHISH KESHRI

Ashish Keshri a guy frm Ranchi presently pursuing his MBA from IILM greater noida has a unique dexterity of weaving the words together that quiver with emotions and feelings that will surely remain enshrined in your heart. He has an ardent desire of writing a novel that will give wings to his imagination to soar the skies of success.

Lonely Love

Your name is now etched on my soul,
Want to embrace and never let you go for my heart you stole.
Let me bear your attitude let me alleviate your sorrows,
For who knows in my life there will be no tomorrows.
I may not be around or forever gone away,
Trust me our souls will touch each other in heaven some day.
Don't ever cry for me if I'm gone forever,
To embellish this face with smile will only be my endeavour.
For you deserve all happiness of life but agonies never.
You know how difficult it was to write with drenched eyes,
With trembling fingers and heart full of sighs.
As the sadness engulfs me emptiness shattered my life,
Whom should I listen to when mind and heart are in strife.
All the pain will vanish and I'll be absolutely fine,
Just walk along with me on the path of life holding hands of mine.
I know you love me but I love you more
Eyes overwhelmed with tears rolling straight to the floor.
When I'll leave this world the last thing I will do,
Holding the pictures of yours, I'll be waiting for you.
I'm holding back my tears but deep inside I wanna cry,
When I'll meet the Almighty I'll ask him why?

Mother's Glory

The basic calculation perhaps my mom never knew,
I ask her for one roti she'll always give two.
You understood what I want, long before I could talk,
From rocking my cradle you made me to walk.
When down with fever her caressing hands run through my head,
Mom your lap is much cosier than flower embedded bed.
Where to get those words which can describe
a mother's sacrifice gives everything her child asks for however may be the price.
Of all the relations, a mother child relation is best, robust and pure
Is there any suffering for a child which a Mother's love can't cure?
Always there for a child no matter how much she herself endures.
The pious feet of a mother even the Almighty adores.
With the blessings of a mother, the whole world will be yours
Nothing can compensate the pain you felt at my birth.
You are the reason behind my every breath, you brought me on this earth.
Whenever I'm distressed your cuddle make all the troubles go away
I know you do feel pain though you never say.
Your arms are the safest place I can ever find.
I know in all my success, you were always behind.
Words can never explain your worth
however I may extol,
My dear mom I owe you my life,
I owe you my soul.

If I make this ocean ink and the earth a paper,
Even then it's difficult to describe a mother's glory ever
ever ever....

Farewell

As you took your first step in college,
The pinnacle of fun; the abode of knowledge,
Nicknames for all; who remembers friends' names,
Never worry for the punishment when everyone is ready to take the blames
Always on the look out for uninvited parties to attend,
Much time in theatres students love to spend.
Attending lectures of professors is the useless thing they find,
Never find it their business then why to mind.
During school days every girl seems to be our sister,
Now breakup and patch up is a tradition of every trimester.
Procrastination is in the blood till the deadline knocks the door
Less of assignments and holidays we demand is more.
Sleeping till 10; to break their slumber you need water to pour.
Some find it a nightmare and fun and thrill for others,
Never know 1st year strangers will be best pals like brothers.
Tussle and scuffle; love or hate and betrayal or debate,
Mess food always sucks; less in stomach more you'll find in plate.
Finding students in class so funny it sounds,
Girls' hostel is their temple; students will circumambulate around.
Will go to any to extent to get the concert passes,
From the excuse of high fever to bunking classes.
College life is about loudining the cheers;
facing the fears and also for the tears ,

As the gear of time accelerates, arrives the farewell, though everyone celebrates it;
but with anguish their hearts yell.
At that moment everyone wishes to stop the time,
Wanna be life prisoners of college; if it is a crime.
But the tradition continues and we drift apart,
Embracing the precious memories with drenched eyes and sobbing heart....

Girl Of My Story

"All the fantasies you hold will surely come true,
for the girl in my story has always been you".
" You listened to my laughter you listened to my cry,
you pacified the sobing heart and let the tears to dry ".
" My heart is full of scars; people gave ,
nothing else it can store.
The pain is becoming unbearable, can't endure anymore".
" I miss you every moment every second of the day,
you know the pain of being apart or do I need to say?"

MEHERE DARAKSHAN

Mehere:

Uncomplicated girl with amorous thought born in quitest bittercold january, Energetic, kind, happy, naughty.Daughter of her baba. Lover of freedom, fun and fantasy, Believer of love and humanity, Who enjoy to play with words, explicit her hearty feelings and strength of her conception, Who wishes that every person she loved always blessed with happiness, Who dreams to see her mumma's ecstasy, Resident of silver City , Cuttack Possessing lucid thoughts

-Darakshan-

Devastating Society

Our hearts were enclosed separately
The keys were lost...
Our religion were different,
Was it's our fault???
He used to worship in temple.
She used to pray in mosque.
The way to temple, mosque were same.
But just ALLAH and BHAGWAAN were different by there name.
Both hearts cried to be together.
Knowing that there fate doesn't allow it further.
Now, society had a smile.
But both wanted to go a mile.
As it's time to be together and fearless.
Let's prove the society they were not shameless.
Society tried alot to divide their hearts into two region.
They were willing to fly like free pegion.
Her ami claimed that he manage to learn the gita.
His maa said that she recite the quran.
How silly was the religion??
Although they were out of these vision.
All these matters were always discussed by everyone.
But to remove these rubish tradition there stands no one.
Theme of the content was still missing.
Why don't we try to solve it as blessing.

Khayal-e-Bayaan

Khamosh laab hai,
jhuki hai nazree,
dilo mein yeh arzoo nai nai hai.
Yeh haal jo dil ka hai,
mohabbat ke izhar honese rosan hua hai,
dilo mein yeh ahsaas nai nai hai.
Abhi to khamoshi guftagu ke beech thehri hai,
jo gehri hai,
dilo mein yeh chahat nai nai hai.
Khusnuma mahol hai bahar ,
khusbu se bhara hai gulsan yaha,
dilo mein jasbaat nai nai hai.
Abhi na aayegi ninde,
nahi sukoon milega,
lehza bata raha hai,
dilo mein yeh mohabbat nai nai hai.
Kudrat ne kya nawaaza,
jo chehre per tabassum chai hai,
dilo mein yeh ulfat nai nai hai..

PRAGYASHREE CHOUDHURY

A sixteen year old teen from Assam who's just learning and growing and is yet excited to bring out the thoughts and expressions of her that are in actual related to all of the same age .

Have A Break!

Thoughts, jumbled up!
Words,fumbled up!
Voices, always letting you feel low,
So, you too are going through the same thing?
Yeah, I know.
Your pace, that got lost in the race,
Your actions, that turned feeble in this age,
Your mind, that's somewhere lost in the maze
Your spirit, that isn't able to come out of the cage.
But, that's the fact and that's the sign
, Everyone out there is in the same line,
A bit broken, and with some type of ache,
But hold on and calm down,
Just have a break!!
Sit under the clear sky and talk to the stars,
Maybe that's how you can know,
that life has much more to count.
The clouds that adds prettiness to your soul,
the moon that might tell you about all your goals,
The entire universe that'll smile back to you,
Knowing the importance of your hue.
And then you'll stand up again,
you'll bloom again, you'll grow again
, You'll swim across the seven seas,
Leaving behind all your pain.
Just hold on for a second and take a break,
As destiny has got a lot to give
and a lot for you to take.

Dear Long Lost Best Friend

There were a lot who came and went. There were a lot who lost and gained. Some tried their best to mould me while others never left a chance to break me. And then, there was you. There were 'we'. Who were we? Friends? Best friends? Lovers? Neither of us actually have the answer to it. Maybe, we were more than all these. Just more than all these tags. Maybe, a bond that actually can't be defined in words. From sharing laughters to cries, from sharing desserts to fries, we were together, just in all ways we could know. From discussing sorrows and pains , to ending with the pleasures of achievements and gains, yes, you were there. You of course were my main. Did you even notice your own way? The way you are created? The magic that you got had always attracted me towards you. You knew my mental traumas as well my physical scars and of course you were the one who always used to say me "Stop studying all the time you nerd!" Remember the days when we talked about forever, even after knowing it as a wrong concept? Remember the days when we planned to get old altogether? Remember the times when you crushed every problem of mine with just a smile? Do you even remember, that "we" too existed? We did, we of course did. Rather, we once had the most beautiful bond that everyone could even share. But, we too fell apart, those promises too turned out to be fake, the sounds of the laughs faded and you drifted away. I won't blame you this time. Maybe, I was just not been able to cope up. The way we fell apart , maybe, my efforts were not enough to let you stay with me here. I couldn't explain neither could I express anymore. Maybe somewhere, this is something not fair. Something unwanted, something undone, just much more than a heartbreak. You knew my broken parts, you helped me to pick up my shattered life, but,now? See, I am still living, um yeah, without you to be honest. But, there isn't anyone anymore who could easily catch my fake happiness. Who could actually make me grow again, who could actually make me flourish again. To be a part of joy and happiness again. I still miss your voice, your 'lame jokes', your smile and your eyes, the shitty crush talks that once did shy. You are now there somewhere in your own world, in your own fantasy. But, you know what? The soul that's here resting In my body still prays for your well being. I still hope you'll be back one day and also bring back me to myself. I still hope we'll turn into kids again, dreaming of our dream land, our fantasy. And maybe someday, we'll shine bright again with you opening your shoulders wide, calling me to rest in that home inside. Maybe someday! You are missed. You are loved. Take care ~Your long lost....

Swati Priya

Swati Priya an idealistic, ambitious girl born in Jamshedpur in the late month of winter.She is too expressive, motivating girl with full of calibre. She's kind of girl who puts up her everything into writing. Being a student of English honour's she gives all her efforts in order to express herself in finest manner.Yet she is also a charismatic personality with full of creativity .She said"Don't bend, don't get suppressed,just be flawless".
##Be Creator
##Be Flawless.

Raise Your Voice

Raise your Voice!Raise your voice asked my soul,
Stop being insane foul.
Show up your humanity;
Vanish all others vanity,
Boycott others cruelty.

Can't you hear me! Can't you hear me!
Every man seems glowing and growing in them;
Only pushing themselves into their materialistic muddle.
Slowly and steady they are giving rise to violence,
Ignoring them becoming so indifferent to other's silence.

How can they utter so cold-hearted?
Can't you see females are the one who gave you birth
,voice!
Serve you as her son, Adulthood to maturity and now you
all be as 'so called Gentleman',
Showing your capacity.

Damini!Nirbhaya!Ashifa
Victim of cravers brutality,
Violent shades of insanity.
Melting the hearts of humanity,
Reducing the faith of generosity.

Burning women/girl with bottle of acid;
Their skin starts to leave their bone,
How can a men be so placid?
Ruining an ambition of a girl
How can they act as a hurl?
Turning Lakshmi the victim into Lakshmi the warrior,

Leading her life without any shiver.

Women's are the blessed being by almighty,
If they can teach you wisdom as Saraswati Maa,
You can also perceive them as kaali Maa.
Being so alluring,adding up her shrewdness
Serving the whole world as:
"Maa","Mummy","Beti","Behen",by her jubilance;

Stop taunting women!
Don't threat their dignity;
Don't tear apart their
soul with your disgusting malignity.
"Raise Your Voice!Raise Your Voice"!

Nand Kashyap

Nand Kashyap a Guy With Extra ordinary Talent With His Words From Janjgir (Chhatisgarh).His Words Are Like Pearls And Whole Poetry Is Like Garland Basically They Are Beautiful.

A Passionated Writer As Well as Awesome Storyteller Everyone Can Connect with him easily. His Words Are Like "It's Mine Story". The words directly touches the heart & soul sometimes I am feeling like my inner feeling convert into words throw which I can tell my pain, happiness, sorrow and joy everything. He is very optimistic and kind his words are just unique and in a way of parody like a heart has its rhythm of lub-dub.His One Of Best Lines Are

"Sard Raat Maddam Hawa,
Ek Hath Me Jaam Dusre Me Kalam Bahoo Me Tum
Esay Me Ek Ghazal Likhna Hai Hume...."

Your Messed Up

All Problems I faced
Although Everything Was Going Well But You Messed..
. I Was Happy In My life Your Presence Made Me More Happier,
When I Am Sad You Are Not Near
Why You Did Fake Promises Dear...
Making You Smile Not Letting You Cry,
Dancing In The Dark , Laughing Under The Blue Sky...
Everything Was Fine Suddenly, You Turned Like Another Face Of Coin..
All Problems I Faced
Although Everything Was Going Well But You Messed...
Everything Was Transparent Between Us ,
No More Secrets To Discuss,
New Friends And You Got Changed...
You Are On Cloud Nine,
Ah Don't Ever Worry About Me I Am Fine...
But Sometime I Miss Our Silly Talk's,
Sometimes I Miss Our Long Walks,
Sometimes I Miss Your Habit Of Teasing Me,
Sometimes I Miss Your Habit Of Missing Me ,
Sometimes I Just Miss You...
It's Not About Love Hurts,
It's About Our Friendship Didn't Worked..
All Problems I Face Although Everything Was Going Well But You Messed..

Accha Hota

Kuch Waqt Aur Theher Jate To Accha Hota,
Chai Bana Rakha Hai Humne Pi Kar Jate To Accha Hota...
Rango Ko Bhi Lagta Hai Waqt Diwaro Par Dhalne Ke Lie,
Hum Bhi Sath Theher Kuch Waqt Bitate To Accha Hota...
Sarfarosh Hokar Maine Tumse Sare Raaz Keh Die,
Tum Bhi Apna Kuch Raaz Batate To Accha Hota...
Hawao Ka Fasala Bhi Mujhe Munasib Nahi,
Humare Darmiyaan Ye Hawaye Bhi Na Hoti To Accha Hota ...
Log Chand Ka Pata Puchte Rahe Jaana,
Log Tumhe Khidki Se Jhakta Dekh Lete To Accha Hota...
Tumhare Akho Me Alag Hi Noor Hai,
Kash Hum Tumse Akh Mila Pate To Accha Hota...
Shrab Nahi Pi Hai Maine Aj Tak,
Tumhre Hoto Ka Zaam Lagate To Accha Hota...
Tum Itminan Se Meri Ghazale Sunte Jao,
Tumpar Likhi Hui Ghazalon Par
Tumse Hi Wah Wahi Luta Pate To Accha Hota...
Tumme Bachpana Besumar Hai aur Khubsurti Bhi,
Tum Thoda Muskura Aur Dete To Accha Hota...
Jana Tumse Ishq Hai Hume
Alfaz Thaam Jate Hai Zuban Par
Tumhe Dekhne Ke Baad,
Kash Ye Alfaz Zuban Se Riha Ho Jaye To Accha Hota...

Chai Bilkul Tum Si Hai

Thodi Garam Thodi Kadak Thodi Sawali Si Hai,
Ye Chai Na Bilkul Tum Si Hai...
Kabhi Chai Ki Patti Ko Doodh Me Uchalte Dekha Hai,
Maine Sukoon Ko Bs Ek Pyale Me Bharte Dekha Hai...
Maine Safar Ki Tayari Kr Li Hai ,
Haa Jaana Tharmas Me Maine Chai Bhi Rakh Li Hai...
Kisey Bs Ek Cup Meri Puri Jannat Sama Jati Hai,
Jab Bi Chai Dekhta hu Mujhe Tumhari Yaad Ati Hai...
Jaana Kaise Hui Thi Humari Mulakaat ,
Kya Tumhe Humari Peheli Chai Hai Yaad,
Tumne Chai Mere Lie Banaya Tha, Aur Maine Tumpe Gawaya tha...
Tumne Na Meri Zindagi Sawar Di Hai,
Jaise Kise Ne Chai me Elaichi Dal di Hai...
Jaana Ye Humre Darmiyan Ye Fasle Kam Kr Do,
Cup Khali Ho Gyi Hai Zara Kettli Se Tum Chai Bhar Do...
Kaisey Btau Ki Tum Meri Kya Ho,
Jisey Chai Me Ghuli Cheeni Sa Mitha Ehsaas Ho....
Talab Tumari Hoth Ki Ho To Chai Se Bhara Pyala Choom Leta Hun, Log Khete Hai Bs Ek Se, Mohabt hoti Hai ,
Pehele Tum Aur Dusre Me Mai Chai Keh Deta hu...

Endlessly

I Care About You And Will Care Endlessly
Loving You Is Ok But Your Ignorance Hurts Endlessly...
If U Feel Hungry I Will Get U Packet Of Chips
If U Cry I Am Gonna Kiss Your Lips...
I Want U To Smile All The Time,
If U Need Take All Of Mine..(All=Smile)
Before Touching Your Hands ,
I Want To Touch Your Soul,
Love Is Not About Body And All...
Before Kissing You Lips I Wanna Kiss Your Forehead,
Love Is Not About Using And Moving Ahead...
Love Is All About Caring Endlessly,
And I Care About You And Will Care Endlessly...
Our First Meet I Got My Final Love,
I Give You My First Priority From All The Above ...
Forget Your Dark Past Let's Make A Bright Future
Not Everyone is Same U Should Remember...
You Are Childish And Dumb As Well,
I Don't Want Ppl Push U to the Hell...
I Want To Care You In Every Situation ,
Don't Feel My Love As Infatuation...
I Love You And Will Love Endlessly,
Whether The Ocean Dry Or The Moon Gets Disappear
Eventually, I Don't Care Am Gonna Love You
Endlessly......

Maa

Barish Ki Bundoo Ko Zameen Par Girte Dekha Hai,
Maine Maa Ko Sirf Bindi Laga Kar Sawarte Dekha Hai..
Aksar Wo Mere Lie Papa Tak Se Ladti Hai,
Kabhi Kabhi Papa Ki Jeeb Se Chori Kar Wo Meri
Khawaishe Puri Karti Hai..
Aj Maa Ka Pallu Unke Hath Me Kuch Jyda Dhaka Hua
Tha,
Pas Ja Kar Dekha To Unka Hath Jala Hua Tha..
Wo Muskura Kar Wo Apne Sare Dard Chupa Leti Hai,
Aye Khuda Esi Kitab Bta
Jisme Maa Bayan Hoti Hai..

Pen_The_Creative

An 18 year old girl struggling to make a place for herself in this world full of people who likes to put up a pretense. Since people failed her pen and paper became her best friend and that's how it all started.

The Beautiful Dark

The crimson red sky
Which was illuminated by the setting sun
The twilight adding more colors to its beauty
Mesmerised, people vowed awestruck
And their movements halted to admire the nature.
Then, the sun came down and darkness enveloped the sky
The stars shined brightly,
Gladly portraying another shade of beauty
But sadly, it was just darkness that the people saw
Because to them dark was not beautiful.

A Mirage of Love

Once I thought you were mine
But, you showed me that you weren't
I was fine with it and ready to move on
But, you came back to give me a ray of hope.
Lighting up my entire world I lost myself yet completely,
waiting for you You came again...
But to dig my grave
This time I was firm not to fall
Still you managed to push me off
I fell! Killing all my sweetness
And I lost the innocence I had.
I thought you teached me how to be brave
But, little did I know that you were breaking me down
I looked up to you for your support But,
like a mirage you deceived me of all.

Devil's Love

He devoured her whole Out of jealousy,
Tasting his jealousy Her heart skipped beats,
Like that of a young girl.
He marked her his,
Both knew that the possibility was zero
But still, she promised him To always stay his'.

Difficult To Get Through The Times

Difficult to get through the times, when no one was by your side.
The entire world has fallen apart into pieces and we are clueless as to where to begin.
Life was hard yet moving, we were soft but still standing.
Never ending ripples of emotions arouse, no matter what we tried,
the calmness was never restored and chaos descended as a friend in our lives.
Hard to believe yet the truth of life, it taught us to keep moving on.

SOHINI GHOSHAL

Sohini Ghoshal, born to the land of Tagore has an immense attraction towards short stories and novels. She has completed her schooling from Loreto Convent,Asansol and is currently pursuing her graduation from Amity University,Noida. Apart from writing, she also takes immense interest in music. She is the only child of her parents and aspires to become a writer and a singer.

The Unheard

The Proposals

Mrs. Sharma was extremely worried and almost desperate now to get her only son married, as he has already come of age as per "societal norms". Vaibhav Sharma, an IIT Delhi graduate, now working in an MNC in New Delhi, is the all hyped up groom being talked about and also owing to his current situation the most eligible bachelor of Champaran. From matrimonials to local pandits to random neighbours, none left unattended. Mr. Sharma passed away when Vaibhav was fifteen, liver cancer it was. The house seemed more like a placement cell taking interviews of a plethora of candidates. All this takes place when Vaibhav was on a fifteen day visit to Champaran. He was that panel member of the interview board who is forced to be a part of this otherwise tedious process, alongside his mother and uncle. He was almost lost throughout the whole process and his family was too busy to notice this. He kept himself either buried in his cell phone or a newspaper or magazine, not actually consuming the content , rather covering up his feelings. Finally, his stay comes to an end and Vaibhav leaves for Delhi, with a sense of content and relief hovering over his face. His mother obviously urged him to stay longer, at least until their project hits the finish line. But this could not be done, even if possible.

The Dilemma

The Champaran-New Delhi express is delayed by five hours and this was making Ishaan so anxious that it was his seventh cup of cappuchino and third packet of Lay's. Coming from a South Delhi background, waiting in a platform like this was not his thing. He could have sent his driver, but that would be under normal circumstances. Finally the announcement echoes through the station "Train no 413325 Up, Champaran-Delhi Express is shortly arriving on Platform no 13", a sense of relief! Vaibhav climbs down his coach and hugs Ishaan. It was more intense than the usual. They quickly book an Uber and head towards their apartment in Safdarjung. Ishaan was like an over enthusiastic mother enquiring over his child's journey and all other details. Vaibhav was somehow lost, blankly staring at the road ahead with rhythmic nodding, like a four year told toddler. Finally Vaibhav ushers, "Why is it that you keep on asking me the same questions over and over again, it was just a ten hour long train journey, for God's sake!". Silence prevailed thereafter with no follow ups. As soon as they reach their place, Vaibhav said, "I am tired, I need rest. Will catch up later." "Let's go out for dinner tonight, they have a new outlet of Pind Baluchi recently opened across the street", said Ishaan with his everlasting excitement, not dead yet. Vaibhav nods and retires to his room. They are all ready for their dinner outing with Vaibhav in a better mood. May be it was the journey that exhausted him, thought Ishaan. They order authentic Punjabi cuisine, their all time favourite and sat there ,with almost only non verbal exchanges taking place. The food arrives and still no sign of excitement on Vaibhav, this was unacceptable. Ishaan finally breaks the ice.

"So, How's Aunty?", Ishaan asked.
"Oh! She must be great, I'm sure",Vaibhav replied.
The uneasy atmosphere still prevailing.
"V!", Ishaan strengthens his voice "Spill it!"
Vaibhav almost about to cry, speaks in a quivering voice, "My mother wants me to get married. She is actively hunting for girls. Twenty five down and still counting."
Ishaan, with a straight no expression on his face, asked "What do you want?" though he already knows the answer.
"You know what I want!", said Vaibhav, raising his voice.
A veil of defeaning silence prevails again. They finish their dinner within that veil, pay the bill and start walking directly towards their apartment. "Did you tell her?" asked Ishaan, his eyes lifeless, staring straight ahead. "Is it that easy?", glared Vaibhav. The discomfort in the air was visibly bright. "I don't know what to do? I can not cancel, but only delay it", said Vaibhav with that same quiver in his voice. "You are an adult, you can stand for your own decisions and you know I am always with you." Ishaan said with an authoritative voice. "Do you want to me to run away?", Vaibhav asked, almost puzzled. "I don't deny that, either. We always knew this would happen sooner or later and talking to them was not even an option", said Ishaan , still with that blank stare ahead. Vaibhav, looks at Ishaan, almost finding it difficult to register. No further exchanges take place. Both finished their night chores and was ready to retire to their rooms when Ishaan suddenly stopped by the corridor and said, "Our love was never easy, was it?" The following days were almost far from normal with little or no exchanges between them. Vaibhav's phone was apparently filling up with portfolios of female canditates from all over the country. His heart was always crying and eyes lifeless. The daily routine was becoming more

exhausting – get up, have breakfast , office, back home, dinner, sleep and the cycle repeats. One morning, Vaibhav gets a call from his mother that almost make him collapse but he manages to stand. Ishaan rushes to him, comforting him and when he looked at the phone call, he somehow knew the reason behind the reaction. "I don't want to do this. Why do we need to label every thing?", this time Vaibhav cried like never before. They both lay there for a long stretch of time when finally Ishaan spoke, "I will not say anything. Just remember, if you decide to turn back, I'll be waiting for you at the very spot." This time it was just a one-way ticket to Champaran owing to the circumstances. Ishaan as usual accompanied him to the station. Vaibhav boarded the train. This time there was no hug and unfortunately the train was not delayed.

Let's Get Married!

The Sharma family was more busy than excited. The cards were distributed, functions scheduled and yes, a girl selected. "Tara Gupta d/o Ramcharan Gupta (retired IPS Officer), single child, B.A. in Economics, Delhi University, Brahmin, works as a teacher in Delhi Public School, Safdurjung" the portfolio said. The arrangements were at it's peak. The sweet vendors, flower men, music groups, dancers, all decked up for a big fat Indian wedding. Vaibhav was both sad and happy. The shine that sparkled in his mother's eyes, was a long lost treasure. Never before had he witnessed this sparkle. The ceremonies started and Vaibhav was lost in another world where he and Ishaan were leading a happy independent life. The ceremonies were tedious that ended just before midnight and so did his dream. They left Champaran in an SUV with a placard hanging above the number plate. "Happily ever after" it read.

What Next??

Indistinct chattering on a Sunday morning filled every corner of the 3BHK apartment in Safdarjung Enclave road. Its been two years since Vaibhav got married and it is their anniversary today. His family had decided to pay a visit to shuffle up their daily routine. All these years have been just fine. Vaibhav has tried to preoccupy himself with all soughts of extra projects and office tours. He respects Tara and her decisions. Overall a happy family. Despite all naggings, his mother convinced them for a small dinner party at a nearby restaurant. This obviously burst a wave of excitement throughout the whole house, except for Vaibhav. But he anyways does not decline. It was 8 in the evening. The members were getting ready accompanied by all soughts of clitter clatter around the house. Suddenly Vaibhav's cell phone beeps, he did not pay attention. They all climbed up the SUV and Vaibhav reached for his cell phone to turn on the google maps, when he read the message. "Hey V! How's everything? I am flying down to Delhi for an official tour. Let's catch up if you are free. Location – Pind Baluchi, Safdarjung Enclave"

PRANJALIKA SABAT

PRANJALIKA SABAT,is a Physicist by profession,a poet and essayist by passion and an enthusiastic social worker. She has been a member of a zero fund NGO. She has been writing since her early schooldays. She mostly writes on social issues,life lessons,romance and erotica. Being an erotica writer, her words are so crafted that they never crossed the thin line between sensuality and vulgarity. According to her, writing your heart keeps it healthy and less troubled. "Pouring all that is bothering you and moving on" is her matra of life. She is currently pursuing her Masters in Electronics from Ravenshaw University ,Cuttack . She has been associated with Story Mirror as a 'Literary Captain". Her blogs glorify the typical hidden human nature ,the day to day life, teenage romance and relationship issues. You can get to her blog describing the harsh reality of present ongoing lifestyle, with the link given below, http://thepoem9.wordpress.com
https://www.yourquote.in/pranjalikasabat

Kalam-

Mein kalaam hun ,akar chaahein jessa bhi ho,
hota sabke paas hun
Kabhi uss maa ka pehgam utar leta hun jiska beta dur ,
sarhad par desh ki rakshya karte huye mitti mein ghul jata hein.
Toh Kabhi school ke akhri dino mein uss dosti ka lafz ankit karta hun
unn kapdon pe jo ab phir kabhi na pehne jayenge.
Kabhi kabhi khujli bhi bhagata hun,
kabhi kisi bacche ke mathe pe bhi nishan gadd ta hun
toh kabhi haaton mein chotti bachiyon ke mehndi banata hun
Dafter mein logon se khoob kaam karwa ta hun.
Mein kalam hun
Jitne bhi aaye mere pratiduandi ,Kya "keypad" kya "voice keyboard",
aaj bhi ganpatti me uss bappa ke charno mein,mein hi hun.
Kabhi kabhi me uss nai si panapti pyar ka pehla toffa ban jata hun
toh kabhi guru diwas me guru ko bhenth ke liye pehli pasand.
Kabhi mein uss zaalim si mashuka ka dhokha baayan karta hun
toh kabhi uss bewafa darinde ka jisne masum si ladki ko shayeri ka bukhar de diya.
Kabhi kabhi mein ek rishte ki pavitrata ko mohar deta hun
toh kabhi meri ek boond syahi saath janmo wali pratigya ko tod dalti he.
Mein kalam hun
Kabhi kabhi mein uss pati ki kamzor yaadas ki nishani bhi ban jata hun

jo uski patni humesa pyar se uske shirt pocket mein rakh
detti he.
Toh kabhi mein unn kadvi yaadon ka saboot bann jata hun
kyun na rahun akhir uss dagabaaz premi ne
uske premika ko mujhe hi toh diya tha toffe mein.
Desh se desh ka rishta bhi mujh pe hi tikka he
meri ek syaahi ki boond se hi MoU ka safar shuru hota he.
Bhaajji ke hisab se lekar wagyanik ki khoj tak,
mera bhi upyog he.
Par afsos mujhe iss baat ka he ki
aaj bhi aese nanhe haat hein jo mujhe dhund ti he
par mera unn tak ya unka mujh tak pahunch ne me
abhi bhi waqt he. Mein kalam hu....

The Night Before My Divorce-

Language of love knocked in our eyes,
you sucked my lower lips
I felt it was the first time,
your fingers drowning into my clevage.
Your breath made me go crazy,
as if Aphrodite signing us to unite again.
Your eyes took my heart into galaxy of intimacy,
horizon of oxytocin broadened,
letting our egos to be packed in pockets
Smell of your saliva droved me to nurture your neck line
with my lipstick stains.
My incisors unbuttoned your shirt
and yours marked hickeys on my curves.
I felt your warm breath beside my lobe
your hands cherishing my bulks,
soon it took us to the land of holy lust.
Ice cubes sliding on my lower back
left my hatred behind the bars of love.
Once again it felt like loosing my virginity to the man of
my dreams.
A second later, you embraced me tight let my tears fall on
your tender skin ,
engulfed my pain with three magical words and that's what
I searched for years.
With each stroke of love
I screamed your name for I know there's nothing wrong
with us.
Just an illusion it was,not a snap of your infidelity
. I digged my nails onto your back
your screams too had the pain of losing us the next dawn.
With the rising sun

I found my vermilion box being a paper weight
to a note quoted "Don't we deserve a second chance?”

Indian Marriage Proposal:

GROUP DISCUSSION ,PI AND SELECTION:- The best part of an" INDIAN MARRIAGE" is it's the same as that of 100 years back or should I say it never ever changed.The only difference is the way of approach.Years ago we,the Women were questioned about our capabilities & now the same has been in continuation but in a different way .Moreover the wheels have turned with respect to gender i.e Mens are also going through the same procedure.Basically if we compare both the approaches we'll come across the similarities .So here's the complete G.D, P.I & Selection procedure from the earlier times and the latest ones.

- **AS** SOON AS A WELL EDUCATED BOY OF EVERY MIDDLE CLASS FAMILY CROSSES AN AGE OF 28/29,& A SILVER LINING ON TOP OF THAT i.e WITH A WELL SETTLED JOB ,THE GROUP DISCUSSION STARTS WITH WHAT ARE THE FUTURE SCOPES? IS HE ENGAGED ? OR HE HAS A GIRLFRIEND? OR SHOULD WE SEARCH FOR A BRIDE? ,WHEREAS IN CASE OF GIRLS THE ONLY THING THAT DIFFERS IS THE AGE ,THE SAME PHENOMENA HAPPENS WHEN A GIRL IS FINANCIALLY INDEPENDENT(IF NOT THEN ALSO NO ISSUES) AND THE AGE RANGE HERE STARTS FROM 25. WELL,THE PRITTY FINE OUTCOME OF THIS SO CALLED PRODUCTIVE GROUP DISCUSSION IS – "AN EYE ON THE CANDIDATE TO JUDGE WHETHER HE/SHE HAS SOMEONE SPECIAL IN HIS/HER LIFE".

- IF THOSE JUDGEMENTS RESULTS IN NON APPLICABILITY OF ENGAGED TAG,THEN THE 2ND PHASE OF COUNSELLING STARTS WHICH HAS A VITAL ELEMENT KNOWN AS REPRESENTATIVES /MEDIATORS /BROKERS .THEY HAVE BEEN GIVEN THE CONTRACT TO FIND A SUITABLE BRIDE/GROOM OF SOME VERY SORTED ELIGIBILITY CONDITIONS WHICH EVEN THE CANDIDATE IS NOT SO AWARE OF.AFTER SETTING UP A FORMAL MEETING WITH BOTH THE CANDIDATES ,THE BROKER GETS A COMPLIMENTARY LUNCH,BRUNCH AND SOMETIMES AN HONOURIUM.

- FURTHER WE MOVE TO THE P.I ROUND WHERE THE CANDIDATES GET THEIR DESIRED SPACE THAT TOO EVEN INTERRUPTED BY GRANNY LOOKING AT THEM SUSPICIOUSLY.THEN COMES THE SELECTION ROUND WHERE THE CANDIDATES ARE BOUND TO GIVE AN ANSWER EITHER YES/NO? AND IF BOTH OF THEM GOT SELECTED OR ELSE HAVE SELECTED EACH OTHER,THEN THE FINAL ROUND AGAIN STARTS FROM A 2ND PHASE GROUP DISCUSSION.

- PRECISELY SPEAKING THIS GROUP DISCUSSION STARTS WITH THE INVESTMENT IN THE PROPOSAL,LOCATION OF THE EVENT AND THE MOST IMPORTANT

ONE" FOOD" WHOSE FLAVOUR AND TEXTURE WOULD BE A MATTER OF DICUSSION FOR ALL THE AUNTIES AND UNCLES NEARLY FOR INFINTE TENURE. FINALLY THE EVENT TAKES PLACE WITH AROUND 3000 GUESTS OUT OF WHICH KNOWN MEMBERS RANGE FROM 300-400.

THESE GROUP DISCUSSION ENDS WITH RATIO OF THE NUMBER OF ENVELOPES,GIFTS RECEIVED TO THAT OF THE SAME ARTICLES BEING GIVEN TO VARIOUS GUESTS IN THEIR RESPECTIVE EVENTS.

Coming back to 2020, the procedure is the same but in a reverse order.The first phase starts with a group discussion with peers, so as to look for a guy to date with, then comes the selection & p.i which is the cherry on top of ice cream. I mean this is what have changed, at least now candidates are being perfectly interviewed to workout the company called "marriage".If all goes well then comes final selection call and a notice to the family that a candidate has been scrutinised. Further the same group discussion process as that of years ago starts on full phase and ultimately results with a flood of 4000 guests,unnecessary investments,expensive location,etc.But there's one person missing in 2020 procedure ,it is non other than broker/mediator but is it really, I don't think so ,for it has been in a form called social media & dating apps. Moreover the needs of society is different and what we do is a complete waste of our year old savings on those who are well privileged .Secondly, Is this what the young India wants?

ds

Kon yahan nahi he musafir batana zara aey duniawalon.
Kahin pet ki jwala ko bujhane
,kahin dur manzil ki talash mein sabhi yahan musafir he ek hi raah ke
Koi tanhai ko dur bhagane ke liye,
Zamane ki shor mein saathi dhundta he.
Koi betti ke haat mein mehendi lagane ki chah mein din bhar pheriwala banta phirta he .
Koi bette ko awal darja dilane ki asha mein ghanto majdoori ke raste par chalta he
Chanchal si premika ko ek jhalak dekhne ke liye,
Deewane ko har gali maholey mein chakar lagana hote he.
Kon yahan nahi he musafir batana zara aey duniawalon
Din bhar mandrati pakhsiyan ho
Yaa ho woh birj se bhhrun tak ka safar kon yahan nahi he
Musafir batana zara aey duniawalon sabhi yahan musafir he ek hi raah ke.

MAITRI LAL

Emotions that is echoed in form of words. Let emotions reach you, she being anonymous.

Heal Or Deal .

How to heal ?
Or even how to deal?
The only 2 things that we are never taught .
"Don't cry like an idiot."
" Don't laugh like a fool."
Stay quite & try being an intelligent one ,
As that is very cool.

It's not okay to fail,
You have to score the first position anyway,
You are absolutely worthless,
And here still ,
I am wasting ,
money on you no less.

Why are you late half an hour
You have to reach home fast ,
Even if you die on the road
That dosen't matter .
You are a slut ,
Be obedient & dont utter a word ,
As you will always be hurt .

Staying quite is the best thing ,
And that is actually your dignity ,
Dosen't matter whether you are : A male or a female ,
The place for your emotions ,
WILL ALWAYS BE HAPPILY,
RESTING IN HELL !

And still one question arises, Heal or deal ?

Neither of us knows the answer,
Nor even the procedure nor formula ,
To how to solve the mathematical structure!

Confusion it creates ,
Even causes destruction of emotions,
My dear elders ,
they are your children with a beautiful heart,
Please don't make them bleed ,
As even growing up they fall apart!

How To Believe In Your Existence?

Every single person , worships you
Every single person fights for you
They pray creating your idols in different form,
But today I want ask you a question:
Do you actually belong in any form?
If your existence was true ,
Then where were you?
When injustice to innocence was at it's height of its peak ,
Where were you when: gita , nirbhaya and many others needed you indeed ,
Where were you when innocent animals were killed by cruelty,
Where were you when humanity was losing its dignity,
Everyone says you created the world.
The supernatural power that exists,
You are the source of it all
When hiccups gets suddenly stopped people thank you as they believe ,
you did it all .
When someone gets saved from any small mishappenings,
They believe it was you who was seeing.
They perform so many rituals,
To please you in every way possible,
It's not that , that I don't have any faith in you,
But my mind question me ,
When someone actually needed you ,
where were you?
And how do I believe in your existence?
As I felt every time the lack of you needful presence!

BARNALI PRIYADARSHINI

Barnali Priyadarshini, just like her name she believes in painting the world with her poetries. She loves poetry, music, nature and everything that gives her peace. As She said- "Poetries are like elixir to this world and to our little criminal heart, heart that is fairly capable of destroying ourselves"..

Destiny

Time made best friends out of strangers,
It made us stronger,
Hope it will not make us strangers again,
Hope it will not break our hope again..
I want a old school romance,
I want you to hold my hand,
Go wherever you want,
Make friends with whoever you want,
But,But,But..
Remember not to leave my hand,
Just remember to hold my hand..
Love is not easy,
Neither it should be,
It's the best feeling in the world,
And best things comes with high price tags,
You gotta burn yourself in flame,
But love is not to be blame,
When your love is true,
You walk,
With all the pain you keep on walk..
Time will break us,
Then time will heal,
It's all in our destiny,
That's how I feel..

माँ

अब अक्सर आईने में खोई रहती है वो,
जब से सुना है अपनी माँ सी दिखती है वो।।

मोहब्बत

दुआओं में है मेरे वो, साजिशों में नहीं,
क्यों कि ज़िद नहीं वो मोहब्बत है मेरी।।

आंखें

अपनी आंखों को छिपाया न करो अब,
कि खुद को देखे जमाना हो गया है।।

उलझन

मेरी ये लटें उलझने को बेकरार है ,
एक बार फ़िर तेरी उंगलियों से सुलझने के लिए।।

ख्वाबों से हक़ीक़त

मेरे ख्वाबों को हक़ीक़त में बदलने लगे हो,
तुम मेरे जुल्फ़ें सवार के, मुझे बिगड़ने लगे हो।।

क्या ज़िन्दगी

जो ज़िन्दगी साथ छोड़ दे तो कोई गम नहीं,
जो ईसमे तू नहीं तो क्या ज़िन्दगी!!

रूह

ये मोहब्बत है जो रूह का प्यासा है ,
इंसान तो अक्शर जिस्म पे मर जाया करता है।।

रूहानी मोहब्बत

ये मोहब्बत है जो रूह का प्यासा है ,
इंसान तो अक्शर जिस्म पे मर जाया करता है।।

सूरज – चंद्रिका

अर्ध चंद्रिका सी में,
तू जलता हुआ वो सूरज,
खत्म होना मेरी किस्मत
और ढल जाना तेरी चाहत।।

गम- ए- हिज्र:-

गम-ए-हिज्र बेहिसाब थे,
आंखों में अश्क कम न थे,
होठों पे शिकवे अधूरे से थे,
पर गलत वो न गलत हम थे।।

PRIYANKA KUMARI

Priyanka is born in Patna , Bihar and raised in Jamshedpur, Jharkhand. She is a commerce student. She is passionate about writing quotes and poems. She uses them as a medium to express her love and pain and the social concerns. She admires Amrita Pritam, Robert Frost and Gulzar. And also likes art, crafts and designing. She loves her solitude and peace and dreams of visiting hill stations and cold places specially in northern India.

Tujhse Durr Jane Kie Soche Kyun

Tujhse durr jane ki soche kyun
Abhi to kitne hi khwabon ko sath mil kar pura karna hai,
Abhi to tujhse judi kayi armaan baki hai,
Abhi to hasraton se bhari kayi shaam baki hai,
Tere sath jo sunkoon or azaadi se guzre abhi
wo zindagi baki hai,
Abhi to khwabon ka jahan sajana baki hai,
Sukh dukh me har dam tera saath dena baki hai,
Abhi to manzil tk pahunchne se pahle safar ko khubsurat
banana baki hai,
Tujhse durr jane ki soche kyun?
Abhi to mere naam ko tmhare naam ke sath jodna baki hai.

Kya Mujhe Kabhi Samjha Hai Tumne?

Meri awaaz me jo hichak thi,
kya kabhi mahsus kia tha tumne?
Mere bezubaan shabdon ko,
kya kabhi samjhne ki kosish ki thi tumne?
Kya kabhi mujhe smajahne
ki kosish ki hai tumne?
Ye kaisi uljhan hai jo suljha nhi rahi ,
Ye kaise faslein hain hmare jo khatam nai ho rahi,
Muskurana chahti hoon ,
magar muskura nahi pa rahi,
Yaad to Bohat aatey ho tum,
Magar ab tumhe ye kah nai paa rahi,

Tumhe Jane Se Rokte Bhi To Kya Kah Kar Rokte?

Dil to kabka hi tut chuka tha,
use jodne ki kosish kab tak karte,
Rishta hmara tikha ho chuka tha,
usme hum mithaas gholne ki kosish kab tak karte,
Tum to pahle hi durr ja chuke the,
Ab hum tumhe paas rakhne ki koshish kab tak karte,
Tumhe jane se rokte bhi to kaise rokte ?

Samet lene do mujhe in haseen yaadon

Samet lene do mujhe in haseen yaadon,
in lamhon se kuch pahle kuch pal churane do ,
shaam hone se pahle udd ne do mujhe is neele gagan ke tale
, meri aankhon ke nam hone se pahle
thoda sa bas mujhe muskura lene do.

SOURABH JALAN

A Freelancer pursuing CA

Unwanted Change

As the storm will pass by,
A lot within and around will shatter.

The unwanted rat race will come to an end,

Whereas the importance of human survival will only prevail.

A lot of myths will definitely gets burst,

That it's not only money which can relieve human thirst.

Humanity though lately, but finally experience,

Ultimately it's nature whose will is final.

Entire world will be compelled to believe,

Some mysteries are there beyond human reach.

Now happiness should be the vision for future,

And it's Almighty's will where humanity surrendered.

BIDYASWINI SAHU

A medium sized fair girl with curly black locks and tiny brown eyes , precisely incarnated with abundant endurance and tranquility. Bidyaswini Sahu is a biology graduate from Utkal University, Bhubaneswar and currently pursuing her post graduate. Show casing her talent with meticulous attention to every stroke of her paint brush and every word from her pen, she proved herself to be a hopelessly realistic painter and deligent writer as well. She owned a number of certificates and trophies in field of knowledge and creativity which is now shinning like a crystal in her showcase. Atlast her respect for family and love to her friends adds like a cherry on the cake to her personality.

My Dad.

Scrolling down my memory lane,
I found one of the best man.
Since the time heading towards hospital,
Yet celebrating for a little girl...
Holding me possibly very close
Yet acting like mine adipose.
With some tears of joy in mind,
He loves me unconditionally like a blind....
Although he runs through out the day,
Still he waits for me to awake.
Sorry for all those sleepless nights,
But I always seen him fresh and bright....
Giggling at my small falls to weeping my fear,
I grew up seeing him sacrificing all that he bear.
Thanks for everything that you gave,
Thanks for knitting my dream wave....
You're the one who held me up and never let me fall,
You're the one who saw me though, though it all
Building my faith to letting for a flight,
You are the only one whom I love infinite....

मेरे दोस्त

दिल की किताब में कुछ तस्वीर लिए ,
जब झांका मैंने अपनी तकदीर में,
कुछ अजनबी मिले नसीब से,
मानो फरिश्ते उतरे हो ज़मीन पे।
कुछ अलग ही उनका नूर रहता,
मानो ऐसा लाखो मै वह कोहिनूर होता,
जस्बात के रास्ते मेरा दिल पिरोये वह अजनबी मेरा यार कहलाये।
बाते रखा करते है बड़ी तशाली से,
जुबा की नहीं आंखे पढ़ा करते करीब से,
तेज्जीब उनका रवैया रहता,
हर खुशी का यह मेरा जरिया बनता।
गीरू अगर तो आंसू उनके भी आए,
मेरे हर दर्द की मरहम वो बन गए,
फक्र नहीं घमंड है यह मेरे ,
कहा मिलेंगे दोस्त जैसे मेरे।
नादानियां इनका फितरत है,
लगी जो मुझे उनका आदत है,
खुदा उनका हर दुआ कुबूल करे,
शुक्रिया जो ऐसा दोस्त मुझे मिले।

ये दुनिया का दस्तूर ।

ये दुनिया का भी अजीब दस्तूर है
जहा चांद पास और अपने दूर है।
यहां बस पैसों का खेल है,
भाई भाई मै भी कहा कोई मेल है।
यहां बिकता हर एक एहसास है,
क्या कोई किसिका खास है?
लोग मानते उनको जिनका खिताब है,
सब तो यह समय का मोहताज है।
पैसों के पीछे तो सबने नींद खोई है,

एक गरीब बाप भी कितने सपने बोई है।
पेट के लिए सब रोते है,
आशु दिखता उनका जो खाली पेट सोते हैं।
दर्द तो वसीयत मै मिलता है,
खुशियों के तो मोल चुकाना पड़ता है।
मुस्कुराता तो जहा है,
खिल खिलाता तो बस वो नन्ही सी जान हा।

Some Quotes Of Life'

1. Fake love is just like a premature decision which makes us mature to have a true relation....

2. One that hurts you is not that he doesn't loves you it's just that yet he doesn't knows you....

3. Love is not what you lost or gain, It's all about what you leaned and faced....

4. The day you will stop understanding yourself, Is the day you will start loosing yourself...

RABEYA SARBAR

Rabeya sarwar Daughter of SA Raheman and sabera bibi Who enjoys reading,writing and teaching Who hates negative attitudes Who dreams wining the every competition Who is determine to make a difference in the live of as many people as possible Who values close relationship with her family,friends and students Who postgraduate in political science from utkal university Who live in salipur but truly misses dharmasala Lover of justice Who gives friendship easily Who is dedicated, creative and caring Who dreams that this year all her students will discove the joy of reading Who lovers of great book

Chicken Masala

Aaj.mamiji ki pair jamin per lagti nahi hai kuen ko unki nanad ki beti unki ghar ku arahi hair.mamiji use apni beti se v jyada pyar karti hain.oh jaldi se jhapat kar kitchen main kam main masgul hojati hain.daining table per khane ki sajawat karke oh unlogonki intejar main raha takti hain.thode dair main oh agaye . mamiji ki khusi ki thikane na samati.unlogonki swagat me liye oh apni anchal sambhal kar bhage bhage unke pas pahanch jati hain.phir kya kabhi damadji se sawal karti hain to kavi beti we.phir aisa ke khusi se ek hi sawal barbar puch baithti hain.isitareha kuch samaya bit jata hai phir mamiji khane ke liye jab dono ku bulati hain to beti bolti hai mamiji ap damad ku pahele khilado phir hum dono sath main khayenge,e sun kar mamiji sar ke isare se mangaye.jab damadji khane se farig hogaye to ab ye dono v khane my chal baithe.beti boli mamiji khane main kya banai hain? mamiji boli jo tu pasand karti hai jaise lemon rice, dahi ,chiken kasha, salad, amki achar bana hai.e sunkar beti ekaek bol uthi chiken kashaaa----.our phir uske ankho main ansu bhar aie.oho kuch sal pahele ke ghatna main kho gai.aisa lagta tha e kal ki bat hai, un dinon ki bat hai jab mamiji ehan biha hokar ain thi tab mama ki salary lakhon ki thi parantu mamiji ekek rupiya ke liye tarasti thi sach mano to oh bahat hi bure samaya ke sath chalti thin ghar badi se jal kuta se khana banati thi, oh v kya bhat our alu ki chatni se mamiji ki gujara hoti thi usper main unper bojh ban gayi thi isper v mamiji khus thin.mamiji bahut bar e samjhati thi ki beti tum apne ghar chali jao kuen mere sath is jahnum main raheti ho.per main har hal mamiji ki sache pyar ki khatir kavi nahi jati thi.phir ekdin main ne mamiji se jid kar baithi ki mujhe chiken kasha chahieye.mamiji Ku malum thi unke pas paise nahin hai phir v unhone mujhe dilasa diya ke bhagwan chahega to kal tum zarur khaogi.lakin mujhe yad hai mamiji ki ankho main tab ansu agai thi.phir subha hoi to mamiji hardin ki tarha apne kam main lagi thi tab v rajmistri ne akar bola ki sidi ghar ki kam hogi.mamiji han bolkar chali gain.per dimag main ek hi bat thi ke he bhagwan main Kahan se is bachi ku chiken kasha khilaon, tab v mistri ki awaz aie ki helper nahi aya hai , our oh cement, main balu milakar pani v dal chuka hai ab oh kaise akela e kam karpayega sar main hath rakh kar puchraha tha.mamiji is bat ku sunkar khule asman ki taraf dekhkar boli he bhagwan tu to meri prarthana sunli meri bachi aj zarur chiken kasha khaegi.phir kya mamiji akar mistri se boli mujhe tum per daya ati hai, dekho tum gali na suno babu ke pas se isiliye main ek idea sochi hun kind tum ku main kam main help kar dungi.per is bat ki bhanak kisi tak na pahunchegi , phir boli chalo oh jo helper ki rupaya tumhe dekar gaye the use mujhe dedo.mistri ne unhe helper ki rupaya mamiji ku lauta diya.tab mamiji khusi khusi se mere pas akar oh rupaya mujhe dekar boli ja jaldi se chikeh lea main banadungi the jaldi khalegi.usdin main v bahut khusi thi phir main our mamiji dono milkar chiken kasha banaye our main khub paith bhar kar khai thi.achanak se mamiji ki awaz per main apni duniya ku wapas aie mamiji bol rahin thi Kahan gum hogai thi? main mamiji ke gore gore chehere ku dekh rahithi our mere ankhon main ansu nikal rahe the tab oh phir se boli Pagli kuen rarahi hai , main boli mamiji kya tum us chikenwali bat ku bhul gayi ho . is chiken kasha mujhe khilane ke liye tum ku ek din mistri ke sath helper ka kam karna padha tha our aj bhagwan itna diya hai apku ki ap har din garibon Ku khana khilati hain . khud ki mahenat se aj ap lakhon main khelti hain,e sunkar mamiji uski ansu mitate mitate khud v ropadi our boli bhagwan ke sath raho Sav kuch thik hojata his.

Ek Saheed Ki Beti Ki Pukar

Ring ring ring baje landline ki ghanti
Khusi Khusi se munni daudi sunke Phone ki ghanti
Hello Papa! Mein tuhmari munni
Jo Kehti hoon Kyun samajhte ho
ki mein tumse Naraaz hoon
Aaj hume bahut siddat se yaad ati hai tuhmari
Tuhmari judaai se bimar hai yeh Munni
tuhmari Munni ko pakde roti hai mummy
Zarokatar Ankhon ki ansoon ki jharna nehi rukti
Ek Baar Ashcharya se munni mummy ko Dekhti rehjati hai
Aakhir baat kya hai munni sawal Karbethti hai
Dhadakte Dil kampkampte zubaan se mummy kehti hai
Aaj kewal Tu nehi Sara desh papa ko Yaad karta hai
Simant me chinna se ladai karte karte Saheed Woh ho gaye
desh ko Surakshya dete dete Apni Khun ki aakhri bund tak
Woh Ladte hi rahe Garv se
yeh desh unhe saheed karar Diya hai
Mujhe Kuch nehi samajh me ata hai
mummy apki baat Sidhe sidhe ish waqt mujhe Karni hai
Papa se baat Dhundo mat munni Papa bahut door Chale gaye hain
Phir Kabhi hamare paas laut ke anewale Nehi hain
Aahein bhar Kar roo ro Kar Munni boli
mummy ko Kahaan gaye papa
mere Yaad Kya nehi ata unko
Dress, khilone, chocolate bhare bag kahaan gaye
Humme bhulake khayal kahaan aapke kho Gaye
Papa Apne wada jo Kiya tha mujhse
Corona se nipat Kar miloge mujhse
Per mere samajh me ata nehi Koun sach bol raha hai
Nehi Chahiye mujhe Kuch Bas aapko laut ke ana hai..

Guru ki Mahima

Guru ki bhumika hamare jivan mein ek gurutva Purna mahatva rahte aaye hai. kahate Hain Guru ke bina Gyan nahin hai aur Gyan ke Bina koi mahan nahin hua hai Sabse pahle Guru to hamari pita Mata hai ham log har pal kuchh Na kuchh Sikh paate Hain Guru Keval ek hi nahin hota balki hamare jindagi mein Jo bhi hamen kuchh sikhate Hain hamare Guru vahi hote hain chote mote durghatna usse bhi hamen kuchh sikhane milta hai sach kaha jaaye to Guru ke bare mein vyakhya karna Keval kasht nahin balki asambhav hai. Guru hua hai jo hamesha ke Marg par chalna sikhata hai hamare Priti ko vah murchit karte hain anjane mein hume Manavikta sikhate hai. Kumbhar ki tarah hamen achcha Insan banate hain Guru jo hai jo hume hire ke bhanti hume chamkate hai. Guruva hai jo hamen Prerna dete Hain hamari atmavishwas ko badhate Hain bipadda mein aage badhane ka sahas dete Hain. Sare duniya Ko Roshni dekar uski Kiran dikhakar Jo hamen jeevit Rahane ki Shakti dete Hain vah hote hain Guru. Har EK Chhatra Apne Guru ke Aadarsh mein Anuppurnit hone ki koshish aur Safal vahi hote hain jisse hamare Dev Bhumi Bharat varsh ki RAM Nara se Narayan vah Guru Vashisht ke liye Shyam Puja Pi the Guru Sandeep pani ke liye Bal Prahlad Ishwar prapti Kiya Guru Narad ke liye Arjun aparajay hua Guru Dronacharya Dronacharya ke liye Vivekananda Vishwaprasiddh hue Guru Ramkrishna paramhans ke liye Indra Devta vah Guru brihaspati ke liye plateau bane vishisht darshanik Guru ke liye aur Scotts bane biral vyaktitva Apne Guru Aristotle ke liye srichaitanya Bani avtari purush Guru Keshav Bharti ke liye Sutaranj Guru ke Aashirwad Bina kuchh bhi sambhav nahin hai. Hamari Arya Bhumi Bharat varsh mein sapne safalta ke liye khush ho jaate Hain parantu teen vyakti aise Hain Jo Apke har har per bhi Khush hote Hain, vah hi pita Mata guru jab pita Mata guru apna Santan Jeet jata hai vah log bahut khush hote Hain. Pita Mata Shishu ko Swarg se martya ko lete hain lekin Guru martya se Amartya sthal baikunth dham Ko le jaate Hain.

Guru hamare samaj ke merudand Hain. "Guru Rastra nirmata shishya bhagyavidhaata". Jo sadguru prapt karte hain unki Jeeva dasha se samaj Ko anek digdarshan milte Hain

NITISH KUMAR SAHOO

Nitish Kumar is a person of determination and conviction. As his name defines not only his attitude but also his personality. Being a follower of Swami Vivekananda, he is optimistic and broad minded who believes in detachment mode of humanity. Always self motivated, enthusiastic and a person of humility with positive vibes. His presence bring warmth to anyone around him & always has a nature of challenging himself to any task laid before him.

Concept of Relativity

Recently this topic has stated to be one of the fascinating subject on which very less discussion has been done and yet subconsciously accepted by all. It not only talk about the frame of reference of the observer but also the frame of reference of the subject as well. Both the observer and the subject are part of one single entity have two distinct and unique characteristics but single functionality. It depends on the Relativity that states its actual role with most acceptable form. In terms of Father of Indian Space Science Dr. Vikam Sarabhai, "We learn the importance of the frame of reference of the observer and how the results of observation depends on this relative states of his frame with respect to that which he observes".

Now allow me to explain what Dr. Sarabhai has said. Suppose we take a simple example of our Indian caste system without being bias. During ancient times say Indus valley civilization the first settlement that came into being forming society to inculcate the very idea of self sufficiency. Some were farmers, some traders, potters, hunters, builders etc who used barter system to trade. With time they became proficient in their profession and their gathered knowledge were passed on through generation hence profession were assigned as their titles hence the advent of caste system. Specialized persons where called for specific job without any discrimination or prejudice. Here in terms of Relativity, then people had liberty to choose any job in which they obtain optimal result. With changing times and growing complexity new profession were created along with decline of some old ones. This profession were complex which required a chain of command line hence again division of caste into sub-castes and forming hierarchal society. Some were manual, some intellectual and other spiritual, where spiritual persons were given higher priority followed by intellectual and lastly manual personnel. It depends on observer who takes best decision for his life. Here everyone is dependent as well as independent of each other yet their is division of class, inspite all of them hold equal position to an outsider. So what went wrong in present context of our caste system. Well the answer is simple, We went from flexible job structure to rigid social caste system cementing it with our generational lineage and inter/intra caste oppression. Thus, we get three different point of view for above scenario. First the one who is oppressing or has higher standard than the rest. His view would be, "this is what we were created to do because our ancestor taught us practised it for generations". Second the one who is being oppressed by the first. He will say "this is what our text says or we were told to do so by the first". Thirdly the one who belong to neither but influenced by both to certain extent. He is a mixture of above three profession and also who is limited on his own. Technically speaking all are equally right and equally wrong in the present context when seen from a third observer. That's Relativity.

Another perspective of Relativity is that one can't state absolute truth or false of any statement. Time has a considerable weightage in this matter. Any statement is interpreted in terms of person's depth of understanding. Again this understanding depends on person's education, experience, learning capacity and his upbringing environment. So it is wise to say everyone will have different opinion which is deeply rooted to his core values. Which is why we have different text, philosophy, thesis and anthesis for same religion depending upon region and time. It may look awkward for any first time reader because we have whole-heartedly accepted the theorem which were taught since our childhood. This is a static concept but Relativity is a dynamic one. If gives you freedom to choose what is best for you than to stick with one dogma for rest of your life. In my opinion one shouldn't be too attached to one's philosophy but try out variants to his salvation. That is why Dr. Sarabhai again said "absolute right and wrong do not exist in the values of those who have understood the Upanishads or those who have followed the Concept of Relativity."

Chaotic Stability

First I thought this as an absurd hypothesis but after deep analysis it turns out to be true to its very nature. And that's what we have a 'Chaotic Stability'. Just to elaborate what this hypothesis is all about one needs to be a keen observer and mindfulness to its surrounding. Right now we may either be sitting cosy in our chair or be lying down on bed but with ease in a static position. Are we really that static? Infact the earth is revolving around the sun in our solar system which is moving with the milky way galaxy while the universe is expanding @ 72Kmps. So I just took away your cosiness.
Point of writing this article is make you understand the dynamic nature of our surrounding and make you adaptable to it. Starting with a simple observation of present era of "Work-Life balance" (WLB). Some regard it to be a modern terminology for IT professionals who tends to unable to cope up with their professional and personal life. The fact that has been missing out is the practicality of modern complexity of competition and globalisation. The craving lies in desire to achieve and outstand everyone else on a common platform while beating around the bush. With multiple things at hand to conquer in a short span of time many tend to lose their mental stability and miss the fine line to work out things with existing ones. This lead to physical and emotional deterioration with their well being, hence a disturbed bondage. But the catch here is, in such imbalanced situation they become so habituated to such condition that if they don't persue it then also they find themselves in a termoil of underachievement. This is how a 'Chaotic Stability' occurs. The solution to get out of such situation is to prioritise things

as per condition required. But this is just one of many such instances whose answer may or may not be that simple.

After giving you a glance what it is all about let me prepare you to a higher level of complexity. Without being critical and adhering to 'Concept of Relativity' let us pick pace from personal to public sphere. Look around your social sphere that includes your friends, family, society and even your government, one will find that everybody is trying to persue something or other. Sometimes this lead to benefit us and in other times leads to clash and conflict. Some accept it and some reject it, those who reject it always makes a difference. There are so many things working together in sync with eachother from local to national that people can't possibly know until told. There is always a small wheel which when misplaced leads to cascading effect on other system until a new balance is found. For example the device on which you are reading this article, it definitely consumes electrical energy. Since our school days, we have been told that electrical energy are non polluting clean & green fuel and this misconception have been taken forward to promote more consumption in electrical energy through invention of new devices that makes our life easier. Although comparatively speaking this is non polluting but certainly not clean & green. It's because staring from its generation, transmission and distribution, lots of resources are consumed in terms of land, water, mining, construction, deforestation etc which ultimately leads to carbon emission into the atmosphere which would otherwise been sequestrated in the soil. In terms of economics, as the demand increases so does the supply which implies the more we depend on electrical equipment to 'make make our life easier' subsequently we are deteriorating our environment, hence our lives. This is a vicious cycle which cannot be stopped but can only be slowed down. On one hand where NGOs, civil societies and some governments are demanding to take action to mitigate climate change, while on other hand the means they use also have environmental impact.

Finally, the most complex form of 'Chaotic Stability' lies not outside but inside us. All that we do is because of our powerful mind and sheer will power. Our mind tends to be in constant struggle to get on going, finding new paths and mending old ones. The consistence ability to indulge in something and other, keeps us busy which may leads to satisfaction or dissatisfaction. Everyone encounter with their own problem and the way to deal with is also different because of its background and experience. It's not possible to find an optimal solution until worked upon according to the suitable condition. All that can be done is to have a general awareness and understanding of internal condition and also regular checks if any deviation occurs. This chaos live with us for lifetime like a shadow and the only way that showed by the Lord Sri Krishna in Bhagavad-Gita to deal with it is through practice of *Sthitaprajna*. In conclusion, this new type of stability is not casily attainablc in any sphcrc but with timc and practice it is possible.

The Lost Realm

Today we have so many scriptures, epics, textbook and doctrines to attain salvation. Many gurus or spiritual leader that have come by in different religion at different point of time. Everybody have their own philosophy and so called institution to preach their religion with or without full length analysis of their doctrine but accepted by numerous followers. In this article I am not here to comment whether their doctrine is true or false, just or unjust but to show a larger picture that yet not been discovered/missed. In many of religious seminar and lecture of these godly men one must have heard that he or she is communicating or transcending God's message to human. Is this really so? In order to understand and realise the following doctrine just pay full attention. Sit calm and discard all your thoughts I will try my best to walk you through it.

We know Humans are different from other species because of their reasoning and analytical skills. If ever their existed any god or philosophy as deciphered by our ancient sages then because the presence of higher intellectual property. Let say there is a grand repository of knowledge in that domain like a cloud server and we have a fraction of that receiver in our brain or soul who can at any moment download and transmit that information as per our necessity. Earlier these sages were able to tap into that higher domain to extract information or circulate these information to commoners. They communicate these information in such a manner as if there is a bidirectional communication. And over considerable amount of time there information have accumulated and transferred to different disciplines who pass it on to others according to their level of understanding or interpretation. This has some how eroded the base knowledge and objectives through which such doctrine were propagated. Now what we have is just the gist of actual philosophy. As we have heard "Little knowledge is dangerous" but partial knowledge is also dangerous. In present world so much other data are generated that it becomes nearly impossible to distinguish between actual knowledge and propagated information.

The solution to this problem and to attain salvation is to discard all other information and make clear path to find out the relevance of that philosophy. At any moment if a new thought comes into our mind let assume it has been transcended from that repository. We need to identify, verify and justify its relevance in our society. Adhering to Relativity, it need to be crossed checked with equally intellectual personalities through debate and discussion before it's propagation. To connect with that higher realm of eternal bliss such path can be cleared through meditation and relate those feeling into oneself. Since this is a bidirectional process only few people were able to capture such knowledge which is extremely important to humanity. Although these passing thought may not be relevant to every human at a time but at certain time people will tend to follow it. This grand repository of knowledge what can be named as God and their messenger called priest communicate such information to peoples. Though the expression and way of representation may vary from person to person but the idea behind it remains the same. Almost every religion have some interlinking and overlapping characteristics which denotes the grand sharing of idea and yet only the tone of it varies.

Here's a simple technique to transcend such knowledge without any mediator. Start with the basic human intuition from "Wh" questionnaire. Formulate these question in such a manner that it can connect every aspect of yourself at small to the society at large. Every question is a relevant question no matter how small or invaluable it seems. Revise that question until it stores itself at subconscious level in your mind. Then pick a suitable place and optimal time most preferably open space and early morning when the mind is less disturbed. Choose your meditating position, close your eyes, breath slowly & steadily, and focus on any particular object, subject, symbol or philosophy i.e., a pen anything that you like. Stay Focused on it. After sometime you will realize that your "Wh" questionnaire are getting answered automatically without any effort. If a little more concentration can be applied then you will also realize the flow through which you connect with that supreme knowledge termed as "God". In this sphere any question can be answered and also new ideas can be extracted.

This is how our sages were able to decipher & answer the most difficult question of life, society, metaphysics etc in most easiest way and showed us a path to lead a better life. Hence in existing busy schedule it will take some time to practice such steps, which will ultimately lead to our salvation. Thus, *"The Buddhists or the Jainas do not depend upon God; but the whole force of their religion is directed to the great central truth in every religion, to evolve a God out of man."*

RITESH BEHERA

Ritesh is although not a professional writer but loves to write out his feelings. He consider his pen as his best friend, with whom he can share anything.

मेरा पेहला प्यार है वो।

मेरे प्यार से अनजान थी वो,
लेकिन मेरे दिल की मेहमान थी वो।
हसीनों की भीड़ से अलग थी वो,
मेरे लिए कुछ ऐसी खास थी वो।
तौल नहीं सकता इतनी खूबसूरत थी वो,
बोल नहीं सकता ऐसी चाहत थी वो।
सांसें रुक जाती थी जब पास होती थी वो,
खामोशी चीख उठती थी जब दूर जाती थी वो।
तब पता नहीं था कि चीज़ क्या थी वो,
आखों की सुकून तो दिल की मोहब्बत थी वो।
पर अब हालात कुछ अलग है नज़र से दूर पर मेरी शायरी का अल्फ़ाज़ है वो,
अब तो मेरे ज़िन्दगी का एक हिस्सा है वो।
भूल नहीं सकता एक ऐसी याद है वो,
भूलना भी नहीं चाहूंगा मेरा पेहला प्यार है वो।

आज आँसुओं को थोड़ा बहने दो

आज आँसुओं को थोड़ा बहने दो
आज जज़्बातों को थोड़ा कहने दो
कल तक जो दर्द सिर्फ तुम्हारा था,
आज उनको भी थोड़ा सहने दो।

चोट

बिना चोट खाये हम कहां चीख पाते
बिना दर्द सहे हम कहां लिख पाते
ये तो बेवफाई थी उनकी,
बिना जिसके ये अल्फ़ाज़ कहां सीख पाते।

मंजिल

धुआं था मगर आग नहीं,
फूल था मगर खुस्बू नहीं,
मंजिल था मगर राह नहीं,
चाहत था मगर प्यार नहीं।

कुछ हालात थी जो हम मोड़ नहीं पाए

कुछ हालात थी जो हम मोड़ नहीं पाए,
कुछ बेड़ियां थी जो हम तोड़ नहीं पाए,
यूं तो बिछड़ चुके है तुमसे सदियों पहले,
पर कुछ यादें थी तुम्हारी जो हम छोड़ नहीं पाए।

मुस्कान

तेरी खूबसूरती का दीदार करने ये आसमान भी झूक चुका है।
तेरी समंदर जैसी आंखों में डूबने ये लम्हा भी रुक चुका है।
था जो कभी निशाना अर्सों से मेरा,.
आज तेरी मुस्कान की वजह से वो भी चूक चुका है।

कहानी

अल्फ़ाज़ों की खोज में हर रात जागता हूँ।
तुम्हें बयां कर सकूं ऐसी शायरी काफी लिखता हूँ।
हमारी कहानी अधूरी रह गयी ज़रूर,
लेकिन इसे एक मुक्काम देने की कोशिश आज भी करता हूँ।

क्यों

जब अंधेरा पसंद हो तो रौशनी ढूँढू क्यों?
जब कांटे खूबसूरत हो तो फूल चाहूँ क्यों?
ना समझना ये मेरा गुरूर है...
क्योंकि जब तन्हाई हसीन हो तो किसीका साथ मांगू क्यों?

एहसास

सोचा जुबा से इज़हार नहीं कर सकता
तो कलम से उन्हें ये एहसास दिला दूंगा'
जो आवाज़ वो कभी सुन नहीं पायी
वो कागज़ में चीख कर बता दूंगा।

आज किसी ने

आज किसी की दोस्ती ने एक अरमान सा जगाया है
आज किसी की हसी ने पूरा दिल में समाया है
बुझ गई थी जो दिया कभी किसी की नफरत की आंधी से,
आज किसी की साथ ने उसे फिर से जलाया है।

RAKESH BEHERA

O forgetful, Immerse yourself in your self for that is the secret of life. Break free from the binaries of good-bad, virtue-vice, right-wrong, light-dark and become immortal.

किसे नहीं होती तलाश !!

इस आसमान को अपने गोद में
कभी चाँद तो कभी सूरज की तलाश है
डूबने को तो ये समंदर भी है
पर इश्क़ में हारे को अश्क़ों की बारिश की तलाश है
बिडम्बना देखो,दुनिया में इतनी संगदलि है
की इंसान को ही इंसानियत की तलाश है
बढ़ना हर कोई आगे चाहता है
पर जाने क्यूं नाम इतिहास में तलाशता है
चलते फिरते इंसान पर हमें ऐतबार नहीं
और पत्थर की मूरत में हमें भगवान् की तलाश है
मजहब ने इंसानियत को यूँ बांटा की
किसीको आरती में भगवान् तो
किसीको अजान में खुदा की तलाश है
किसे नहीं होती तलाश
पूछो उसे जिसके ख्वाब टूटे
उसे भी जीने की वजह की तलाश है
अरे वो जो कहता है की नहीं है
मुझे ज़िन्दगी में कोई तलाश
पूछो उसे,उसे भी मौत की तलाश है
ख़त्म तो एक दिन ज़िन्दगी हो जायेगी
पर तलाश नहीं क्यूँ
मुझ पर यकीन नहीं तो सुनो
तुम्हारे मौत के बाद भी तुम्हारे अपनों को कफ़न की तलाश है ।

Raah

Raah me hum mile kahan, Bazm me wo bulaye kyun
Khayal unka aaya kaise,bojh ye dhoe kaun

Haadsa ye hua kahan, Zakhm hai hara kyun
Gunaah-e-ishq hua kaise, Sitam ye sahe kaun

Gumshuda hain jane kahan, tafteesh koi Kare kyun
Hum yun khoye kaise, fasana ye kahe kaun

Hum uske ho kar bhi uske kahan hai 'Ejaz'
Darakht ye kate kaise,dast ab saware kaun

Yehi Hota Hai Zamaane Me Kya

Yehi hota hai zamaane me kya
Kho jaate hain log talaashne me kya

Faile hain kitne mayus chehrein yahan
zehmat hoti hai ek haath badhane me kya

Bikhre pade hain kitne kirdaar
Toot jaate hain log banane me kya

Haath me jaam liye karte aqili ki baat
Bekhudi nahin milti ab maikhaane me kya

Takleef nahin hoti ab kisi ko kisi ke jaane se
Mashroof hain log ab bhulane me kya

RIYA KUMARI

Riya Kumari born and raised in Jamshedpur , Jharkhand . She is a student of class 10 studying at RKMES , Bistupur ,Jamshedpur. She loves to write poems , stories , horror stories and quotes . She uses them as a medium to express her feelings , thoughts and her desires . She is idealized by Ramdhari Singh Dinkar , Siddhartha Deval, O Henry and Nitesh Tiwari . She also loves to make people laugh . Her hobby is writing and cartography . She loves her solitude and touring and travelling new palaces . She uses her humour to make people attracted towards her . She believes in the saying " make your hobby your passion " .

नमस्कार दोस्तों। मेर नाम रिया कुमारी है। आज की जो मेरी कविता है वो शहीदों पर है वो भी महिला शहीदों पर है जिन्होंने हमारे लिए अपनी जान की कुर्बानी देकर स्वर्ग लोक का आवाहन किया। जब भी हम शहीदों की बात करते है तब हमे कुछ गीने - चुने लोगों की ही याद आती है जैसे की भगत सिंह , राजगुरु , सुखदेव , मंगल पान्डेय आदी। लेकिन जब महिला शहीदों की बात होती है तब सबको सिर्फ एक ही नाम याद आता है वो है रानी लक्ष्मीबाई का जबकी ऐसी और भी महिलाए है जिनके नाम हम नही जानते है जैसे की मिथाली मधुमीता , पुनीता अरोरा , किरण शिखावत और न जाने ऐसे ही कितने नाम है जिन्हे हम नही जानते । तो मेरी जो कविता है वो इन्ही वीर पुत्रि पर है। मैने इस कविता का नाम " तुझको कसम है माँ मेरी की रोना नही है " रखा है। इस कविता के माध्यम से मैने उन बातो का व्यकत किया है जो एक जवान शहीद होने से पहले अपनी खत मै लिखती है । पंक्तियाँ सुनिएगा ।

तुझको कसम है माँ मेरी की रोना नहीं है

पहली पंक्ति मे मैने उस दृश्य का चित्रन किया है जब उस जवान की लाश उसके घर तक आती है और उसका खत जब उसकी माँ को मिलता है । पंक्तियाँ सुनिएगा।

सीमा पर एक जवान जब शहीद हो गई
संवेदनाओं के कितने बीज बो गई।
तिरंगे मे लिपटी लाश उसके घर को आ गयी
तरप उठी हवाएँ उदासी छा गई।
तिरंगे मै रखा खत जो उसकी माँ को दिख गया
मरती हुई जवान उस खत मै लिख गई।
बलिदान को अब आँसुओ से धोना नही है।
तुझको कसम है माँ मेरी की रोना नही है।।

क्या याद आ रहा है उस जवान को । पंक्तियाँ सुनिएगा।

मुझको याद आ रहा है तेरा ऊँगली पकड़ना
कन्धे पर बीठाना मुझे बाहों मै जकड़ना ।
सहेलियों के संग खेतों पे मै तेज भागती
सुनने को कहानी तेरी रातों को जागती ।
पर बिन सुने कहानी तेरी गुड़िया सो गयी
सोचा था तुने और कुछ और हो गया ।
मुझसा कोई तेरे घर मै खिलौना नही है।
तुझको कसम है माँ मेरी की रोना नही है।।

उसकी माँ उसके लिए डोली सजा रही होती है ताकी जब वो युद्ध से लौट आए तब वो उसकी शादी करवाएगी पर वो नही आती उसकी खत आती है सुनिएगा उस बेटी ने क्या लिखा ।

सोचा था तुने अपने लिए दामाद लाएगी
नाति को अपने हाथों से झूला झूलाएगी।
तोतलाती बोली नाती की तू सुन न सकी माँ
आंचल मे अपने कलियाँ तू चुन न सकी ।
न रंगोली बनी घर पर न डोली पर मै चढ़ी
पतंग पर सवार हो यमलोक चल पड़ी।
वहां माँ तेरे आंचल का तो बिछौना नही है।
तुझको कसम है माँ मेरी की रोना नही है।।

हमेशा अपने भाई से लड़ती रहती थी लेकिन आज वो अपने भाई के लिए लिखती है। सुनिएगा।

भईया से कहना उनकी दुलारी चली गई
बचपन की दोस्त और एक साथी चली गयी।
अब कौन उनको पापा से डांट खिलाएगा
कौन राखी का बन्धन निभाएगा।
कहना की बहन बनके अबकी बार आउंगी
सुहाग वाला सेहरा अपने संग लाउंगी ।
अब भाई और बहन मै मेल होना नही है ।
तुझको कसम है माँ मेरी की रोना नही है।।

अपने पापा की रानी अपने पिता के लिए लिखती है । सुनिएगा ।

पापा से कहना बेटी को याद न करे
किस्मत को न कोसे कोई फरियाद न करे ।
अब कौन उन्के कन्धे पर गाना गाएगा
कौन बाप बेटी का रिश्ता निभाएगा ।
उम्मीदों का महल सारा पल मे डह गया
बेटी का सारा फर्ज ही अधूरा रह गया ।
वेतर से निकली बेटी ये सलोना नही है।
तुझको कसम है माँ मेरी की रोना नही है।।

इस कविता के अन्तिम बन्ध मे मै यह बताना चाहती हूँ की सैनिक इस देश के लिए कितना कुछ करता है और बदले मै उसे क्या मिलता है। सुनिएगा।

सरकार मेरे नाम से कई फण्ड लाएगी
चौराहों पे तुझको तमाशा बनायेगी।
अस्पताल, स्कूलों के नाम रखेगी
अनमोल सहादत का कुछ दाम रखेगी।
पर दलालों की दलाली पे तू थूक देना माँ
बेटी की मौत की कोई किमत ना लेना माँ।
भूखे भले ,मखमल पे हमको सोना नही है।
तुझको कसम है माँ मेरी की रोना नही है।।

PALAK DAS

15th year old Lives in Tuiladungri Golmuri Jamshedpur, Jharkhnd

Is It That Easy?

Whenever you will ask for advice, they will ask you to let it go as if it's so easy.

I want to talk about the situations that lead a relationship to it's end

. It is scary to even imagine living a life that we have dreamed of living with someone. It is difficult to imagine it without the person. These are the situations of a dilemma when you don't see clearly what is right for you Sometimes we don't get the chance to choose We are left with no choice. They leave us in the middle of nowhere.

This is when we hear from everyone to stop worrying and just let it go. " Take a deep breath and let it go". As if we don't know it already. But what about the heart that is bleeding continuously? What about the beautiful memories that are haunting us every night? What about the broken dream! It takes years of pain.

Missing them becomes a part of our lives . It hurts. It is a gradual process. It is easier said than done. Forgiving is easy but forgetting isn't. We can do everything that is in our hands. We can stop stalking them, we can stop looking at their pictures, we can delete the number and chats; But the heart wants what it wants. We cannot stop ourselves from missing them in the middle of the night. We cannot stop ourselves from dreaming about the time when everything was alright. We cannot stop those automatic tears.. .

Only hope helps us at that time. Only the belief in ourselves. I agree that it's not easy, but it's also not impossible. And just because it is though, it doesn't become a bad choice. You took the right steps! You can do it! You aren't alone, I'm with you Trust yourself!

KAUSHAL SAO

An analogous description of Kaushal Sao can be made through the description of a Phoenix. Just like the mythical bird, Kaushal might fall down to ashes but then again would rise up, in no time. This signature quality of this CA Aspirant helps him grow in every wake of his life as he strives to quench his ever growing thirst of knowledge. He might've been born and brought up at chaibasa, a small town in Jharkhand but his heart also beats for the city of joy - Kolkata. He started writing and performing in Open Mics in the English language but gradually after each open mic, he grew fond of Urdu and Hindi content. With each new write up, he yearns for criticism more than compliment which he believes, will make him a better writer one day.

Humanity Is Defiled

Watching from his tranquil heavenly abode,
He Gave a serene smile,as humanity bowed.
Neither the golden haloed Angels,
nor any incarnation
But the almighty adored humanity - as his best creation.
Consumed by jealousy, Lucifer unleashed his evil temptation,
To save humanity - his precious child,
God banished him, eternal damnation.
But is Humanity really worth saving?
Breathing violence, consuming the lust and raving.
Embracing demons of racism, bullying and killing,
towards doom we are waving –
A Highway to Hell is what we've been paving.
But then fate slammed the last nail in the coffin,
When for mockery, humanity betrayed an innocent elephant,
Losing its sanctity - All in.
God had the devil exiled
But it was humanity who had the sanctity defiled.
Lord almighty gave a sigh, while Lucifer - smiled.

Bird With A Broken Wing

Amidst the party of nature – serene spring
Latched to the darkness, to grief it'd cling.
Happiness became a facade, tormenting –
To the bird with a broken wing.
Like a ghost, drifting through days Head held down,
society's piercing gaze.
Lost within the mental maze
Where Expectations & Frustration - Continue to chase.
She sung her pain to the nature Judged & ridiculed,
was labelled a failure.
She did not choose such a behavior –
Prisoner within, her mind the jailor.
Harsh is the truth,
But this is what communication brings
To the birds with the broken wings.
And that is why they choose to hide
Carrying fake smiles, hurting deep inside.
You swallow the regret, You misbehaved
Now you wish they could be saved!
They're gone, yet you ask around
While their corpses wither in mental battleground.
They did not need to be saved, But to be found!

संक्रमण का दौर

संक्रमण के दौर में,
पढ़े लिखे पंडितो को,जाहिल बनते देखा है
ग़रीबी देख रखी है मैंने मगर –
रोता ग़रीब फिर एक बार देखा है।
खाली सड़क में घूमती उस कार को देखा है,
पैदल चलते, थकते- पड़ते, बेदम गिरते, बीमार को देखा है।
भूख तो देखी है मैंने भी,
सड़क किनारे निवाला लेते, एक लाचार को देखा है।

बड़े सितारों को समारोह में जाते देखा है,
राजनेताओं को कीचड़ उछालते देखा है।
विवाद तो रोज़ ही देखे हैं मगर –
देश हित में परोपकार भी शानदार देखा है।
त्याग भी देखा है मैंने मगर - अपनों के लिए,
अपनों से दूर, उस जवान को देखा है
Virus से जूझते - लड़ते डॉक्टरों को, गवांते जान देखा है।
दूरियां बहुत देखी है,
भिन्नता भी देखी है
संक्रमण के इस दौर में भारत को एक साथ आते देखा है।

SRUSHTI PRAJANA MOHANTY

Miss Srushti Prajna Mohanty is pursuing her Post-graduation degree in Botany in the Department of Botany and Biotechnology, Ravenshaw University, Cuttack, Odisha, India. She used to express her views & thoughts in her blog 'Voice of heart' at Wordpress. She is an active writer in the mirakee. Her writings mostly include human emotions, our culture & value system. She has also taken interest in writing articles about environment, its present challenges and the ways forward.

Biodiversity : Issues And The Action Plan

This paper is concerned with the ongoing discussion on the issues faced by Biodiversity & need for a comprehensive action plan.

Theme for the year 2020's World Environment Day is declared as 'Time for Nature' which reflects the need of the hour. Therefore, our vision & mission should be clear & strong enough to protect the biodiversity of planet earth from degradation.

Biodiversity refers to the variety & variability of life forms on the earth. Our biosphere constitutes all the flora & fauna, whose survival provides smooth living for all the species. The term 'Biodiversity' was coined by Walter G.Rosen in 1985.

In nature, biodiversity can be observed at three levels,i.e., genetic level, species level & ecosystem level. About fifty thousand genetically different strains of rice are the examples of genetic diversity. The greater amphibian diversity exists in the Western Ghats of India than that in the Eastern Ghats is an example of diversity at the species level. At the ecosystem level, India, with its deserts, rain forests, mangroves, wetlands, coral reefs, alpine meadows has a greater diversity than a country like Norway.

All species play complementary & supplementary role for the survival of all living entities. Man, being the Homo sapiens should restrain from actions that would erode species but do everything to protect them from extinction.

Indian Biodiversity

Being, one of the 17 declared mega diverse countries, India has 10 biogeographic zones altogether, harbouring 8.58% of mammalian species, 13.66% of avian species, 7.91% of reptiles, 4.66% of amphibians, 11.72% of fishes & 11.8% of plants as documented so far. In the recent past, government's work on environment conservation has kept India among the top 10 countries in the Climate Change Performance Index (CCPI). As we know, forests are the repository of biodiversity & play a vital role in maintaining climatic equilibrium. Increase in forests & tree cover by 5100 sq.kms is a remarkable achievement as reported by ISFR, 2019 (Indian State of Forest Report).

ISSUES

The insatiable hunger of the new civilisation has threatened the diverse & healthy biological order as it is consuming resources at a much faster rate than their rate of replenishment. This has led to the extinction of approx.15,500 species worldwide. Some recently extinct species are Indian cheetah, Sumatran rhino, Indochinese tiger, Thylacine, Stellar's cow etc. Major causes of such biodiversity loss include overpopulation, industrialisation, alien species invasion, over-exploitation of mines, climate change & pollution.

LOSS OF BIODIVERSITY MAY LEAD TO PANDEMICS

Ecosystems naturally restrain the transfer of diseases from animals to humans, but this service will decline if ecosystem gets degraded. Thus, maintenance of ecosystems & their associated species is key to prevent the emergence of any new pandemic.Preservation of nature & natural resources are needed to have a sound environmental & economic policy making. Lessons from the Covid-19 pandemic have given us above stated findings.

ACTION PROGRAMME

As we all know, there are two basic approaches for conservation of biodiversity; in-situ & ex-situ. In-situ or on-site conservation involves protection of species in their natural habitat. This system includes biodiversity hot spots, protected areas, sacred groves etc. Ex- situ conservation or off-site conservation involves placing threatened animals & plants in special care units away from their natural habitats. These are like zoological parks, botanical gardens, wildlife safari parks, gene banks etc. Besides these traditional methods of conservation, efforts should have been made by Govt. & NGOs (Non Govt Organisations) to create awareness among public regarding the conservation strategies. The recent news regarding plantation of more than thirty five lakhs saplings by students across educational institutions under the 'one student one tree' campaign is a welcome gesture.

GANDHIAN APPROACH

The onset of Covid -19 pandemic has made us to remember Mahatma Gandhi's words like, "Earth provides enough to satisfy every man's needs, but not every man's greed."

RITU ROUMYA SAMAL

RITU ROUMYA SAMAL The author is an example of the curious writer about the social issues, beauty of environment, cherish the human relations with society and she is an ingenious displayer of the mother earth. The author is not only of a creative sentimental but also a successful academician with Gold medal in Masters in science from Ravenshaw University, Cuttack, Odisha. She is the owner of her self blogging site in wordpress, "VENERATION TO WRITE" and "KUCH UNKAHI BATEIN"
https://rituroumya.wordprcss.com/author/rituroumya/
https://rituroumya824277688.wordpress.com/author/riturou myasamal/

The Reminiscences Of Lord Jagannath:

The life of every living being, the love of every devotee;
The smile of every face, the hope of every alacrity;
The affection of every enthusiast, the lust of every devadasi;
The passion of every poor, the devotion of every rich;
The tender heart of every lady, the strong soul of every man;
The childish playful love of a child, the real heart desire of an old;
The aroma of mahaprasad, the spice of Indian tradition;
The way to the great dham of India, the path of eternity;
The lord of the universe, the part of the jannath sanskriti;
The trio deities of lord Balabhadra, lord Jagannath and their sister Subhadra whose assimilation gravitate to moksha (salvation).

The dexterity of the Badadeula (Lord Jagannath temple), the heart of the bada danda (Great Grand road);
The great Meghanada Pacheri (The temple's high wall) and the entrance through the remarkable mukhashala (Frontal porch);
The admirable garba griha (Sanctum Santorum), the magnificent ratnavedi (The throne of pearls);
opening of singhadwara (The lion gate), the steps of baisi pahacha (The flight of twenty-two steps);
The great surveillance of Jaya and Vijaya, the colossal stand of Arun stambha (Sixteen sided monolithic pillar);
Along with all the exalted temple's confession, we cannot forget the hatidwara (The elephant gate), vyaghradwara (The tiger gate) and the ashwadwara (The horse gate);

Decorated with Lord's bless and expressed with love and devotion, the great grand road of India leads to the assignation of every devotee;
Irrespective of caste, creed, religion, tradition, culture, rich and poor, the great grand road gives shelter to every striver.
The juggernaut of the great grand chariots of the royal triads spreads ecstatic ordain of bada danda (The great grand road).
The land of Odisha is blessed with the obsessed devotion of Lord jagannath and the whole universe is blessed with the sinuous grace of the great trios.

एक मिलन

यह कैसी लीला है!जो सुंदर हो उसके ओर मन ढल जाता है।
यह कैसी लीला है! जो दुर हो उसे छुने कि इच्छा बढ़ जाती है।
यह कैसी लीला है! इस जहांन में अपने इच्छा से मिलन होना रब कि दुआ है।
यह कैसी लीला है! जिंदगी में कुछ पाना हो तो बेशक कुछ खोना है।
आखिर यह कैसी लीला है!
ज़मीन पर यह सुंदरता लफ़्ज़ों से नहीं कह जा सकते, महशुश करना हो तो ज़मीन को नजदिकि से एक बार देखो।
रंगों से भरे ज़मीन के बदन रंगे होते हैं न जाने कई तरह के फूलों और पेड़ों से । चादर सा जैसा लपेटा हुआ धुल से, जो चमके सोने के जैसे।
अलग-अलग प्रकार के लोग और अलग हि उनके अंदाज। जैसे एक बगीचे में खिला हो रंग बिरंगे फुल।
जहां कई सारे मौसम आते हैं मेहमान बनके, ठहरके अपने ढंग से रंगते है ज़मीन को कुछ इस तरह। लेहेरें बेहती है यहां कई सारे नदियों और समुंदरो का।
उज्वल होती है हर रोज़ शाम को इसकी चेहरा जब दीया जलती है मंदिरो के आंगन पर।
आवाज़ गूंजती है यहां, जब जोर से सुनाई देता है नमाज़ का पुकार।
नि:शब्द होने लगती है, जब बजती है चर्च की घंटी और सुनाई देती है बाइबिल की धुन।
खुशबू आती है यहां, जब गुरूद्वार में पकते हैं कई सारे पकवान।
रात के अंधेरा डरावना नहीं मगर एक निरवता का आभास कराती है यहां।
ज़मीन की खूबसूरती जैसे जन्नत से उतरी एक परी की कल्पना करवाती है यहां।

यह बेहकती सुंदरता आसमान को अस्थिर करने लगती है। मिलने के लिए एक बार आसमान बादलों को संदेशा भेजता है, "जा बादल जा धरती को छुके आ, ज़रा मुझे भी तो बता करीब से यह धरती कैसे दिखती है!"
गरजता हुआ बादल दौड़ के जाता है.......
मिलना है जो ज़मीन से दिल को नाज़ुक होना ही है ....
गरज गरज के बादल पिघलता है बारिश के बूंदों जैसा, जाके चूमता है ज़मीन के होटों को,
बाहों में लेकर वह धरती को आहें जब भरता है देखता है यह धरती चमकती है बारिश के बूंदों से और खिलती है देखकर बादलों का काला रंग।
जैसे कई दिनों से धरती को इंतज़ार था कि कब मिले उसे आसमान और बनजाए वह भी भरा पूरा।
धरती थी अधूरी आसमान के बीना, आसमान था अधूरा धरती की ख़ूबसूरती के बिना,
हो गया जब मिलन दोनों का तो बनगया यह जहां......
तो बनगया यह जहां.......
कायम रहे यह मिलन, धरती आसमान.....
जीता रहे हर हस्ती और खिलती रहे यह जहां.....

BHAVIKA ASMI VERMA

Bhavika Asmi Verma, a Sagittarius born Indian, is a writer,avid reader and a patron of learning, Much like her father, she believes in Zodiac signs and planets. She's a fierce Phoenix with an unnerving sense of judgement and it's safe to say that her arrow always hits the spot.

Apart from Hindi and English, she has a fair knowledge of Gujrati-having spent her girlhood in Gujrat- and French,Spanish, Korean and Russian.

She enjoys playing piano and coding and aspires to pursue a career in astrophysics with a degree from MIT. She's teaching herself ISL and ASL and hopes to do good for the deaf and blind and LGBTQ+community. She wants to share her story through a YouTube channel,like Ali Abdaal and Nathaniel Drew (her favourites).

You can connect with her on Twitter(@asmi_verma), on her Wattpad(@Sammantha01Rowling) or @sam-ro on Terribly Tiny Tales.

Boundless.

She sat over a bridge, One fine evening;
Her hands on the ridge Of her nose,stroking.
She peeped down on the river,
And surveyed the yard; Not a single man thus far,
But behind her, she forgot the boulevard.
"Oh how I wish I were content-Of his grace
Which, upon me, he spent-But I can't! I can not!
"Dear God! Is this our end?
With his love all spentAnd I, forever discontent?
She did not notice the strange company,
As she was drowning in her melancholy;
No fault of the maiden,
Ignorance is what makes us human.
The stranger,
Marched with shallow feet;
Curiosity on face, And pity in heart.
Because anyone would ponder,
Over a celibate's sorrow;
But little did they wonder
Of the Apollo's alpenglow.
The young lady's eyes were swollen,
And her poor heart was sore;
Thus the stranger decided,To wait no more.
It rest its palm
On the yoke of her dress;
And felt the sparks
Too hard to suppress.
The former felt them too,
And jerked her head up;
And witnessed a heavenly blue.
Beautiful, would be an understatement-

And exquisite too-
For the eyes that bore into hers,
Were the bluest of all blue.
"Why must a beautiful Eve- Such as thee-must bawl?
There must be a man involved!"
"Yes, ma'am.", she replied this time;
Blushed,but couldn't hide.
The lady only gave a smile
For she knew of the tornadoes in her mind.
She sat beside her;
As they glanced at each other
When the saxon bellowed from the church.
Neither decided to leave, Though it were late
For they couldn't possibly rest
Without exchanging names.
"They call me Ellen", she chimed.
"What is thoust name?"
Asked and passed a smile.
"DeGeneres", the older said,
The other one gasped.
"Mine,too!"
The younger exclaimed and laughed.
She held her knuckles,
And said in whispers:
"You are sixteen, paired with Bridgers."
The maiden was shocked, yet inquired,
Bht was simply ignored;
As the lady continued to tell,
What no-man should ever have heard.
"You thought it was,but no love it is.
And you accepted,but now, don't want to get married."
Certainly were they simple words
But not for the girl,

As cheeks were moist again,
Welcoming a new wave of floods.
She held her hand in hers, And wiped the fallen tears.
They held eyes intently,
As she continued boldly.
"Fear me not,I shan't tell a soul,
But speak up,you and fear no foul.
"Silence will yield you no solution",
She said and reduced the distance Between their chests.
"State your mind; give no second option."
Ellen held her hands tight
And claimed her lips in a surprising kiss!
Without spending a moment's thought.
For the older, 'twas no surprise.
Thus, he fastened her fingers, On the drape of the other's
And closed her eyes.
They melted into the kiss;
Their pleasure flair Filled the air,
Whilst they experienced the heavenly bliss.

RATAN PRASAD

He is Ratan prasad. An adventurous boy of 6th April 2002. He has been Persuing Std 12 from Kasidih high school. And an ex student of Sdsm as he had completed his studies till Class 10th from there. He is an excellent athelete and a great football and voleyball player. He loves to write poems and stories in his leisure time. We feel happy and proud to share his thinking in our book. Its been an month since he is working on this. And we hope and pray that his dedication that is shown in this will be appreciated by you.😊

Kuch Rang Zindigi Ke

Ek daur tha meri zindagi mea
Jb ham andhoro mea jeetea the
Na koi khowish thi na koi makshad
Bs moot ki talsh thi
Moot ko dudnea jb hm nikley sadko pea
Mulkat zindigi sea hui,
Tutey dil kea purjey mea halchal c mach gai
Tujhey dekh kr kuch asa lga jaseey mujhey sarri kayant hi mill gai
Jaha zindigi mea andharo ka raj tha
Waha roshni c diknea lg gai
Moot ko bula kr tujhe paaney ki cha thi
Meri zindigi mea ab na koi raah thi
Tujhey paya tho lga ki khuda millgaya
Andhari sea nata tuta sawara millgaya
Har dua mea ab tri salamati mangu
Rab sea yahi faryad ha
Tera hissey kae saarey gum mujko dea de
Teri saari khawisho ko purrey krnea ke parr mujhey dea
Or sarri kushi tujhea dea Or srai umr Tu mera bn kr rahey.

Pyar Ki Talash

Kushi ki talash me umr guzar gai
Par ek pal na milla
Moth ki talash mea
Sases chal pari pr mot na milli
Bura socha na kisi ka
Pr duniya ne humey buriya hi di
Pyr koja hm ne jha
Wha bhi digga bajiya milli
Bikher hm the dube the gum me
Ek shara milla dosti ka gubbra milla
Zamin ko chor kr asman ki saar kra gya
Dil ko gum sagar sea
Kushi ka kinara dila gya
Dosti bhi asi thi ki jaan tk de dea wo
Salo na akley jeeney na rasta hi hta diya
. Pyr ki ab zarurt hi niii
Pyr unho nea itna diya.
Tanhai ki zarurt hii ni thi
Sath apna dilla diya.
Dil ek jagha bna
Dosti itni ghari kr di
Ki ma ko apni ma or bhn ko apni
Bhn bna liya.
Zarurt kea samey bin bulay
Aajet par jb wo khud dukh mea ho .
Dil mea chupa muskuratey.
Har pal teri dosti ki yaad aagai
Is dosti ko kudha bhi alag kr payagi.

AVINASH MUDULI

Avinash Muduli is a content writer, public speaker & problem-solver. He dedicatedly solves people's problems sent to him on his Instagram, and makes videos on as many as he can. He defines it as the purpose of his life.

Individualism

What is Individualism? Individualism is nothing but taking responsibility for our own 'self'. This 'self' is the real you. We often suppress this 'self' most of the time in our life by seeking approval, acceptance& commonness from the external world.

Let's say, I appeared an exam & I know very well what I have done, but I judge my skills based upon my results or the marks evaluated by the teacher. I never consider that may be the result evaluated had a complete influence on the teacher's mood or thinking while she was evaluating. By solely relying on the marks or results I am killing my 'self' skills or the actual skill of my 'self' is neglected.

Let's take another example, you are in a relationship. You fulfill all the needs, wants, and spend all your time with your partner. Without even questioning or thinking whether those needs, wants & time investment is actually worth or not. When you do so by completely dedicating your whole day for your partner, there only you lose your 'Individuality' or your 'self', by not giving importance to your work, skills, purpose or even your own problems. These things are very important as they shape you as a person. So, have a bargain skill whenever you are or indulging in a relationship. No need to stay available all the time for your partner or any other person. Take care of your 'Self' first.

Always remember 'self love' is the greatest form of love. Everyone in this world loves themselves & give importance to themselves first. There is a famous quote by Mark Twain,

"The world owes you nothing."

Lastly I would like to highlight some important points that are necessary to make your 'self' or 'Individual' stay alive :-

•Never let your 'Self' be compromised because it will make you think & make you realize what is good for you in the long run.

• 'Self' makes you realize what you think about yourself not what people think or believe.

•Most importantly, 'Self' helps you to provide knowledge about the things that are within your control & let go of the things not in your control.

AVISEK ROUT

Student of pharmacy From-Aul, Kendrapara, odisha

हां मैं लड़की हूं इसलिए पढ़ना है

हां मैं लड़की हूं
इसलिए पढ़ना है
कई ग्रंथों को रचना है
इसलिए पढ़ना है
मुझे खुद को गढ़ना है।
तो मुझे पढ़ना है
अब किसी बंदे की क्या औकात
जो मुझे रोक के दिखाए
सारे कांटो को कर दिया पार
अब मुझे छू के दिखाएं
हां मान लिया मैं नारी हूं
पर अबला तो नहीं
कभी आंख उठाकर हमको भी देखो
हम भी मर्दों से कम नहीं
हां मैं लड़की हूं इसलिए पढ़ना है ।।
कभी ज्वाला से उत्पन्न आग
तो कभी शीतल से बहती नीर लोग पूछते अस्तित्व तो हमारी
तो हम भी कहते हैं कभी सती तो कभी भवानी छीन लेते हैं हमारे
जीने की जुनून
काट के हमारे पंख
क्या यह है हमारे देश के कानून
आंख होकर भी हमेशा बंद
नए कानून बनाना है
तो पढ़ना है
अंधों को रोशनी दिखाना है
तो पढ़ना है
हां मैं लड़की हूं इसीलिए पढ़ना है ।।
ना रुकने की चाह
ना खोने का डर

लड़ती थी और लड़ती रहूंगी
चाहे चले यह युद्ध जीवन भर सारे जहां को बदलना है
शो मुझे पढ़ना है
हां मैं लड़की हूं इसलिए पढ़ना ह

SUCHARITA SAHOO

Sucharita is a prolific writer from Cuttack... She is also a die hard MSDIAN... She mostly writes about love and tries to pen down romanticism beautifully with very simple but ornamental words... Let's check what she writes about...

हाँ में मोहब्बत करती हुँ

हां, माना कि तुम मेरी नहीं हो,
फिर भी तुमसे मोहब्बत करती हुँ,
चाहे तुम मुझे सिर्फ अपना दोस्त ही मानो,
फिर भी मैं तुमसे मोहब्बत करती हुँ।

तुम्हारे खुशी का हिस्सा नहीं चाहिए,
पर अपनी मुस्कुराहट तुम्हारे साथ बांटना चाहती हुँ,
तुम्हें पाने की आस नहीं है,
फिर भी तुम्हें खोने से डरती हुँ,
हाँ में तुमसे मोहब्बत करती हुँ।

तुम आसपास हो तो सब कुछ खास होता है,
तुम परेशान हो तो, वेवज्हा तकलीफ मुझे होती है,
तुम्हारे अनजाने में ही,
तुम्हारे छोटी छोटी खुशीयों का खयाल रखती हुँ,
हाँ में तुमसे बेइंतेहा मोहब्बत करती हुँ।

तुम्हें बस एक दिन ना देखुँ तो, दिल बेचेन सी हौती हे,
पर तुम्हें जी भर के देखना कहाँ मेरी नसीब में हे,
इसलिए सबकी नजर से बचके, अकसर चुपके से तुम्हें देखा करती हुँ,
तुम पर हक तो नहीं है, फिर भी तुमसे मोहब्बत करती हुँ l

हाँ खुदको तुम से दूर रखने में दर्द तो बहुत होता है,
पर आंखों के आंसूओं को गिरने से पहले पोंछ देती हुँ,
वेसे भी उस दर्द की अब आदत सी हो गई है,
क्योंकि सारी दुनिया से छुपाके जो तुमसे मोहब्बत करती हुँ।

Ms Dhoni : The Untold Story

Cooler than the moon, brighter than the star,
The one man army of the Indian cricket war.

When the top orders fail to score,
seems like setting of the sun,
You are the one and only person,
the whole nation can rely on.

With either holding the bat or making the lightening stump,
Everytime you make impossible things to possible,
giving us goosebumps.

You not only brought the golden era for Indian cricket,
But also made India no1 in T-20s, ODIs and in test.

The one and only captain to win all the ICC trophies,
Your charming smile is just like the cream in cookies.

Learning from the mistake, to the best decision you take,
Leading the team like a boss, guiding them in their worse.

Coolcst among the bestests,
fastest between the wickets,
Sacrifice a lot to make the new comers best.

From taking all the responsibilities of young Indian team,
To face the criticism silently as the eldest of the team.

Playing with back pain and injured finger,
But never loosing your calmness under pressure,
You are proving age is just a number,

Your passion and dedication is what matter.

SOURAV KETAN SAHU

A tall dusky guy with glasses enriched with creativity in every possible aspect of life. Sourav Ketan Sahu has completed his +2 from Ravenshaw University, Cuttack and currently pursuing his graduation in Bhubaneswar. Apart from being a MBA aspirant and inducing professionalism to be accepted in market, he also dreamt of achieving perfection in the fields of cooking, baking, painting, doodling and mandala art, photography, graphics designing and cinematography. He is a keen observer which is showcased in his writings as well. In addition to this, he is a well known student in his college for his professional attitude and oratorical skills. Last but not the least, he is adored by his family and friends not only because he affectionate, but also for his crazy sense of humor.

वो college के दिन भी कितने अनोखे थे!

सूरज की पहली रोशनी के साथ,
चाय की एक प्याली के साथ,
आखों में नमी लिए,
और ख्वाबों में कुछ मीठे पल लिए,
चलो शुरू करें वो दोस्तों का सफर, जो बहुत अनोखे थे,
वो college के दिन भी कितने अनोखे थे!

तेरी दांट से रूठ जाती थी मै,
तेरे मनाने से मुस्कुराती थी मै,
College में late से entry हो,
या security guards और teachers का गुस्सा हो,
याद आ जाती है हर वो सैर, जो बहुत अनोखे थे,
वो college के दिन भी कितने अनोखे थे!

मेरे साथ झगड़ा करके, एक Chocolate से मान जाती थी तू,
नखरे तो बहुत थे तेरे, लेकिन मेरे लिए सबसे प्यारी थी तू,
प्यार तो करती थी तू हमसे कुछ ज़्यादा,
और दिल में रखती थी हमारा साथ ना छोड़ने का वादा,
सीने से लगाकर रखूं तुझे और जी लूं वो पल जो बहुत अनोखे थे,
वो college के दिन भी कितने अनोखे थे!

जान जाती थी क्या है मेरे मन में बिना बोले दो शब्द,
हर problem का solution होता था तेरे पास बिना लिए कोई वक़्त,
असली चेहरा देख कर भी दिल से अपनाना कोई तेरे से सीखे
और खुद से पहले हमेशा औरों को रखना भी कोई तेरे से सीखे,
तेरी हसी से याद आ जाती है वो लम्हें जो बहुत अनोखे थे,
वो college के दिन भी कितने अनोखे थे!

हमारे पास है ये यादों की लड़ी,

लेकिन सेह नहीं पाऊंगा मै जब आएगी वो farewell की घडी,
अलविदा कहना मुश्किल होगा,
लेकिन साथ रहने का वादा तो निभाना होगा,
ये 3 साल भी कितने अनोखे थे,
वो college के दिन भी कितने अनोखे थे!
वो college के दिन भी कितने अनोखे थे!

आसूं की कीमत

हर आसूं की कीमत जानने के लिए, मां का सपना तो पूरा करना ही होगा!
ज़िंदगी को जन्नत बनाने के लिए, इससे तो हकीक़त में बदलना ही होगा!

कलाकार - ए – मोहब्बत

आशिक़ को दिल मत देना, कहीं फूलों से खुश्बू कम ना हो जाए,
दोस्तों पे जान मत छिडकना, कहीं हर दिन रंगीन ना हो जाए,
कभी कोई कलाकार के आखों में झांक कर मत देखना,
कहीं पूरे कायनात से मोहब्बत ना हो जाए!

कुछ तो खास है

कुछ तो खास है तेरे इन यादों में,
याद आती है जब आंखें नम हो जाती है,
कभी मुस्कुरा उठती है ,
तो कभी गम ले आती है

NAJMUS SHAHEDA

Najmus Shaheda is a student, currently pursuing master degree in computer application, born and brought up in Odisha. Apart from being a tech enthusiast, she also has interest in the field of literature. Her inclination lies towards genre fiction. She has also been appreciated for her work in her institute. Besides that, she also runs a page sharing micro tales in social media.

In The Blink Of An Eye

Everything stopped, people were stood like statues all around me, people in cars, men on bicycles, babies in pram all lifeless, frozen in time, while the devil held my hand and asked "Are you ready?" "For what", I questioned. "For our wedding, princess", he said taking my hand into his and vanished into his underworld.

It was a bitter cold winter morning of December. The Sun was hiding behind the clouds, making it appear as if it was early morning. I got ready and made a dash for the front door, but nearly ran head-first into my mother. She puts both hands on my shoulder and said smilingly, "There you are my Erina, mommy wants you to return home before sunset after school without loitering around." Only if she knew I dropped school and worked as a waitress in a pub to lessen my family's burden. After waving goodbye to her, I walked to work. On the way, I heard something rustle in the bushes next to me. The hair on my neck stood up. I murmured to myself "Is someone following me?". I creep of the sidewalk slowly and searched for the source of sound, but found nothing. I checked time and was late for work. I hurried.

Reaching there, my coworker informed me of a man, who was looking for me and has been waiting by the table. I looked over the direction she pointed, and it was true. There was a man, who looked like he had just walked out of a fashion magazine. His shoulder bulge out of a perfectly tailored Italian suit, and not a strand of hair out of place. He peered out of the window with his beautiful thick-lashed blue eyes, lost in thought. I grabbed my order pad and strolled over to the mysterious man, acting professional. "Hi! Welcome to the Roxy.", I said. The man adjusts his cuffs and looked up with stormy eyes. "Hello Erina, I am Dylan", he said giving a heart-melting smile. "What would you like to have Sir?" I asked concealing my surprise of him knowing my name. "I can't say I am hungry, and I don't need a drink either", he said with a slight devilish grin playing across his lips. I questioned him politely as to why he was here then, and was taken aback when he uttered "You, I suppose". I noticed a strange marking on his forearm while he adjusted his tie. It was raised and almost seemed as if it was burnt into his skin. I stared at him in utter disbelief when he laughed and said "Get me whatever you think I'll like", with a devious smirk. I marched into the kitchen and when I returned, he was nowhere to be seen, instead on the table there was a note saying "See you around."

After my shift winds to an end, I headed home. Moonlight gleamed in the sky. Streetlights illuminated the ground while I heard some leaves rustle off in the distance. I looked around, feeling the pressure of someone following. It was like the morning incident in repeat. It became creepy and for safety I took a cab home.

As I swung opened the front door, the house was cold and still. "Mom, I'm home!" I shouted walking towards the kitchen. I found my mother collapsed on the ground. She was completely still, one arm outstretched across the cold floor. I ran to her limp body and dropped to my knees, frantically searching for signs of life. I leaned and checked her pulse. It was faint. I grabbed her forearm gently, noticing something strange. And to my shock, it was exactly the same mark as of Dylan's.

The moment I knew there was something wrong going on. I was intrigued and worried at the same time. I rushed to the hospital. Nurses wheeled her to the ward. Doctors said that her blood pressure dropped and everything was just fine as usual. I went to check on her, after she regained her senses. She was crying when I entered. Wiping her face she said "I am sorry for keeping things from you, keeping you in dark, just for the sake to save you, but I think it can't be delayed, not any longer." I perched down beside her bed as she explained that 21 years ago when I was a newborn, we met with an accident, in which I died and my mother made a deal with the devil to save me. He transferred half of his soul into mine giving me a new life. By doing so, I became his soul mate and in return he would take me to his world after I turned 21.

Stunned with her words, I ran out of the room, out of the hospital, to the streets. I tried to process all the information, the existence of another world, demons, my death, and all manner of madness. Then all of a sudden, in the blink of an eye, my surroundings froze and a man appeared in front of me - Dylan.

Micro Tales:

1. They thought burning her alive is wise,
unknowingly gave a way for pheonix to rise.

2. 'She' loved 'him',
'He' loved 'her'.
'He' was 'him',
but 'she' was not 'her'.

3. with teary eyes :"But why?"
"Girls aren't allowed to !", exclaimed father.
Shattering of dreams filled the room with silence.

4. He grabbed her by the neck and smashed her against the wall screaming: " You ruined my life!".
The alcohol bottle shattered into thousands pieces

5. "My son will fullfill my dream, he'll grow up to be a fighter!", said father with joy.
And the creativity of an artist died

RAJESWARI OJHA

Rajeswari Ojha born on cool winter like her nature . She is a passionate writer and dancer . An extrovert ambitious girl who loves to be adventurous . A carefree damsel who always wears a smile to lightup the darkness surrounds her and leaves a bit of sparkle of positivity. How she writes is a reflection of how she feels about the world . let's connect with her words .

कोरोना एक बदलाव

बिन बुलाए मेहमान बनकर जिन्दगी में वो आया था ,
कोबिड -१९ नाम से रुबरु वो कराया था ।
चीन के वुहान अपना ठिकाना बताया था ,
जग को मुठी में करने का मंसूबा बनाया था ।

पता ना था हम सब पे इतना भारी पड़ जाएगा ,
दौड़ता जिन्दगी की गाड़ी पटरी से उतर जाएगा ।
सोचा ना था चेहरे की मुस्कान ऐसे छिन जाएगा ,
उड़ते परिंदे को पिंजरे में कैद ऐसे कर जाएगा ।

कोई ताबिज नहीं अब सानिटाईजर रक्षाकबच है ,
कोई मुरत नहीं अब डॉक्टर ही भगवान है ।
मास्क अब जिवन का अभिन्न अंग है ,
ना मानो तो पुलिस लाठी का खौफ है ।

वो जो दौड़ के आते थे कभी गले लगने ,
आज हाथ मिलाने से कतराते हैं ।
कहीं हो ना जाए कोरोना ,
बिच कि दूरियां अब वो बनाते हैं ।

वो मोमोज की चटनी और गोल-गप्पे का पानी ,
वो चिकन विरयानी और दहीबड़े का घुगनी ,
सोचा करके ये जुबान लाल टपकता है ।
वो चाय कि प्याली , आवारा दोस्तों का गाली ,
याद करके ये दिल अब रोता है ।

पब में रात काटने वाले ,
आज घर के कामों में हाथ बंटाते हैं ।
रेस्टोरेंट में चाईनीज खाने वाले ,

आज मां के हाथ का बना परांठे खाते हैं ।

दरार पड़ गई थी जिन रिस्तो में ,
आज वो जूडने लगें हैं ।
छेद हो गई थी जिस ओजोन में ,
आज वो भरने लगें हैं ।

प्रदूषण का साया घटते ही ,
हिमालय कि चोटी आज फिर से दिखने लगी है ।
मैली पड़ी थी जो गंगा घाट अर्जो तक ,
आज फिर से आंखों को झलसाने लगी है ।

जिन्दगी के भिड में भाग-दौड़ करते थे जो कभी ,
आज घर में बैठे पाए जाते हैं ।
चाहे दफ्तर का काम हो या स्कूल कलेज कि पढ़ाई ,
बच्चों से बुढढो तक आनलाइन के भरोसे है ।

एक तरफ प्रकृति का स्वरूप बदल रही है ,
और दूसरी तरफ कोरोना का उप्तीडन है ।
एक तरफ परिवार से मिलने की खुशी है ,
और दूसरी तरफ बेरोजगारी का मातम है ।
यह बदलाव जिन्दगी को एसी मोड दिया है ,
जिन्दगी की गाड़ी को फिर से पटरी पर लाने में ,
आत्मनिर्भरता और स्वच्छता अनिवार्य हो गया है ।

SUBHASHREE MISHRA

Subhashree Mishra is a girl of odisha inspired from her grandfather's devotional poems and decided to pursuing the same path. Nd inspired from her fathers extraordinary writing skill, her writtings are always a fusion of her special feelings and words.. She is As strong as mountain, agnate soft bridge Bright as sunshine, alike snow the freeze... Dark like darkness, wide alike heaven.. Image of Almighty deep as ocean..

The Stormy Path; A Story Retold

DEV, a naughty little boy from rural India, is the youngest son of his parents among 6 other siblings. His father is a hard working farmer and from childhood Dev had complete faith that he can do anything & that came a bit true as well. He could climb a coconut tree, he could cycle 60 Kilometers continuously. He could swim, could fish, knows farming and a bright student as well. But from the very beginning he was interested in machines so he was very keen about mechanics. Sometimes he knowingly broke his toys to know how it worked. He was always curious about it but nobody was there to answer his questions. After observing his curiosity , his head master approached him and said “DEV, if you study well then you might become an engineer & so will you find your answers and you will also get an opportunity to learn more about machines. After hearing this his heart was filled with joy and happiness as he got his ultimate life goal that he dreamed of. So he started studying with strong determination. His one& only ambition was to be a good engineer.

With growing age, he came to know about people's condition and decided to help the people with his available knowledge as per his strength. Days passed, and he also passed out school and got selected by a known university and decided to take admission in science stream.

His family couldn’t afford for his study so he started to work as a fisherman, paperboy and sold palms and coconuts to earn some money for his essential study materials. Somehow he passed 12th standard with good marks. His father wanted him to run a tea stall to earn money for his family. But he wanted to join engineering as he worked hard for that. His dream to be an Engineer faded as no one in the family supported it. Then having no support, he decided to learn some techniques of engineering on his own with a little education on them. That commitment & enthusiastic approach towards engineering didn't get along with his father's idea. So he was discarded from the family by his father. Having nowhere to go he just spent his time roaming around the city.

"Fortune Favors the brave" proverb came true about Dev when accidentally he met an engineer who offered him a job to teach his son. Knowing about his situation, he offered the boy a place to live. One day he approached the engineer & requested him to lend him some books on engineering. The engineer gave 5-6 books to dev. After 2-3 days Dev returned those books. The engineer was keen to know what Dev had learned in those 2-3 days. So he asked Dev about the books for which Dev replied "I have completed all those books". The engineer was surprised to hear that & to know the truth, he asked some random questions to Dev from the books. Dev answered all the questions which astonished the engineer. The engineer was cheerful about that and appreciated Dev for his dedication. Some days later in an unfortunate accident the engineer passed away. That put Dev back to start again where he had left.

Thinking about all these and about life he reached a station and boarded a train. He was deeply affected by the death of the engineer and while standing by the door someone pushed him from behind & he fell out of the train. While bleeding heavily he somehow reached the nearest station where he came in the eye of the station master. After reaching the station master he fell unconscious. The Station master took him to the nearest hospital & helped him in his treatment. After the heavy injury & bleeding he went to comma for 20 days. Slowly he started to recover after a month. After recovering he gave a heartily gratitude to the station master for whom he was alive. The station master then helped him to get a job of radio repairing. Dev learned all the works within just two weeks & stayed happily there which included food twice a day. Due to some loses in the radio business the owner started to treat the workers very badly so Dev left from there. He never had enough money to eat so he used to smoke cigarettes to get away with hunger. He made a hut on the top of the hill in a unknown location and started fishing from the nearest rivers and sold them to earn a living.

Once he saw some people throwing megaphones (BULLHORNS) as they were not working. Dev had the knowledge on how to repair those so he took them and started repairing and made them useful again. People started to know Dev as an electronics repairer and offered him electronic equipments to repair. He started to love that job and after some time build his own shop for those works. May be he wasn't that educated but his dedication and observation skills helped him to grow his business to a new height as he establishes his own company. Now he could work as he wanted. He also helped people by opening a college for poor kids in his place.

So, "Believe in yourself and work hard to achieve success. Value yourself irrespective of the failures, you have to stick in that determination and be patient. God's delay is not his denial; wait & you will see the glory of God.

RISHI VINAYAK

Ordinary lad from Ranchi, learning to express, learning to explore, opportunity is just needed, I'll strive to accomplish even more.

Favour-

It was late night coming back home,
journey was way too long.
The day went completely seismic,
filled with wax and wane,
sometimes miracle, sometimes efforts go barren.
Having doleful thoughts to stay fruitless,
or finally know where to look in the flow,
or need just a favour or something more.
Collecting lot of impressions in that humanless road,
Suddenly a vehicle came out of blue asked me home,
man seemed generous,
on way back wanted to convey his thoughts of the day,
"In this nefarious world better be a naive other than hard
work or you are nothing worth"
It's still unknown was it just a favour or something more.

Today-

It wasn't us who were running out of time,
it was nature.
At this hour of time where world is at halt,
we need to see our future.
In this era of tremendous work and pressure,
we need to take measure.
Earth is healing with pace,
humans stopped depletion,
we saw nature's new face.
Rivers are clear and fresh,
birds are returning home.
Grasses are green than ever,
while people are learning to live alone.
It's rather to believe what we see,
than to believe what is yet to come.

Better Place

Better place, better people,
We try to find ourselves in near future,
we were able to settle,
the situation of the world is now stable.
Discrimination was fading out of humanity,
mankind was unleashing a great opportunity.
people with their lives were able to cope,
we all together saw a new hope.
That night I was too lost in myself,
I completely forgot,
we were still dealing with the present.

The Wind

The wind from the past always ignites the fire for tomorrow,
finding rhythm in the work,
let the destiny be followed.
Learn from the day,
peruse every moment.
Facing bigotry people is common,
what matters is rising from the bottom.
Till the last second there is hope,
the question is are we able to cope?
The wind from the past always ignites the fire for tomorrow,
another day comes,
there is no place for sorrow.

ARPITA PRIYADARSHINI

Arpita Priyadarshini is a budding writer, who has been associated with many schools and college events and has been able to convey her vision towards making the youth to 'make a move' in a present scenario. She received her exemplary schlorship in high school and now is pursuing her bachelor's degree in BIOTECHNOLOGY honours from MITS School of Biotechnology. She has preserved to build a vibrant community of followers who actively engross with her artistic skills as well.

एक बेटी कि अनकही कहानी

बड़े नाजुक से मेरे पिता ने
मुझे पाला था,
मेरी हर मांग को अपने दिल के
संदूक में डाला था,
एक बूंद आंसू आंखों मैं
आने नहीं देते थे,
मेरी एक मुस्कान के लिए
पूरी दुनिया से लड़ जाते थे,
कई थे दिल मैं अरमान लाएंगे
अच्छे इंसान को चुन कर,
पर बेटी तो उनकी फस गई थी
एक दरिंदे के चक्कर में
बिना सोच समझ कर,
मुझे जो इतने प्यार से मेरे पापा ने
संभाला था,
कुछ हिं महीनों में तूने मुझे सौ गुना
रुलाया था,
तेरे लिए मेंने अपने पापा का
दिल है तोड़ा,
तूने मुझे किसी और के
लिए है छोड़ा,
शर्मिंदा हूं पापा हो सके तो
करना अपने लाडली को माफ़,
धोखा देके किया है मैंने ज़िन्दगी का सबसे बड़ा पाप।

CORONA:एक प्रेम कथा

देखना चाहती हूं तुझे
पर ये social distancing ने रोक रखा है,
तुझे करीब से ना सही
पर वीडियो कॉल मैं तुझे देखने का शौक पाल रखा है,
और ये कोरोना क्या जुद्दा करेगा
सची मोहब्बत करने वालों को,
ये पुलिस वालों के डंडे ने हमको डरपोक बना रखा है।

इस क़दर प्यार करती रही

मैं आंखों मैं आंसू और दिल में प्यार छुपाती रही,
तुझे तेरे खुशियों से मिलाकर तुझसे दूरी बनाती रही,
तुझे पता तक ना चले ऐसी कोशिश करती रही,
तेरी एक मुस्कान के लिए अपने सारे सपनों को कुचलती रही।

SRISTI RAJ

Born on 19th of March of the year 2005, a young and aspiring writer with scientific interests, to be brief. She is a dreamer and a citizen of Jamshedpur, Jharkhand. Her write ups include mostly Poems and micro tales covering different genres. A friendly, ambivert and optimistic person and an active volunteer in several events. She believes in in the power of words and thats her speciality to use them to portray her message. She strongly agrees with the fact that life is not a fairy tale with happy endings, but its all about success and failures.

Bloody Pages

The little bird flourished at her abode,
To measure the sky, and claim it own.
Fluttering her pennons, she planned her flight,
But they were restricted and she was confined..
Was this designated to be her halt?
Trusting the falsifiers was her fault;
Who were indisguised as her blood relatives,
And her alleged In-laws.
How well played those mortals,
With her dreams and emotional calls.
She thought her ambitions to be a burden on all...
And so between her and those dreams stood a wall
This intangible wall was built by her parents,
Mum and dad to whom she called.
Cementing was pleasingly done by her insuing family,
And the final touch was added by her artificial gaity.
The heart in flames was freezed,
As she stood at the graveyard of her dreams..
And saw the murder of her ambitions,
With an adorned knife of 'marriage and fusion'
Made a lot of attempts to find,
The love and passion in the people around,
But always faced the demons inside,
Sitting quietly in the human's hide.
Then one fine day she found,
Her way out of this bound;
And opened a book, dusty and dark,
Which turned out to add the misplaced spark;
She turned those crisp pages,
And sipped the words one by one,
Sniffing the page gave the desired satisfaction,

For she would read 'em in a minute's fraction.
Wistfully, the book along with her heart was torn
And in her room she was thrown.
She looked at a blank page with her teary haze,
Which was similar to the dissolution on her face.
With the draining bloody drop of red,
She wrote, inkling the pain she was fed.
'Bloody Pages', the poetry title read,
And with this simmering hope, now she was led.

Lover's Graveyard

He laid there freezed,
She sat there stiffened.
Their hands in hand, clasped together,
And the world seemed to give a pacific gesture;

She remembered those sweet hours,
But now things have changed.
Sweet memories turning her sour,
She was standing at his graveyard;

Those pearl tears from her chocolate orbs,
Fell on his cheeks arid and dry.
Her lips drained with silent sobs,
Her body tired of sorrow vibes.

The night was gloomy and rimy,
Even the moon was curtained,
Behind the sky dark and cloudy,
And the weather manifested the maiden's dolour;

For the last time she laid,
Her delicate fingers on his apathetic lips.
And finally sunk in oblivion,
Taking her leave;

To the world she was indebted to,
Where she met him and was attached to.
And lied on his holy relics,
Cursing death who pulled them apart;

The next morning was a day bright and fair,
The bodies of the lovers together.
And for their souls I wish,
May hail in heaven, resting in peace!!

DEEPAK PANI

Deepak is not a writer by nature but he feels comfortable to share his feelings through writing. His writings are inspired by his experience in life.

The Feeling Called LOVE

Love, the word itself is complete.
It is enough and it's pure.
so let's take a stroll down the memory lane,
to the first time we loved someone .
It never matters how you end up.
what matters is the sense of being together
and the fact that someone is watching over you
gives you confident and you know that she will bring you back on your feet if you fall.
It's like a wave of sea which washes away all your pain and sufferings;
it's like a bolt of lightening running through the veins
It creates a sense of sacrifice and it is always worth it .
You just know it.
It is about a person to whom we would come home to.
It just complete us.

सावन

बिखरे हुए हैं फूल
महक रही है सुगंध
सुन्दर लगने लगी है ये दुनिया
कहीं ये जन्नत तो नहीं।।
हर तरफ हैं खुशियां खिलने लगी हैं कलियां
कहीं ये सावन का महीना तो नहीं।।
हो रहा है एक एहसास अजीब सा
चड़ने लगा है ये रंग खुशियों का
दिल में मेरे जग रहा फिर से
ये प्यार तो नहीं।।

अब मैं और लौट के नहीं जाऊंगा

अब मैं और लौट के नहीं जाऊंगा
फिरसे अब में पीछे मुड़कर नहीं देखूंगा
पंख कटे तो चल लूंगा
पैर टूटे तो तेर लूंगा
दिल टूटे तो सह लूंगा
तेरी याद आए तो चुपके रो लूंगा
कुछ भी करके खुदको संभाल लूंगा
अब मैं और लौट के नहीं जाऊंगा

अनजानों के सहर

अनजानों के सहर में
किसी अपने की तरह
वो आई है हमारी जिंदगी में रोशनी की तरह ।।
अब बस चाहत यही है कि
जिंदगी के सफर में वो दे मेरा साथ
एक हमराही की तरह ।।

कुछ ऐसा हाल हुआ

कुछ ऐसा हाल हुआ उन्हें देख के।।
ना पलके झपकी ना आवाज़ निकली जुबान से।।
बस दिल ने कहा दिमाग से की
मिल गई तेरी मंजिल जिसे तू मांगता था तेरे खुदा से

ANKITA SAHOO

An ambivert girl, chasing her dreams, struggling through circumstances. She loves to follow her heart and intuition as it gives her courage and confidence. She believe in making difference as well as create notions and norms of own. She quotes her life as; "Don't waste your life on one goal, make it broad"

Call of Fate

I woke up this morning to millions of thought in mind. My eyes could barely sleep last night. The watery pupils were staring at the ceiling, urging the sun to never dawn.

Adjacent room reside another soul, who also happen to emerge with infinite dreams to this sunrise. As curtains were raised his face glittered with exhilaration.

Tears rolled down while turning my side in bed and my lips murmured, "I wish I could endure this pain and torture."

Back in the kitchen my mom screamed, "Do you people get the time ?." Be quick! Arrange the tables soon.

He headed towards our room with heavy steps.

Wake Up! Wake Up!, he yelled.

The younger one was dragged out of bed. Poor fellow, his 4am sleep with 69th uncompleted chicken dinner match was disturbed. With a drooling mouth he was handed an empty bag and 500 rupees.

The clock ticked half past 12pm. "They must be arriving soon",father claimed.

Every corner of the house was decorated with flowers and fluorescent lights.

Delicious food, sweets and all sorts of beverages were served in nice set of crystal crockery and glasses.

Mom wore a beautiful banarasi saree and Father was in his nicest pair of shirt and trousers. They both looked jaw dropping.

“It's time! It's time! They must be arriving”, Father bawled out of joy. His words trembled in excitement.

“Give them a call.”, mom said.

“I think they are troubling themselves finding their way”, she added.

At once the cellphone flashed light and rang. It was them. Father answered the call.

“Hello! It's Gangadhar”, they addressed and chatted. Few minutes later the call went disconnected.

Father's face went pale. He was unable to utter a word. He went traumatised and shocked. His body collapsed down to the chair.

“They denied”, Father replied.

They found someone more better than our daughter for their son.

The whole atmosphere went numb.

Deep inside I shattered, not because the alliance broke, but I never wanted my parents to face this nightmare.

Again my lips spoke, “I WISH YOU WERE HERE,SWEETIE”

MAHESWARI TARAI

This is Maheswari Tarai. A girl who is deeply committed to the cause of serving the people of her motheland.
#Student
#From Cuttack, Odisha
#One man with courage makes a majority.

The Focus Pinned Behind A Dream

Here is a small story about a student who deserves any kind of struggles in her life.

In this position the generation has been totally changed and a woman can do everything as compare to a man. So here we discussed about a girl who deserves all the problems and her family situation for her success or her bright future.

Every student has their own dream. So here is a girl whose family background was so poor. And her aim to help peoples to become a doctor for doing some social works for poor people since her childhood. She was thinking that becoming a doctor is only path by which she can provide free health checkup to all peoples. Due to deficiency of proper guidance her aim for doctor was remain break.

But her target for helping peoples was continuously upgraded. And she wants to do some other works for which this work has been helped for the peoples and her country. And she searched for the paths to reach on her goal or future that she wants to do something special for her nation.

Walt Disney said that:

"Times and conditions change so rapidly that we must keep our aim constantly focuscd on future.

She saw many options for doing some works for the nation. For reached in this position she faced many struggles and she prepared herself both mentally and physically. School and college life passed away. She will get this situation that she won't take a proper decision and we know very well that the quality of thinking matters a lot during the hardest time of your life. In this moment she will face her family situation that family members said something and she has to do this. In this matter she has to choose both her passion and her family words. But she gave her passion to more priority because she has to do something for peoples. She gave a small priority to those peoples by whom she was reached on this level. She was trying her best to become a special person for her family and her nation. She was trying and till trying now. For becoming or reach on this level she gave an art on her work. By a dream this was not possible this work has been done; we have to do some special works on this how this dream can be achieved and give a proper direction to achieve this. She is trying to do her best and reach on her goal for doing works for peoples. Let's see what happens. Is this girl can achieve her goal?

THE GREAT MAN Bruce Lee said that:
"The successful warrior is the average man, with laser-like focus."
Is this girl can achieve her goal!

RAKESH KUMAR NAG

इनका जन्म 1976 में झारखंड के राँची जिले में हुआ । इनके पिता का नाम नंदकिशोर नाग और माता का नाम तुला देवी है । पांच भाइयों और एक बहन में ये सबसे बड़े हैं। मैट्रिक की परीक्षा इन्होंने संत पौल स्कूल से की और फिर मारवाड़ी कोलेज से इंटर और कॉमर्स I स्नातक की पढाई शुरू की फिर बीच में पढाई छोड़ दिल्ली चले गए । वहां उन्होंने जवाहर लाल नेहरू विश्वविद्यालय में रशियन भाषा में स्नातक में दाखिला भी लिया था और परिस्थति वश उसे भी छोड़ दिया और अकाउंट्स की ट्यूशन देने लगे फिर एक निजी स्कूल में भी पढाया और वहीं के प्रिंसिपल भी उसी दौरान उनके मंझोले भाई का निधन हुआ और वे राँची वापस लौट आए । उन्हें लिखने का शौक बचपन से ही था । उन्होंने अपनी पहली कहानी " पितृभक्त " 14 साल की उम्र में ही लिख डाली थी । जब वे आठवीं कक्षा में पढाई करते थे ।वर्तमान समय में वो अपनी जीविका चलाने के लिए अनेक कामों में व्यस्त हैं फिर भी लेखन जारी है ।जो एक समाजिक आडम्बर को कटाक्ष था ।

उलझन

बड़ी उलझन में हूँ सुलझाऊं कैसे?
एक बात जो दिल है दबी, बताऊं कैसे!
चंद ही दिनों में मेरी नींद मेरा चैन छिन लिया, तुमने ।
ये समझाऊँ कैसे!
जुबां खामोश है, मगर आँखों से सब कह दिया है मैंने ।
ये बात समझती तुम भी हो ,पर बताऊं कैसे!
करके हंसी-गुनाह बनती हो नादान ,पर बताऊं कैसे!
बड़ी उलझन में हूँ, सुलझाऊं कैसे ?

आखिर इंसान चाहता क्या है

कृष्ण के आगमन से लेकर, ओशो के प्रस्थान तक।
कुरुक्षेत्र से लेकर हिरोशिमा तक,
बह्मास्त्र से लेकर नाभिकीय शस्त्र तक।
आखिर इंसान चाहता क्या है?
धरती से लेकर पाताल तक, जन्म से लेकर मृत्यु तक, विज्ञान के सहारे हर भेद को खोल रहा है। आखिर इंसान चाहता क्या है?
अब, तो इंसान को बनाने वाला भगवान भी उससे डर रहा है, क्योंकि इंसान ही इंसान का "क्लोन " बनाकर उससे भी प्रतियोगिता कर रहा है ।
आखिर इंसान चाहता क्या है?

जमाने के बहाने ।

हम स्वंय जानते तक नहीं है,
क्या है सही, क्या है गलत ।
बस,दे देते हैं
तर्क- वितर्क हम अपने-अपने हित का ख्याल रख।

स्वंय कभी न खोजा है, न खोजेंगे, तभी तो पहचान पाने में रहते हैं असमर्थ ।
क्या है सही और क्या है गलत ।
जब करते ही नहीं प्रयास, इन्हें ढूढने का।
हल इनका निकाल पाते नहीं, तो पलायन भी छिपाते है, बड़ी अदा से।

कहते हैं आराम से यूँ ही
अरे! यही तो जमाना है यारों ।
और निकल लेते हैं ,थोप कर बहाने से ।
सारी चीजें जमाने को।

क्या ढूढता हूँ !

गुजर गया वो कल,
उसे आज ढूढता हूँ ।
हर किसी में तेरे एहसास ढूढता हूँ ।
जानता हूँ कि सब कुछ धोखा है फिर भी गैरो मे अपनों का साथ ढूढता हूँ।
जल गया है सबकुछ मगर राख में कुछ ढूढता हूँ ।
सचमुच मैं पागल हूँ ,ठंढे पानी में आग ढूढता हूँ ।

AWADH

झारखंड प्रदेश के रांची में मांडर थाना अंतर्गत सुरसा गांव में एक साधारण परिवार में ७/१/१९५२को इनका जन्म हुआ। पिता श्री भूनेशवर सिंह, माता लाखों देवी के घर दो लडके एक लड़की मैं सबसे छोटे थे।दस माह के जब हुए तो पिता का साया उठ गया, ससुर जी की ताड़ना से परेशान इनकी माता श्री इनहें लेकर मायके चली गई। वहां से इनके छोटे भाई जो जमशेदपुर में कार्यरत थे उनके पास रख कर इनका पालना की। अवध भाई दसवीं तक की पढ़ाई के बाद रांची में. I T I में मोटर मेकेनिक का टर्निंग पास किया। लगभग एक साल नौकरी के लिए भटकना पड़ा फिर एक्स चेंज के माध्यम से सी सी एल में एप्रेंटिस ट्रेनिंग के लिए बहाली हुवी १९७५__७७ तक ट्रेनिंग पुरा करने के बाद वहीं पर इनकी नौकरी हो गयी। पागल बड़े भाई, भाभी तथा उनके चार बच्चे , गरीब बड़ी बहन, बहनोई तथा उनके चार बच्चे और मां तथा अपने चार बच्चे मीलाकर कुल२१ परिवार की गाड़ी खींचते आगे बढ़ते रहे। अपनी छोटी बेटी के जन्म के पहले कविता लिखने की प्रेरणा जगी

जीनदगी की गाड़ी

जीनदगी की गाड़ी
समय के रास्ते पर
रात दिन रूपी पेड़
गीनते नजराने कहां पर
जायगी या रूकेगी
मंजिल का कोई भी
ठीकाना ना हो
यूं बेकार चली जायेगी
समय के रास्ते पर

अंजना राही हूं
अंजाने राहों का
जाउंगा वहीं पर
जहां कोई ठिकाना हो
सोचता हूं।

सोचता हूं कभी कभी
भागजाऊं
सवाल है कहां पर ?
उत्तर है
जीनदगी की गाड़ी
समय के रास्ते पर
रात दिन रूपी पेड़
गीनते नजाने कहां पर
जायगी या रूकेगी

मंजिल का कोई भी
ठीकाना ना हो
यूं बेकार चली जायेगी
समय के रास्ते पर
यूं बेकार चली जायेगी
समय के रास्ते पर।।

परिवारीक बोझ के साथ भारतीय मजदूर संघ के बैनर तले शाखा सचिव से लेकर एरिया तथा प्रदेश तक पदाधिकारी बनकर खदान में कार्य रत अनपढ़ सोसीत पीड़ित मजदूरों की भी सेवा करने का सौभाग्य प्राप्त हुआ। भ्रष्ट समाज,देश, तथा दुनिया में जबकि परिवर्तन की जरूरत है वहां लोगों को हमने सीते हुवे देखा तो उसे एक कविता के रूप में लीखा

घीसापीटा जिंदगी सब जी रहे हैं
बेहतर फटे को सब सीरहे हैं
कहने को क्या नहीं है जो यहां पर
चुल्लू से पानी सब पीरहे हैं।

कोई चाहता है हंसना यहां
हंस नहीं सकता,
कोई चाहता है रोना यहां
रो नहीं सकता,
कोई चाहता कुछ कहना
कुछ कह नहीं सकता
कोई चाहता है कुछ करना

कुछ कर नहीं सकता
कोई चाहता है मरना
यहां मर भी नहीं सकता
क्या काम है यहां
क्या कररहे हैं
घीसा पीटा जिंदगी सब जी रहे हैं
बेहतर फटे को सब सीरहे है
कहने को क्या नहीं है जो यहां पर
चुल्लू से पानी सब पीरहे हैं
चुल्लू से पानी सब पीरहे हैं

गीत लघुकविता लीखने का क्रम चलता रहा इसी क्रम में मैं आध्यात्म से जुड़ने लगा और नौकरी से सेवानिवृत्त के बाद घर परिवार से बैरागी मन फरीसता बनगया

फरीसता का रीसता
होता नहीं है
वो उड़ता ही रहता
यहां फीर कहीं है फ-----+

जहां भी वो रहता
उड़ता उड़ाता
हंसता हंसाता ही
रहता फरीसता
चिनतावों को
मीटाने वाला
फंसता नहीं है

कहीं भी फरीसता फ------

ना खोता ना रोता
फरीसता बना जब
बाबा से बातें ही
करता ही रहता
रहता नहीं वो
किसी घोंसले में
बंधकर नहीं
जंजीरों में भी रहता
फरीसता का रीसता
होता नहीं है
वो उड़ता ही रहता
यहां फीर कहीं है यहां-----
फरी –

ANUPAM DEVJYOTI JENA

Student of +3 1st year,SN college Rajkanika, Kendrapada.

YOGA : An Internal Piece Andmental Bliss

Today in the materialistic world we are running after money,power and prosperity inspite of living a healthy and peaceful life. In this race we are going farther away from peace and healthy life and inviting various physical and mental. diseases. In order to get peace and real success we have to follow the blissful path of yoga.

Now a day despite of knowing the appropriate meaning of yoga, we are in a missconception about yoga. So let's analyse the real meaning of yoga : yoga is a part of Sanatan Dharma or the eternal way, which is the ancient wisdom tradition of South Asian subcontinent India. The word yoga comes from Sanskrit word YUJ which means union, yoke or mastery. "Yoga is the union or integration of body, mind and spirit or in ither words body, breath and mind." Swami sivanand of rishikesh used to say, yoga is the union of head, heart hands." So that what we think, sat and do are in harmony. The expansive state that is yoga comes from this unification.

In a more mystical sense, yoga is the unification of individual soul with the supreme soul. When the body, breath and mind are aligned, our energy system vibrate at the same frequency as the universal vibration represented by syllable "OM". There have been many articulation of yoga is a path begining with Bhagbad geeta in about 1500 BC. Krishna speaks of different path to the state of yogs, harmony, peace and beingness.

The paths are :

(1) Jnana yoga (the path of contemplaton)

(2) Bhakti yoga (the path of devotion)

(3) Karma yoga (the path of action for its own.)

Yoga is a state of being not a doing. These paths are routes to yoga. Yoga is not a doing but it is a state. In 300 AD Patanjali codified what was know of yoga until that time in a collection of 926 aphorisms called " Yoga darshan" or " Yoga sutras". Patanjali defines yoga as ' yogas chitta vritti nirodha.' The fluctuation in consciousness or the release from the patterns of habits etched into consciousness.

The thinking of human can be measured as thought wave by EEG machine.

1. Beta - It is a rapid fluctuation if active thinking.
2. Alpha - It is the calmer state of mind achieved when we take few deep breath or do relaxation.
3. Theta - It is an intuitive, stiller state like that between waking and sleeping. It is Avery meditative for which Yogi's practice meditation after waking
4. Delta - It is another state of thinking which is naturally occuring state of mind. It very still like during deep sleep meditation.

Yoga is an weapon to capitalise on natural meditative state to come into an integrative state and act from that place. In yoga seven chakras which are very important. They are

1. Throat chakra
2. Root chakra
3. Sacral chakra
4. Heart chakra
5. Naval chakra
6. Third eye chakra
7. Crown chakra.

Patanjali is most famous for his eight fold path that comes from chapter 2 of ' yoga sutras ' in which he outlines a whole technology for coming to this state of integration and enlightenment. This is called astanga yoga. Following this path we can reach in that state.

Though the origin of yoga is India, we the youth of India have to popularise and spread this mysterious way of living all over the world and in order to get peace, real success we have to follow this blissful path of yoga. .

TUHINA CHOUDHURY

This is Tuhina Choudhury,A Writer Poet & musician,Currently a student of English Honours,professional Singer

Choice Is Yours

It is not necessary
That a man should only date a woman,
It's His personal choice.

It's not necessary
That a man should take all the responsibilities after marriage,
Man and woman are equal.

It's not necessary
That a child should score 99% and top the school,
Every child has their unique qualities.

It's not necessary
That a couple should expect their baby after couple of years,
Parenthood is a choice not compulsion.

It's not necessary
That a girl should get married before 30,
It's nowhere written,neither she is bounded.

It's not necessary
That a transgender should be treated as untouchable,
They too are human beings.

These things are really not necessary
But it's necessary for the society where we live.
And the most important thing which everyone lacks is,
What is necessary for "US"

SO START LIVING FOR YOURSELF BEFORE LIVING FOR THIS SOCIETY.
WHAT MATTERS THE MOST THE CHOICE IS YOURS.

ANWESHA BAHINIPATI

The writter is 20 year old girl persuing her career in Integrated master in science mathematics and computing,love to express herself,quite straight forward and pragmatic by nature.her content are basically related to human behaviour,peace, ongoing problems in life and explicit way to tackle it. She is also interested in attending humanitarian committees.

A Good Life Is One Inspired By Love And Guided By Knowledge

First of all let me share my views on relating love, knowledge and a good lifestyle.Love for oneself or for anything surrounding you gives ideas to maintain a comfortable life and knowledge helps to implement those ideas which ultimately makes life worth living and better.

Good life means a balanced lifestyle with a positive attitude to live today and plan for tomorrow.having a thought to work for others and finding peace in other's satisfaction all these will make life worth living. Self satisfaction and inner peace are the two important component of a healthy lifestyle. Good life means when you have money but you don't need it to buy peace and happiness. When you realise everything in this life is temporary only the love and respect gained,the satisfaction felt and the happiness spreaded is permanent you start leading a optimistic life then after criticism doesn't affect you ,you start learning from everything.

The way you like the bitterness in chocolate start liking the disappoints you have related to yourself.

Life will become too simpler to understand,love yourself the way you are because all those matter is self-love.

Love is immortal it can be for anything , starting from your pet to the small flower in your garden,it can be for your friends, family or anyone who makes you feel better and also it can be for chirping sounds of bird to the wind carrying positive vibes the only thing matter is your perception of considering things going around you. All these changes around you will give a sparkle in your life and will make it exciting to live.

Love demands comfort, happiness, satisfaction and most importantly peace and we need our knowledge to achieve all these from nothing to everything.

Now how knowledge will help us getting all these?

We can say knowledge is a simple combination of intelligence and Wisdom and a person having both knows how to make life better.Intelligence ismaking others useful for yourself and wisdom is making yourself useful for others both of these will help you gain love from others which will lead to a better life. Knowledge not only concerntated around study but it can be physical which deals with exploring and noticing stuff and happenings around you, social which deals with small gestures that makes other happy for example a thank you for the gift you received and it can be logical which says everything around you happens for a reason you only need to find that to feel complete and satisfied with your life. Each of these will make you a better person and understanding everything and accepting it with love will help you lead a pragmatic and a good life

SANGEETA PRASAD

Her name is Mrs Sangeeta prasad, she was born on 16 september1975. She has completed her education form bihar .she is an amazing teacher and mother of 2children . She loves tho write stories and has an interest in singing. Overall she an amazing personality

Ek Thi Reema

Wo kehte hai na,

zindagi mein kabhi kisi mazbutt insan se bhet karni ho,
toh bss ek bar sanghrash karti hui aurat ki dincharya ko dekh lena!
Aapke kitne hi adhure sawaalo ke jawab,
naa jaane aapko mil jaaye aur aap khud-naa- khud,
uss devi ki murit ban jaaye!!

Yeh kahani hai ek aise ladki ki, jo bihar ke ek chote se gawo mein janam leti hai. Maa- Baap garib hone ke karan padhai- likhayii adhuri chor bohot choti umar mein shaadi ke bandhan mein bandh dete hai.
Jinhe shayad nahi pata ho, unke liye mein, yeh batana chahungi ki aaj bhi bihar ke kaayi aise sheher hai jaha sikhsha ka aabhav hai, rozgaar, weyabsahi, rehen-sehen, jeene ke torr- tarike, inn sab mein aapko ek alag hi dirtapan nazar aayega.
Inn sab wevasthao ki maari "REEMA", jisne toh abhi aapna bachpan bhi sahi se nahi dekha, usse jeevan ke ek aise bandish mein jakad diya gaya, jaha se nikalna uske liye aasambhav sa tha. Nahi pata tha ki uske sath kya kiya ja rha hai? Shaadi ke baad, reema ko aapne sasural jana pada
Sasural mein wo anya baacho ki tarah khelti- kuddti, parantu yeh sabhi uske saas ko bikul pasand nahi tha. Wo usse ghar ke kaam shikhati, ghar ke logo ka khayal rakhne ko kehti, ya yuh kahu ki use ek purna- roop se bahu banane ki koshish ki jaa rahi thi.
Hamari saamaj ki ye ek aise widambanna hai, jisse humara desh aaj bhi ubhar nahi paaya. Parantu inn sab mein "uss bacchi reema ki kya galti thi"?!!

Samaye bit ta gaya, reema ka paati ramesh aab wayasakh (18yrs) ka ho chuka tha. Aab reema- ramesh ke tin baache bhi the. Inn sab ke beech ramesh ko ek gandi addat lag gayiz wo nasha ka aadi ho chuka tha. Wo rooz sharaab peeta aur ghar par aakar hungama karta, baacho ko - aapni patni reema ko marta-peet ta.

Yeh saari ghatnaye reema ki zindagi mein ek aisa aadhya tha jiska kahani- saar kaafi dukhdaayi tha.

"Ek aurat ki zindagi tab narak jaati hai, jab uska swam-saathi, jeevan-rakshak, uska hi dohan karne lage. Reema ke saas sasur bhi ramesh ko daat te - faatkarte par us sharaabi par inn sab ka koi aasar nahi padhta.

Kehte hai na ki:

"Vikataao ki naadiya jab beheti hai
toh aapne sath bohot kuch baha le jaati hai.
Bus reh jaati hai toh bhuli barsi yaade!!"

Reema ki zindagi mein ek gehera mor tab aaya jab uske saas-sasur swarg sidhar gaye. Aab ramesh aur bhi zyada kuritiyo ka shikar hota jaa raha tha, aab toh uske aanya mahilao ke sath aaved sambandh ki bhi baate samne aa rahi thi.

"Dusri oor reema aapni tin nadan baccho ke saath aapni futi kismat ka rona roo rahi thi."

Tabhi reema ne nirnaye liya ki wo aapne baacho par inn sab ka koi bhi bura aasar nahi padhne degi. Wo aab ramesh ko uske haal par chor, aapne baccho ki sunheri bhavisya ke sapne liye dusre seher ko chal di.

Waha, wo logo ke gharo mein kaam kar, aapne baacho ka kisi vidhyaale mein dakhila karakar rehne lagi. Uske baache bhi kaafi samajhdar the. Aur aapni maa ko itni kaadi mehenat karta dekh aache se padhayii karte aur aapni maa reema ka khayal rakhte. Uske baacho ke mann ek khayal jo iss tarah hai ki, kehte hai

" naasuk si cheez hoti hai aurat
maardo ka sahara lena hi padhta hai!
Par maa toh,
Papa ke naa hone ke baad bhi bohot majbuti se khadi hai....."

Samaye beet ta gaya, reema aapne baccho ki padhayii jaari rakhti hai. Aur aapne mehenat karti, baacho se bas padhayii karne ko kehti hai.

Aur samaye ka faal dekho aaj uss ghatna ko beete 20 saal hogye jab reema aapne paati ka ghar chor, ek aanjaan seher mein 3 chote baccho ke sath aayi thi.

Aab uske tino baccho mein ek doctor, ek engineer aur ek shiksak hai.

Reema ke aab tino bacche uske tin stambh hai jo usse sahara de rahi hai.

Aur issi beech reema ka paati bhula bisra reema ke pass wapas lauta hai, uske bacche usse swikaar karne se inkaar kar dete hai parantu reema ka hirdhya shant jaal jaisa swaach awivam pavitra tha wo uss ramesh ko bhi maaf kar deti hai usse aapne parivaar ka hissa maankar khud ke saath shamil kar leti hai.

Wo kehte hai na,
"Maa ki kaami koi pura nahi kar sakta agar koi pura kar bhi sakta hai toh wo swam maa"!! Reema par aadharit kahani sacchi ghatnaoo se prerit hai.

PRADEEP KUMAR SHILL

Pradeep Kumar Shill is an independent and dynamic personality full of confidence and positivity. He is a cheerful, ever smiling and laconic person with a great command over words and thoughts. He has the ability to pen down his feeling and imagination with good humor and moral responsibility that one can connect with.

As he follow Kabiguru Rabindranath Tagore, he loves to write in English, Hindi, Odia and Bengali. He is bengali by birth, but love to write in odia the most. He is an excellent academician, and has true devotion towards lord which is reflected through his work. He is a nature lover and is as expressive as he could be through his poem. He is blessed with a sweet voice and style of narration that could leave someone spell bound.

A Letter To Love

Dear Beloved,
Tis' been a while,
My days are spent, lost in your thought,
My night keeps me wandering,
Neither you knew it,
Nor I had dared to express it.
But today, I feel like
Writing a letter to you,
To express my deep love,
Which I kept hidden since long.
Many times, I thought
To say it, but can't.
The pain, the burden which I carry
Is only to reveal in front of you.
Just once try to understand,
Feel yourself in place of mine,
Whether I am eligible for,
Or I am just not.
If you wish, I shall write,
The pain in which I am living,
A heart filled emotion
And the language of affection.
For whom I live in solitude,
For whom I live alone.
That loneliness, too a bliss,
When memories skim through my dreams.
I have been a lone traveler,
Seeking for a companion.
Whose connection, fervor
Will fill me with desire and aspiration.
Is this why I search for you,

Someday, sometime,
To sit beside me to whisper,
With your hand in mine.
Tell my dear! will you write back
A grinning phrase in a letter,
If you find me suitable to counter,
I'll be waiting for your answer.
Don't forget to respond,
Eagerly waiting with a hope.
The truth being you, love of mine,
I seek you for lifetime.
With this drift in mind and heart,
I wrote this epistle,
A soul and hopeful eye,
Awaiting for your reply.
With love,

KRATISHA SINGH

Writing is my passion as it give words to my feelings , loving, caring, helping in nature with simplicity having less expectations teaching is my profession and ready to make new friends explore new things and see the world according to my own perception

कहे अनकहे सवाल-जवाब

किसी को जानने के लिए कितने सवाल-जवाब चाहिए होते हैं? कितनी तो परतें होतीं है इंसानों मे जो हमारे सवाल-जवाब के दायरों मे दूर -दूर तक नहीं आती I
फिर भी किसी से भी बात करने का सिलसिला हमेशा छोटे-छोटे सवालों से ही होता है, कैसे हो? ठीक हो?
ऐसे ही न जाने कितने सवाल , फिर बीतते वक्त के साथ यहीं सवाल आदत बन जाते हैं और देखते ही देखते एहसास बन जाते हैं,और सवालों का दायरा बढ़ जाता है कैसे हो ?की जगह मिस्ड यू ले लेता है, ठीक हो ?की जगह मैं तुमसे बहुत प्यार करता हूं जानती हो न ? कितना बड़ा बदलाव होता है ये दो लोगों के बीच का जिसमें किसी को दिक्कत नहीं होती है ...प्यार कितना खूबसूरत होता है न ? नहीं शायद प्यार मे पड़ना खूबसूरत होता है वो पल जब सब शुरू होता है हम अपने दायरे बढ़ाते हैं एक दूसरे के प्यार मे , सही -गलत जैसी तमाम दुनिया-दारी किसी का डर नहीं किसी की फिक्र नहीं ,
प्यार कितना बेखौफ खर देता है दो अलग -अलग दायरे के लोगों को ....
इस दुनिया से बहुत अलग और बहुत खूबसूरत एक अलग ही दुनिया होती है प्यार मे पड़े लोगों की .....
शुरुआत होती है प्यार की शायद इस लिए ?
सब कुछ इतना खूबसूरत होता है तो कोई अलग क्यों होता कभी किसी से ?
जैसे मैं और तुम हुए ......
कितने साल बीत गए और इन सालों मे न जाने कितनी सारी प्यारी शुरुआत देखी है और उतना ही बद्तर अलगाव भी देखा है ....

कुछ लोगों को तो मुयूट्यूल अडंरस्टैडिंग के साथ अलग होते हुए देखा है यकीन मानों मुझे बिल्कुल समझ नहीं आती उनके अलग होने की वजह कि बस अब हम साथ नहीं रह सकते ,और उन दोनों मे से कोई भी किसी एक को रोकने की कोशिश नहीं करता है इनफैक्ट मैनें उन लोगों को बहुत खुश देखा है .....

हैरानी होती है मुझे उनको देख कर की कैसे ये कैसे हो सकता है......

और अगर ये लोग कर सकते हैं ये तो मैं क्यों नहीं ?

क्यों मुझे आज भी उतनी ही तकलीफ़ होती है जितनी उस दिन हुई थी जब तुम मुझे छोड़ कर गए थे

जबकि मैनें कितनी कोशिशें की थी की तुम मत जाओ पर तुम्हें मेरी किसी भी कोशिश का कोई फर्क नहीं पड़ा क्यों?

तुम मुझसे अलग हो कर खुश हो पर क्यों और कैसे ?

ये सवाल तोड़ देता है मुझे अंदर तक ...

हम तो आपसी सहमति से अलग भी नहीं हुए फिर कैसे तुम खुश रह सकते हो ?

मैं गलत थी ? पर कहां ? क्या मैं इतनी भी जगह नहीं बना पाई तुम्हारी जिंदगी मे की तुम्हें कभी तो मेरी याद आये जैसे मुझे आती है ....खुद को लाख समझाने के बाद भी जब भी मुझसे नहीं रहा जाता मैं तुम्हें मैसेज कर ही देती हूँ कि ठीक हो न तुम ? और तुम , तुम तो पलट कर ये भी कभी नहीं पूछते कि तुम कैसी हो .....खैर इस दुख और गुस्से मे मैं भी तुमसे कोई और सवाल नहीं करती ....

पर खुद को रोकना , सम्हालना आसान नहीं होता उस वक्त

हमारी शुरुआत भी तो कितनी खूबसूरत थी

न सब कुछ सपनों जैसा शुरुआत तो सबकी खूबसूरत ही होती है न ?

पहले सवाल , फिर एक दूसरे की आदतें , फिर साथ न होते हुए भी एक दूसरे को महसूस करना ये तो हर love story की शुरुआत होती है न

हम बचपन से यहीं तो सुनते और देखते आये है दादी -नानी की कहानियों मे वो जो सफेद घोड़े वाला राजकुमार या फिर किसी अत्याचारी राक्षस से बचा कर ले जाने वाला राजकुमार .....हमारे सपनों की दुनिया प्यार कितना खूबसूरत होता है ये हमें हमारे बचपन के किस्से से ही पता चलता है और जब भी कोई शख़्स जिसमें उस बचपन वाले राजकुमार या राजकुमारी की थोड़ी सी भी झलक मिलती है हम उसको सम्हालने मे अपनी पूरी ताकत लगा देतें हैं .....

अपने दादी -नानी के नुस्खों के साथ मैनें भी तो यहीं किया था बल्कि मैनें तो कोई सवाल भी नहीं किया बस तुम्हारे सारे सवालों के जवाब के साथ तुमसे प्यार किया था या बस मुझे तुमसे प्यार हो गया था मैनें कोई दायरा भी नहीं बढाया तुम्हारे लिए क्योंकि तुम सब कुछ थे मेरे लिए मैं जो भी हूं मैं जो भी थी सब तुम्हारे लिए तुम्हारी वजह से ......

फिर क्यों -क्यों गए तुम ?

हमारी कहानी भी तो कितनी खूबसूरत थी बिल्कुल वैसी जैसे मेरी दादी और नानी सुनाया करती थी उसमे सब कुछ तो था जो हमारे बीच था ....

पर उन कहानियों मे राजकुमार कभी भी राजकुमारी को तो छोड़ कर नहीं जाता था न जैसे तुम गए या वो राजकुमार भी गया होगा और उसको वापस बुलाने का कोई तरीका भी होता होगा पर मैं कहानियां सुनते -सुनते जल्दी सो जाया करती थी शायद इस लिए कहानियों का वो पहलू कभी नहीं जान पाई वरना मैं तुम्हें वापस बुला लेती और फिर कभी नहीं जाने देती .... पर अब समझ आ

रहा है "प्यार" इस एक शब्द मे बहुत भार होता है और इस शब्द के साथ जुड़े वहीं खूबसूरत से लम्हों की दकियानूसी तकरीरें ही हर शुरुआत को इतना खूबसूरत बना देती हैं कितना उलझा हुआ है सब पर फिर भी ....

आज मुझे गुस्सा आता है की मैं क्यों सो जाया करती थी या फिर मैनें कभी कोई सवाल नहीं किया शायद इस लिए तुम्हें जाना आसान लगा है न ?

PRATYUSH JENA

Hello folks! Pratyush Jena is a budding writer from the sand city Balasore. His heart lies in astronomy, exploration, photography & his weird world of imagination. This is his first ever publication as an author. Currently, he is a B.Tech 3rd year CSE student at Silicon Institute of Technology, Bhubaneswar.

We As One

Have you ever thought of exploring this universe? I think, most of your answers would be yes. Okay, let me just rephrase it: Have you ever thought of exploring your universe? Umm, think about it and keep on asking yourself because we dream as our society wants us to dream. From the day we born, we gotta follow a framework, or else you'll get neglected/ignored. For example, from the beginning, we all are framed to focus on studies only, about the marks (those simple two digits) rather than learning something useful, creative, interesting. School to even college we get judged every time according to our marks or GPAs.

Nobody thinks of other things like sports, writing, music, etc astheir profession because we have believed that money is everything for us and becoming a sportsperson or a writer or a musician you cannot survive in this world and that's why all these come under co-curricular activities. But the fact is, we never valued them, never tried to explore our own interests, never thought beyond those digits and got end up with the biggest trap of life, 9 am - 5 pm.

Yeah, it might give you money & momentary happiness but with a huge exchange of 29 days of your happiness. That's not life, it's more like a slow poison. Try to live your life, do what feels good, and makes you happy from inside. The reason behind that frameworkis 'competition'. Yes, I agree competition helps to grow knowledge of a single person at an exponential rate but it also deteriorates other's capabilities, emotional stability & control.

Some people compete with each other without even knowing the reason behind it.They are like " yaar ye kar raha hai toh mein bhi karunga" and no matter what the result will be, they just keep going like that. I think they took Ae Dil Hai Mushkil seriously: “Safar khoobsurat hai Manzil se bhi”. The following example gives more clarity about competition : Just buy a flower pot and put 5 different kinds of plant seeds in it with some fertilizers. Water the flower pot daily for a few weeks. After some days youwill notice that they all will start growing but there will be some uncertainty in it. None of the plants will grow properly as they all will be competing with each other for food. On the other hand, if you take 5 separate pots and put one seed each with the same fertilizer, you will definitely mark the growth of each and every plant. Each of them will show their own elegance, beauty, and capabilities. Learn to compete but not with others, rather compete yourself. Try to beat yourself every day, that is what growth is.

Do not look back, just go on as Newton’s third law says, ‘The only way humans have figured out of getting somewhere is toleave something behind’. Together, without competing with each other we can achieve hell lot of things. The feeling of Oneness is not important, because it’s necessary. We the humans stepped on the moon in 1969 and it’s more than 5 decades now, we are still on the moon. If you look around this world, there are many things yet not explored because we used to compete in that, who will find it first or who will first send probes to this or that planet or which nation will become a developed one. We are competing with each other like a basket full of crabs and if one of the crabs tries to jump off, it gets pulled back by thecrab underneath it. If we grow as ONE, as humans, as one nation with no boundaries, we can make ourselves more advance. There are many questions, yet not answered, such as our origin. We don’t know our past from where it began, who is our creator, or how all these things happened? Yes, we do have a lot of theories but they are only theories. We don't know the purpose, don't know who we actually are, and where we came from. All the answer lies in this vast universe, and we as one can find out everything. Stop competing with each other and start exploring together.

RISHIKESH SAHOO

Rishikesh Sahoo. A Definite Integral with Infinite Limits (Math student).A graduate from The Ravenshaw University, Cuttack. He got awarded for the 29th rank for the Pathanisamanta Mathematics Scholarship. (By the hon'ble Chief minister Mr. Naveen Patnaik, Odisha.) Whatever he writes is nothing but his spontaneous inner reflex; the reflection of true incidents of his life. Besides he is a sketch artist, a guitarist and cook but barely a Writer.

Love To From Life:An Evolutionary Path Accompanied By The Chronology Of Betrayal, Motivation And Success

Chronology of Love:

- Whenever someone would try to find me, I hope they'd discover me no where else but under your eyelids.
- Being a human everyone has a thirst for love. To love and to be loved.
- A face full of joy, and that curvy wavy eye. A slight wry smile and the sparkles never dry.
- Be my alarm. I promise I'll never let you snooze.
- The bond between me and darkness was deadly vigorous. You came in and ventilated me with your own ablaze sparkle.
- Love: [A Phobia] (long distance relationship) You know hundreds of people are around. Still you're lonely because of the absence of that one person.

Chronology of Betrayal :

- Busy: A dramatic word to express, that you're of less importance compared to other things.

- In that deadly extensive desert when I needed water, I thought you were the only waterfall who could save me. After a while you popped out as a mirage.

- Pissing off a good heart is a talent. Rare witches are that much talented.

- I think I was colour blind. She was changing her colours. And I couldn't even notice it.

- Similarity between the heart and hymen is once broken, the further fucks don't hurt anymore.

- Your lie was damn colourful and you painted it very beautifully on the canvas of disloyalty.

- Sorry is not a detergent to wash every fault.

- She was a storm who never stopped ruining even after the end.

- Every betrayal has its own special story that, they are caused by our own special ones.

Chronology of Motivation:

- A flame always leaves behind the scar of burn.

- Love's always been chaotic. And we people clutch chaos deep inside.

- Investment of time for self development gives the best profit ever.

- Don't let your history write your Future-Story.

- Remember the person who teaches you how to ignore unnecessary people, has already mastered that skill.

- Emotions are the fuel for the Life-Vehicle. You either let them burn you or use them to move forward.

- Better turns in to best When practice turns in to hustle.

Chronology of Life:

- Personification of the lifelessthings happens when you are scared or in love.
- The conclusion hurts else memories are exquisite.
- Reflections are always distorted. They never show the real image of you.
- Some people are the heart of your story. And Some are the parts, And some are just Volatile-Words.
- Be the Sun or a Lightening in my life. Stay forever or just vanish within a blink. Clear vision is what you wish. Need is just an illusion.
- You still remain a toy in the hands of society unless until you learn and master "Tolerance, Ignorance and Acceptance".
- Solitude is where you can roam around even without a map and would never be lost.
- Life is an art. Attitude is the pencil. It's on you how to draw.

TANISHA NANDA

Tanisha Nanda is a 3rd year B.sc 'statistics' student who has just started to brush up her penning skills. A pure dendrophilia, her foodie skills are in born and unbeatable! She is diligent and convivial!

It's Ok

It's ok if you don't like sports
You will still be the cool dude whom we will support.
It's ok if blue and red colour are not your favourites
You don't always have to go for the reliable black , you can even choose shades of light.

It's ok to have pimples ; you can be fat or thin,
Hormonal problems are so natural, so you shouldn't really grim.
It's ok if you don't like science
Wait, you don't have to necessarily take commerce, even arts will do fine.

It's ok if you need time to get ready; mirror is something, you too can cling
There is nothing to be embarrassed about, taking time to dress up is not only a feminine thing.
It's ok to have a seat at the end of the day even if there are women nearby standing,
Tiredness takes an equal toll on all genders, now that's something we should be understanding.

It's ok to tell your story, women aren't the only ones abused
Men too are victims many a times, they too have their share of wounds.
It's ok to take break from job, If you feel it isn't working for you
For how long you can subside your passion in the name of responsibility, In this way you will ultimately screw.

It's ok if you are confused regarding the aim of life, it's not
always those with concrete goals ultimately thrive.
It's ok to fumble, crumble and stumble
Doesn't that make you later humble.

Oh my man, it's ok to be man that doesn't fit inside the
definition of society
You are man enough, and if people still don't understand,
then it's their pity.

SRIYA SUDESHNA BEHERA

From -Aul ,Kendrapara,odisha Love to sing dance and write. I am a student of BSc*

कुछ अलग था

इस इट जिंदगी में हजारों भीड़ में करोड़ों लोगों मैं हुई मुलाकात। पता नहीं खुदा को क्या मंजूर था। पर अजीब नहीं कुछ अलग था। अजीब थी, पर कुछ अलग नहीं थी। पापा के साथ रहती थी और मां मेरी बचपन से ही गुजर गई थी। उस दिन से कुछ अजीब सा डर रहता था लोगों को खोले का। ना पढ़ाई अच्छी थी न किस्मत। बस इसी के साथ चलती रहती थी मेरी जिंदगी।

तो कहानी शुरू हुई ,यू खत्म हो गई हमारी vacation। अब पहुंच गए हम टेंथ क्लास में ।खिलते हुए धूप में एक उम्मीद थी नया बाहर निकली उसी उम्मीद के साथ और हमेशा की तरह सीधा नजर गई उस सफेद घर की तरफ। वह घर था उस लड़के की यूं बोले तो मेरे एक तरफा प्यार "रोहन"का । मेरे प्यार के हद बस इतनी थी कि नजर मेरी बस उसके पास मे रुकी थी चाहती थी पर पाने की उम्मीद नहीं थी।

रोहन क्लास में सबसे कौन हर बच्चा था ।वह पढ़ाई में सबसे आगे और उसके पिता एक जाने-माने डॉक्टर थे। हमारे मास्टर जी उसके अच्छे आदत और मेरे बुरे आदत कहते कहते कभी थकते नहीं थे।सारे लड़कियां उसके पीछे पागल थी तो मैं कहांबाद पड़ती बस फर्क इतना था वह वक्त ढूंढते थे इजहार करने का और मैं ढूंढती थी मेरी जज्बात को उसे छुपाने को। एक पल में दिल बोल पढ़ता था ,"जा तोड़ दे अपनी खामोशी "और एक पल मनो दिमाग करता था ,"उसको देख और खुद को देख "पागल है क्या? इस दिल दिमाग के चक्कर में बीत गए 5 महीने पर रह गया सब वैसे का वैसा ।आ गया वह वक्त जब हमें चुनना था आगे क्या पढ़ाई करनी है हाय मेरी फूटी किस्मत ,दिल में दर्द लिए और होठों पर मुस्कुराहट अपने जज्बातों की खेल में उलझी हुई थी।में अचानक एक आवाज आया पीछे से ,"श्री"!वह आवाज थी रोहन का । मेरे पास आया और बोला कि' सर ने मुझे तुम्हें पढ़ाने के लिए बोला है '।आज से जो भी दिक्कत है मुझे बताना ।यह बात सुनकर जब मैं उसकी आंखों में डूबा हुआ था मुझे उठा कर वह बोलने लगा मैं

तुम्हें आज से तुम्हारे घर में भी पढ़ाऊंगा तुम्हारे पापा ने कहा है।और चला गया। एक प्यारी सी मुस्कान देकर। औरों मुस्कान मानव कई सवालों का भंडार खोल दिया मेरे अंदर। क्या ऐ इत्तेफाक था या बनी बनाई साजिश।पर अलग ही था....। शायद में फिर से भूल गई करनी और कराने में कितना फर्क है। उसने तो कहा होगा जरूर होगा फिर से करो पर मुझसे नहीं हो पाया ।अब तो जैसे मेरे शरीर के सारे अंग मुझ पर हंस रही है और उसका दर्द बांटने की कोशिश में भी मेरा आंख से आंसू बह गया ।मैं जोर से रोने लगी और मेरी नादानी उसके सामने खोल दी। वह अचानक मेरे हाथ पकड़ कर बोला चलो, और मैं बिना कुछ बोले उसके कदम से कदम मिलाकर चलती रहे। वह ले गया एक जगह जिसको मैं बचपन से देखती आ रही हो।पर आज कुछ नया था कुछ अलग। रोहन ने आंखों से इशारा किया और बोला ," याद है एक छोटी सी लड़की जो है मिट्टी में घर बनाती थी। वह बार-बार टूट जाता पर वह अपने कोशिश नहीं छोड़ती ।फिर एक जगह पर इशारा किया और बोला वही लड़की जो हमेशा सारे बच्चों की मदद करती बिना अपने परवाह किए डांट खा के वहीं बैठी रहती थी और रोती थी पर कभी किसी का साथ नहीं छोड़ती थी। वहां से खड़ी चुपचाप जैसे मेरी भीगी आंखें कर देता सब बयान कि और लड़की में हूं ।इतने में वह बोल पड़ा अब वही लड़की डर रही है ।श्री ,दुनिया में हर कोई Mr perfect होकर पैदा नहीं होता, हमारी मेहनत हमें उसके काबिल बनाता है ।हमारा अपने अंदर झांक के देखो पता जाएगाyou so much more than you know .....

सब मुमकिन है बस अपने ऊपर भरोसा रखो क्योंकि मुझे तुम पर भरोसा है ।हमेशा तुम्हारे साथ हूं ।keep fighting.... उसकी हल्की मुस्कान ने और उसके एक एक लफ्जों ने मेरे सारे अरमान को छा गया ।मेरे सीने में कभी सुकून से धड़कने लगा और दिल समझ नहीं पाया रोए यह क्या करें। यहां से उसके बातों का कुछ ऐसा असर हुआ जैसे मानो फिर से खुद को पहचान लिया। परीक्षा हुआ खतम। रोहन पहले स्थान में था और मैं उससे बस 30 mark पीछे

थी ।कुछ ऐसा था नया जैसे दिल फिर से बोल उठा हो चल कुछ छोटा नहीं है।

अब हम दोनों एक यूनिवर्सिटी में वेल पढ़ने वाले थे वही सुबह वही धूप कुछ अलग था तो उसे चाहत के साथ उसे पाने की उम्मीद हां अब जो भी हो अब इजहार करना ही है एक दिन मैंने तय किया आज खामोशी नहीं इजहार कर लूंगा जो होगा देखा जाएगा तो शुरू हो गई तैयारी of course पहले प्यार का पहला इजहार और जो कहते हैं ना अगर नसीब ना हो तो स्वयं भगवान भी कुछ नहीं कर सकते किसको पता था सुबह की खिलखिलाती धूप रात को अचानक तूफान में बदल जाएगा और मैं बैठी उस तूफान में भीगते हुए रोती हुई और खुद को पूछते हुए अगला लड़की अचानक पीछे से वही आवाज आया श्री तुम कर क्या रही हो और मैं बस में मैं कर रही गई पर मेरा सीधा नजर गया उसकी हाथों में पकड़ी मेरी डायरी जो पता नहीं उसे कहां से मिल गया और बाद में पता चला कि मेरे दोस्तों ने उसको चुपके से चुरा कर दे दी थी अब मुझे बोलने की कुछ जरूरत ही नहीं थी जब वह काम मेरी दोस्तों ने कर दी वह अचानक मेरी करीब है और उसकी पास आते ही उसकी सांसों की गर्मी मेरे दिल मिनट प्रति 250 बढ़ा दिया मैं कुछ बोलूं उससे पहले ही बोल बड़ा बचपन में जब तुम मिट्टी में खेलते अपनी मनमानी करती अब से तुम्हें प्यार कर रहा हूं हर सुबह जब तुम बाहर आकर हमेशा मेरे घर की तरफ देखती हो तब से तुम्हें प्यार किया जब क्लास में मुझे देखती और अचानक नजर घुमा लेती कि मुझे पता ना चले तब से तुम्हें प्यार कियाand now all I want for love is you because I love you. ...... वह वक्त मेरे लिए कुछ थम सा गया बेशुमार मोहब्बत हो गई होगी उस रात बारिश की गुंडों को भी जमीन से जिसने मुझे तुमसे हो गया नई चीजों से अब नया रिश्ता जुड़ने लगा क्योंकि मुझे तो प्यार पहले से था अब तो उससे भी हो गया था पेड़ों की पहेलियां को देख में यू शर्म आ रही थी जैसे उन्होंने भी मेरी तारीफ कोका पिटारा खोल दिया हो अब तो मेरे सारे आंसू भी बहना बंद कर दिया कुछ

अजीब नहीं था बस वही अलग सा लगता था तू जिसने मुझे मुझसे मिलाया था।

मुझे आज भी याद है वह दिन जब तुमने मुझे कसके पकड़ा था और मेरे कंधे में सर रखकर मेरे काम मैं बोला था पागल कभी नहीं छोड़ूंगा जल्दी वापस आ जाऊंगा सांसों के बीच एक बोतल से लगने लगी थी जिंदगी जब पता चला कि जिस प्लेन में तुम गए थे वह लापता है अब तो मेरी कहानी भी अधूरी लगने लगी तुम्हारे बिना तुम वह घर थे जिसमें एक बंजारे को गाना दिया था तुम वही लड़के हो जो मुझको मुझसे ज्यादा जानता था तुम वही हो जिसने मुझे सितारों के दरियों पर रख आसमान से आजाद बना दिया तुमने मुझे कुछ इस कदर प्यार किया कि जब आंखों में आंसू भरे तुम्हारे तस्वीर को बिहार से हूं अब तो मेरे कलम की शादी भी कोशिश करके तुम्हें बयां नहीं कर पा रही है कुछ बदला नहीं है वही धूप वही सुबह बस तुम नहीं हो यही तो अलग है। रोहन,your love enlighten me

KAUSHAL BUDHADEV

Kaushal Budhadev is a content writer, poet, teacher of chemistry at Narayana group of schools. He creates content related to chemistry & other study material on YouTube. He defines teaching as the purpose of life.

YA RAB...

Ya rab..
Kya fitoor hai tera,
jism ne udi ruh ka liwaz hai,
phir q isse kafan ki talash hai..

Zindagi khud ki hai,
phir q dunia me kisi aur ki khoj hai..

Na koi basera hai mera yaha,
Na kuch leke jane ki raza hai
Phir q har dua me khusi ki talaab hai..

Juda hona ek din har kisi se hai..
Ye toh riwaz hai..
Phir q kisi se wafa ki sikhayat hai..

Manzil har kisi ki ek hai..
Phir q bewaj phirne ka junoon hai..

Waqt kisi ka v nahi..
Usse bewafa ki aadat hai..
Sath reh kar, hmsha ruthi rehti hai..
sab de kar, khud hi chen leti hai...

Risto ka tasur hi kuch aur hai..
Umar ke sath bhadti hi jate hai..
Naye risto ke sath naye pechan bana lete hai...
Kuch sath rehte hai, kuch bichad jate hai..
Phir q kisi ke intezar me rehta hai..

Ek kali raat ke,

subha na hone wali khawab se,
Jaga hu...

Ab na ullzuga koi v tere sawalo se..
Ab waqt nikaluga apne aur apno ke ly..
Ab na rakhuga koi udhar wali zindagi..

Khauga wo, jo mujhe pasand hai..
Piuga wo, jo mujhe mann hai..
Jauga waha, jaha meri chaha hai...

Ab maine khud par bharosa ka hunar sikha hai..
Bahot se kasur hai teri, ye zindagi..
Phir v teri niyati ko qubool hai..
Ab maine jaan liya hai..

zindagi umar se nahi..
Apni karmo se mashoor hai

PALLAVEE DAS

An enthralling writer and voracious reader, Pallavee's writings are a bliss to read. She is a cheerful person who always wears a soul soothing smile. Born in Odisha's northern-most district, Balasore, her editorials also sore high. A post graduate student in Biotechnology, also has a huge craving for literature. She leaves no stone unturned to deliver a cogent script.

The Weird Mind

Being unable to please everybody is never being that pleasing. Not responding to all the parameters that make a perfect person is never being that perfect. Not abiding by the protocols that are always meant to be maintained is never being that accepted one.

It is always difficult to choose between "GOING WITH THE FLOW" and "MAKING YOUR OWN WAY". It is always opposed to be yourself and not to stand on the index created by a never-known element.

And it is the time for her to take a decision, a decision without any contamination, a decision so clean, a decision that may not be appreciated by many. She has broken almost all the rules, protocols, parameters, that are meant to characterize her under the species called "WOMAN", that also according to a hypothetical, illogical, exaggerating nomenclature system. But the most interesting as well as disgusting fact is that most individuals of this species have accepted to be liable and the "Go with the flow" system.

Now, she is none other than an anti-social being, who is going against the society. Everybody stares at her with a suspicious look, some make fun of her, and call her a weirdo... So, should she change her way to be back into the so-called "Social frame"?

She is a self-designed, protesting personality who always stands against all the theories that can differentiate her from a MAN, except those physical dissimilarities. She has some WEIRD kind of thoughts of her own about the world. The terms like "Like a boy", "Like a girl" have no existence for her. The most peculiar thing is that her principles which are always protested by the society, surprisingly are given as examples, praised in speeches and admired in front of one another by the same society.

If we can not do what we speak, then what is her fault?

If we are used to every nonsense, illogical and base-less strategies, then what is her fault?

And if we can not change our wrong perceptions, then why should she change her genuine, logical enough thinking for the sake of society???

Then who is weird, she or the society???

No... She will not be affected by the dubious eyes, hateful words, and the zero acceptance nature. She will always support all the changes that are needed for a new society, a new world, so rejuvenated. And never ever she will discard the self for the sake of others because she has realized that such an enthusiasm, such a heart, and such a determination is found very rare, which she is gifted with and she will never disappoint the almighty.

This time, she decided not to quit, even after many obstacles, even after the contradictions in her mind which often come at certain intervals.

And, this time she decided to "GO AGAINST THE FLOW"...

She has decided to remain that much WEIRD.

PRATIKSHYA DHAL SAMANTA

Pratikshya Dhal samanta has a strong,independent and free flowing personality which she exhibits in her work. This time she showed her thoughtful and a little out of the box thinking. As a reader i always admire her work hope you will feel the same magic while reading and transforming into her realm

Nobody Is Dumb

People are not born with tags such as religion, caste or intelligence. No one is to be judged on the basis of any other individual's intelligence. This is the story of a girl who heard the word 'dumb' more than any other word from other people's tongue. People refereed her as a dumb person just because she was not good at mathematics, did not have good and fluent english-speaking skills and was not able to memorise history lessons. This is all about a little, innocent girl named padmakshi. She was born in a rich family to the sharmas in new delhi. Her father was a successful professor working in a prestigious university. She was sent to kendriya vidyalaya school at an early age of 4. From the very beginning she had developed serious health issues like fever. Thereafter she frequently became absent to school. Hence the fundamentals she required was never gained by her. She lagged behind while her friends moved ahead.

padmakshi soon began to realise that her education line was drifted and that nothing could have been done to undo that. None of her teachers or friends gave support to her. All were carried away by their own loads of work in life. Even her family could do no good to her. Time passed and she grew up to a 14 years old girl. By that time, she had developed complete hatred towards her studies. She was so depressed that she thought "it's better to give up" because to her studying was totally waste of time.

at that time of her hardship something unexpected happened to her.her sister, pariniti happened to visit her. She realised that her little sister was facing serious problems in studies. Since she is a teacher in a high school, she quickly grasped her weakness and decided that it is time her sister moulds her future by herself. All pariniti did was provide some basic help. She decided to change the methods of studying. She started teaching her with at the moment events. For example, pariniti asked her to calculate the money spent for vegetables when her father bought those, she asked her to tell about mother's work in english etc. She showed her animated videos to develop her english vocabulary and conversation skills. She explained geographical situations with day to day life experience. Her hard work paid off. Padmakshi started taking interest towards study. It was like a ray of sunshine in darkness to her. Soon her academic performance progressed. Now she is at her best in solving mathematical problems to memorising historical dates.

Moral of the story: -

One need not to be quoted dumb if he/she doesn't learn through one method. 'learning is everyone's cup of tea' unlike said by most people. The only difference is the technique one uses to improvise. No person on earth is born dumb. They just need to apply alternate ways to exhibit their talents. 'knock knock till the door is open' we all need to keep trying hard with our ways till success reaches us. All these are possible if we think its possible and if we believe in it.

Loneliness.

The night feels lonely
When the moon disappears..
The morning feels lonely
When the sun disappears..
The night sky feels lonely
When the stars disappear..
The garden feels lonely
When flowers disappear..
The river feels lonely
When water disappears..
The house feels lonely
When family disappears..
But,
I feel lonely
When 'Maa' disappears..

ABHISHEK SAHOO

Being a very cheerful boy, Abhishek Sahoo has always been appreciated for his enthusiasm and intelligence in every stage of his life. Born and brought up in a educationally disciplined family in the district of Kendrapara of Odisha state, he was always motivated by his parents to go beyond the imagination, which he does perfectly. Intelligence when meets with his imagination and innovation, the combination leaves a heartfelt impression on any piece of paper and this is what Abhishek does with his talent.

You Will Always Be Mine

You will always be mine,
Till the last sun shines..
You will occupy a huge part in my heart
Even if we are miles apart
Some things are best left untold
Because they exaggerate the feelings too bold..
No matter what happens in future,
We will always share this beautiful bond together

Purane hone par,
log bhagwan ki murtiyon ko badal dete hain,
Tum to theher ek insaan hi..

SORRY

Memories come trodding down
Fresh in the night's dark gown..
On his bed, he turns and twist,
Holding onto those days like a clinching fist..
He who wants to be the reason of everyone's smile,
Has stacked the pain and agony of someone's life like a pile..
Long tales of love and emotion does he talk,
Breaking the same like a piece of chalk..
Sorry for every drops of tear he gave,
Hope you forgive him for god's sake..

Her Face

Her face flashed today in my dreams,
Dazzling in the soft light beams..
Neither of us had any words to speak,
Eyes staring each other & love was at its peak..
Hope this turns out to be real,
I am getting mad under her romantic spell...

Ocean of emotions

Have never seen a face so innocent,
Like a glowing bulb's filament..
All the anger vanishes away,
When your smile reaches my eyes' doorway..
Eyes of yours, black and deep,
Feels like an ocean of emotions ready to unzip..
That innocent dark eyes and smile so sweet,
Feels like I am in paradise on this gloomy night..

Mohabbat

Dikkat ye hai ki,
hame mohabaat ho gaya tha sahab,
Warna bata dete,
aawargi kya cheez hai!!.

MANISHA NANDA

Manisha Nanda, has been a teacher earlier. Recently she is working as an Analyst in Instrument Management and fixed income in HSBC. Pen and papers have been her best friend since she was 11 years old! Kind of good samaritan and a pure bibliophile! Nevertheless a good painter as well. A conscientious woman she is!

Death Becomes A Art

There, on a sill of capricious decisions
Glass splinter sit waiting a wavering hand
Reflective the reminiscence wrapped 'round the drape
Lost in a pane that she can't understand

Chilled calls the breeze through a jagged expulsion
Scenting the air neath a ceiling now stained
Dampening hallucination behind oven doors gaping
Finding the pilot light has not complained

Ripping out pages of scrawled delusions
Day becomes night in the depths of her mind
Chasing the reverberation when no one will answer
Begging each shadow for something to find

Setting a table of rounded persuasions
Watching incandescence fade fast in her eyes
Turning the knob towards a melancholy direction
Why is there none who react to her cries

Loneliness peels back the mounded condition
Voices of reason have fled to her past
Fearing the calamitous will visit tomorrow
Sensing the hour shall now be her last

So many days and the roses need pruning
Nary a manoeuvre is noticed inside
Caught in his thoughts that her words had desideratum
If only those moments ignored would confide

Desperate ink found in fingertip writings
Penned by the fiends left roaming her head
Still abode the question of trepidation never listened
Death becomes art in the stanzas unread

TANMAYA MALLICK

This is Tanmay mallick from jajpur , odisha.Pursuing my post graduate degree from Ravenshaw University,cuttack.Always had a special inclination towards poetry and song composition. Maybe that person made me remember my personal hardship which inspired me to pen it out...

We Must Talk

Life has been a wonderful journey till date. But, there are some dates that are not so easy to forget. Especially, if that day did change someone's life and that change has been brought because of another person who gradually becomes so important that it's kind of difficult to forget.

Sometimes happiness comes like a ray of sunshine and sometimes sorrow looks like dark cloud on the horizon; as human life is neither so easy nor it was. There are many moments where one go through immeasurable stress, emotions, sorrow/grief that one cannot express to anyone but there always exists a thirst of not getting a proper chance to express what we really want to.

After experiencing these random things an incident strikes to my mind that made my day more unforgettable one.

I was returning back to my place in bus after enjoying the entire day with my good old college friends. I was waiting to catch a bus to return home and as usual the bus was late. Finally, bus came; I got in; unfortunately it wasn't lucky enough to get my favorite seat that day as it had some other plans. I got a seat nearby a middle aged man who was engaged with his phone. After few minutes he tried to start a conversation with me but I was bit uncomfortable to start a talk with him. He started to convers by asking me to guess the speed of the bus and I haphazardly told 60km/hr. Then, he showed me a speedometer app in his phone and confirmed me the speed of the bus. It felt like he wanted to talk as he was too bored. He then asked me about my studies and about my whereabouts. I answered his questions but was least interested to ask about his whereabouts but he himself started talking about his life. By profession, he is a police officer and his daughter was studying in medical college and his son was in grade 11. He was very proud of his daughter but for his son he was not the same man. He had mixed emotions for his son and was confused what to do with his son.

Out of curiosity he told me you are like my son and you must have gone through same phase so how did you cope at that time. Then, suddenly I returned to that phase where I always wanted to pursue my career with music but was not able to do because there was a huge communication gap between me and my parents. So, I told him to discuss with him what he want in life and not to force him to do anything that he do not want. Communication is such a thing that can solve anything in one's life. You daughter will going to be a doctor after few years ,its will be the most beautiful moment to cherish but at the very same time if you will just understands what you son really want to do in his life and will support him without comparing him with your daughter ,it will be the best thing you can do as a father . Not everyone is born with the same capabilities so you must know what else he can do and you must not force him to fulfill your demands by looking at the society and by comparing him with others. After this discussion I could see a moment of relief not only in his face but also within me that I finally consoled someone to take communication as a path to solve the problem rather than anything. It was just a moment of some time that should be given to everyone to solve the problems.

DISHA SANKHYASHREE

Namaste and Hello, This is Disha Sankhyashree from CTC, Odisha. I'm pursuing Pharmaceutical sciences at Utkal University. Being an introvert it's difficult to express my feelings verbally, this is when I started to pen my first poetry when I was 13. I believe that connection of a soul with poetry makes it alive. My love for poetry grew with years and now it has become a passion of mine. I always give trust on purity of life and its meaning and imaginations in my writeups. I hope you all will enjoy my work. Thank you.

Mere Andar Ek Zamana Hai

Khudse ladhne ki zid h
Mujhe khud ko harana h,
Mei bheed nahi iss duniya ki
Mere andar hi ek zamana h...

Darpok nahi bekhaof hun mei,
Is duniya se mujhe ladhna h,
Mei bheed nahi iss duniya ki
Mere andar hi ek zamana h...

Sikayat nahi is zindagi se
Mujhe gir ke khud uthna h,
Mei bheed nahi iss duniya ki
Mere andar hi ek zamana h...

Nafrat nahi h iss dil mei
Duniya mei pyaar bharna h
Mei bheed nahi iss duniya ki
Mere andar hi ek zamana h...

Father

Father, you are the silent lover who loved us with your full heart,
You are the one who provides us with everything we want..
I'm lucky to have you as my guide from the start,
You are the first man who loved me with a pure heart...
Holding your fingers I learnt to walk and learnt speaking,
For me you are more than just my dad, 'My king'...
From dropping me at school to my university together,
I'm blessed to have you and thankful to the creator ...
Not only academic but life lessons is all what i learnt from you,
Making you my role model all these years the wiser I grew...
When I'm upset, I just look at the hope of shine in your eyes for me,
They are much deeper and intense than the waves of the sea
These words of love are just very little to say,
Too small compared to your sacrifices for us each day.

Life

So unpredictable life is in here,
live it to the fullest, O dear!...
Life is just a stage of destiny,
don't captive life with just mere money...
Smile to the sun shining so bright,
and sooth your soul beneath the moonlight...
This world is your magnificent home,
the nature surrounds you making you warm...
Don't expect with the heart of a child,
it brings revenge blaze so wild...
Calm your heart with faces of smiles,
your journey awaits you to travel miles...
Connect to different souls and laugh aloud,
but don't lose your originality among in the crowd...
Confront your challenges and smile through your scars,
Great leaders are born out of the wars...
You are just a beautiful soul, Remember,
pressure always creates a diamond out of the coal...

Best friend

You strengthen me by protecting me from my nightmare, You pampered me with all your love and deep care. Sharing my secrets and my problems I found a true mate in you, a true friendship in this cruel world is found very few. Morning starts with you and the day ends with your thought, you freed a butterfly who was once chained and caught. Just like two bodies and one soul we shared beautiful years together, You were the soul I always wished for and I'm so thankful to the creator. Darkness being all around, you entered with a ray of hope into my world, You spread warmth and delights everywhere stealing away the shivering cold. I wish you stay forever till eternity and beyond with me, You brighten up my world and make it blissful glee. I hope you achieve all the success you deserve, On your failure just look aside and you will find my love for you heartly preserved.

BISWASMRUTI MANGARAJ

Biswasmruti Mangaraj is a software engineer, singer and writer who works for Tata Consultancy Services as a Security Analyst with experience in cyber security and automation testing. Writing for him is not only a hobby but also a passion that he pursues whenever and wherever he gets time from his work schedule. He has been passionately pursuing this hobby since last 9 years along with his other passion which is singing. He is a regular stage performer with multiple accolades in singing and frequently uploads music covers in his YouTube channel. He is currently working on a book which he intends to publish in the near future. It all started with reading stories and poetry since childhood which gradually inspired him to create literary content and make it available for the world to read and acknowledge. He first started writing poems in 2011 for a school competition where he was a part of the debate team as well. Ever since then he's continued writing short articles and poetry through Google's blogging platform - "Blogger".

Flower of Hope

I was dreaming in my dream, holding a hand that was rough and kind
In that dream I was a silent watcher, watching around for something to find
I couldn't remember what I lost
I couldn't understand why I searched
What's lost was definitely meant to be lost
Perhaps my very soul needed to be forged.

So, I kept walking in the dream, renting the body of my younger self,
My tiny hands clasped my mother's finger, in an attempt not to lose myself.
She is the woman who gave everything to me
She sacrificed her future to build my life
From a 3 bedroom apartment to a single room,
She taught me how to live and survive.

Next I drifted off to a luxurious bed, only to be woken up by a rude slap.
My father, who slapped me, then kissed me and made me sit in his lap.
He is the man who made me who I am
He is the man who burnt himself to give me warmth
Perhaps the only man who never gave up on me,
When I couldn't differentiate, south from north.

I was then transferred inside a blanket, where a caring hand shielded my body
It was the hand of my brother, who even in sleep wished to protect his buddy.

His memories keep me alive
He is the person I look up to most.
Even if I can never be like him
Still, in his teachings, I place my trust.

Then I landed near a hospital bed, where a tiny baby was crying in her crib.
The baby was a stranger to this world and she clasped my finger tightly in a grip.
The little crying angel was my sister
Who grew up to become my moral compass.
She is perhaps the only person who truly understands me
And she is the water to my anger and arrogance.

Finally, I found myself sitting on the grass, with a gorgeous lady at my sight
I first met her, almost two years back, near the elevator at my worksite.
Her eyes were tiny, overflowing with kindness.
Her mind was her own, filled with colors of life
She is the person who changed me forever,
And she will be a special person for the rest of my life.

In the end I found what I was searching, inside the very body I inhabited
Awakening from my dream, I found four shining gems that my past entrusted.
The first two were strength and support
The last two were care and love
When I engraved all four onto my soul
I found the missing flower of hope.

My Little Butterfly

I was a wanderer sleeping in a distant island,
When I saw a butterfly flutter across my land
Her eyes were bright and cute like a ping pong ball
I loved her button shaped nose and her pink hair band.

She was a breath of fresh hair and that's all I knew,
Her wings were flaming red and it was a site to view
The butterfly's four eyes, sparkled like a star in space
Her hair was like Rapunzel which looked neat and new.

I wanted to catch hold of her and make her mine,
Yet she was a free spirit like a glint of sunshine
Her cheeks turned baby pink, every time she blushed
And her smile was intoxicating like old red wine.

Every time I reached out for her,
She smiled at me yet her heart closed the door
Every time I tried to understand her defenses,
She would conjure a shield and hide her emotions even more.

Butterflies cheer us up and spread happiness
Yet people forget that their life used to be a complete mess.
Before they could fly, they were caterpillars with thorns
Wriggling patiently, they waited for life to bless.

When I fell for such a beauty is still a mystery,
For wanderers sing songs that ripple through history.
Some may say that her pretty face is all I love
Yet, her soul is what created this chemistry.

Every day I wait for that butterfly to flutter,
To experience the wind and frequently drink water.
I see all of this sitting in my lonely island
Oh! how much I want her to make my life better!!

I am a wanderer and wanderers move with their song,
Yet emotions and feelings can even make us wait for long.
Perhaps butterflies feel every fleeting moment is temporary
But even they can sometimes be wrong.

They say, time and tide wait for none,
Once someone has left, they truly are gone.
Still love is the only thing that stretches through time.
If I can't reach her,
then maybe my love will be the one.

JAGANNATH PRASAD

Jagannath Prasad is a 23 years old guy from a small village of Odisha. He is a born writer with the most beautiful handwriting I have ever seen. He has an immense talent in photography, drawing and writing. A man of a great foodie and a travel blogger. He loves to keep his people happy by making fun as he knows the actual value of smile. A golden hearted person with a gem nature and his great aura puts a sparkle on his overall nature. He cares for everyone who cares for him. A soft spoken kind hearted beloved person ever ready to help the needy. I adore him due to his 'Way of talking' and 'Friends are Life' personality which make him so unique and special.

Her First Call...

Those were my graduation days I was literally serious about my studies simply was a sincere student who liked by all professors. I was continuing my bachelor's in Physics.

Everyday I went to college 5-10 minutes before to make my mind stable with the respective atmosphere. That was a Monday morning, I came across a girl at college bike stand. She was on her Scooty listening to music. Suddenly I saw her and my mind distracted and without thinking anything suddenly a "Hii" came out of my heart, at first she was astonished as I was a stanger and replied with "Hello" with her sweet voice and ravishing smile. I was impressed by her smile and voice and fall in love with those from that day. Gradually hii... hello continued for some days and most of the times I stared at her when she was in khatti with her friends at college lawn. One day I randomly scrolling my facebook page and suddenly came across a Facebook account and she was none other than that girl, I sent her a friend request. The very next day a notification popped up and that was the acceptance of my request, that was the first step towards our friendship.Then, we were friends in facebook, then gradually connected in instagram and we then became social media friends. We chatted for hours, shared so many things. Even exchanged our whatsapp number as well as contact numbers but we were very comfortable in instagram inbox. Then I came to know she was a chemistry student of 1st year where as I was Physics of 2nd year. Then we shared some of our college memories as well as past memories and we never dare to share our feelings which spontaneously had in our hearts for eachother still how our friendship turned into Loveship we couldn't know. We had spent many joyous moments but never ever had phone calls. Later I came to know she was also fall in Love with my way of talking. Then I was overwhelmed by knowing that and the happiness gathered in my heart was priceless and quite pure.

One Sunday evening, I was in my evening walk with my friend Gopal suddenly my phone began to ring & came to know, that was from her. I got so excited to hear her mesmerizing voice, which fill my soul with joy, as that was "her first call", I received, with a moaning voice she said, "Hey, I met an accident near Zobra bridge, please come soon". As soon as I came to that place and came to know she was hospitalized at SCB medical, after reaching there I came to know she was no more. My heart broken into pieces and an ocean of tears flew away. I was never expecting the ending of a love story could be happened before it started. I lost a soul who touched my heart and filled my soul with wonders. She was my soulmate.

"Her first call became her Last call as well."

Once A Stranger Always A Stranger...

We all are strangers at first sight. Nowadays there're so many ways for connecting people,in real life and in social media too. Some are only our Hii Hello friends and some are Hi hello friends with a smile. Some are our festive friends, they remember us in some occasions and wishing us the best. Those people are really nice. Some are our whatsapp status friends,they only see our random posts if needed they reply. Those are one type good people. Some remember us in their need, well' you people are really awesome. But those egregious people are so called temporary. And here comes the real people, one day they're strangers then close to us by interaction, gradually leave memories in our life. So many gossips so many memories...we also share all our feelings emotions day to day activities etc etc. Gradually, all are gone in vain with time. Importance decreases, Love, care, affection all those things... only memories are left with teary eyes. Then we can realise the actual meaning of "Hurting". Well...at first we meet those strangers without any hope & at last they leave us with many memories & become strangers. Friendship dies,not friends.

****

We never see the tomorrow which is uncertain, still we hope for the best and dream so many things. Isn't it the beauty of Life? Yes Life is beautiful Just smile &go on.

****

There's always a major difference between the smile of sorrow and the smile of happiness, so just stay calm and the deserving one will definitely mark it.

****

Don't be cheap with the cheapest world. If you will be cheap then you are no more you, you will be one of them so be you always. Stay calm b'coz you can...

SNEHASRITA SWAIN

Here is Miss Snehasrita Swain , a librarian by profession, a lady with great heart and always ready to help others with affection. In this harse pandemic scenario , she did not kill the vacant time and hence accidentally stepping towards the creative world of writing . She understands the zeal to live the life in any situation. Most of her poetries and qutoes express the value of nature, life, relations, emotions hence inspiring and motivational mode of life . Hope the readers will definately enjoy reading, get the healing dose and inspired.

नैना

दो नैना की कहानी
हे दिलचस्प ओर रूहानी
किरदार उनकी है निराली
सबकी विशेषता को झट्से पहचानती

जुड़े हैं दोनों एक दुसरे से
बड़े करीब से जैसे
पानी और मछलीरानी
है तो दोनों असल में पृथक
लेकिन कभी ना होते हैं अबिभक्त

खूब मजबूत है संगति उनका
कभी ना हो सकता अमना सामना दोनोका
फिर भी समझते हैं दिल का हाल एक दुसरेका
बिन बताए , बिन सुने , बिन देखे
कभी ना होती तक्रार ओर अनबन
कभी ना होती संसय ओर जलन
मिसाल बनती हैं साथ उनकी सबके लिए
जैसे जल बिन असंभव जिवन

रिश्ता उनका है सबसे अनोखा
जैसे परछाई हैं एक दूसरे का
सच्ची खुशी दिल की झलकती है
नैनों की कोनेसे हलकी सी लालि चमकती है
जैसे अंधेरे में जुगनू झलसती है
दुख में आंसू छलकती है
रेह नहीं सकते हैं बिन आंसू बहाये
नौछबार हैं हरपल एक दूजेके लिए
यही तो मूलतत्व है अतुट बन्धन के

पता चला असल में रिश्ता निभाते कैसे हैं

जिंदगी की तरकीब

लोग कहते हैं
सबके दुख दर्द को सुनना चाहिए
दिल की अनकही जुबानी को आपस में बांटना चाहिए
लेकिन अक्सर मैंरे मन में खयाल आता है

ए दुनियावाले !
कभी किसिके दिल का हाल जानने की कोशिश की है ?
फिर भी लोग अपने परेशानी को बांटने के बजाए
भाई ! सब ठीक है बोलके बात को टाल देते हैं

कभी सोचा है क्या!!
ऐसा कियुं होता है!!
कितने लोग दूसरों की तनाव को समझनेके लिए सुनते है
लोग तो बस सुनके जवाब देने की दौड़ में लगे रहते हैं

संयोग कोई सुनके समझले भी तो
समस्या का समाधान केलिए उपाय सोचने के बजाए
अपनी परेशानी को विस्तार रूप से व्याख्या करते हैं
सबको एकदुसरे के सहायता ओर साथ की जरूरत है
यह स्वीकार कर सदभावना से सबकी मदद करना है
यह एक प्रयास आज से शुरू होना चाहिए

खुद की परेशानी से जूझ के सीखो
ज़िन्दगी की चुनौती से लड़ने की तरकिब सीखो
संकल्प करो खुद से , मुश्किलों से डरोगे नहीं
मुसीबत आए तो डटके सामना करो तो सही
फिर देखना ज़िन्दगी जीना आसान होगी
सफलता खुद ही चलके तुम्हारे पास आएगी

खुद की तकलीफ भूलकर
दूसरों की समस्या का हल निकालोगे
खुद से पहले दूसरोंके लिए जियोगे
जिंदगी जीने की असली मकसद यही पायोगे
आखिर में जिंदगी के सचे योद्धा केहलायोगे

SARVAGAYA PRASAD

Sarvagaya is a very good boy, intelligent, helpful, down to earth, best cadet of my scouts and guides group, loves to help others and always ready to help others. Obedient, disciplined, has gem of heart. Dibya Ranjan Biswal

Friendship

Our friendship was one of a kind of ,
An example of how two people bind.
You were the gift I treasured most,
Incessantly about you did I boast .
Remember the fun we has under the sun ,
For other mates like you, I had none .
We were close and understood each others moods,
Life for us was perfect - too good .
Destined to be friends for namesakes we are ,

Our story of kinship we were to take far .
But in moment everything shattered ,
As a bitter truth unravelled .
That truth unveiled,
Is the cause of the rift in this tale .
But this separation I cannot bead
For my heart is filled with sorrow and despair .
My sister is no longer near ,
The thought of that makes my eyes well up in tears.
From this sorrow I want to be free ,
For the both of us may happier days forever be .
Forgive and forget and revive our friendship again,
in this , both our efforts will not be in vain.

Remember Friendship

Oh friend !
I remember the days we played and fought,
Had fun together and frightened each other
A lot .

I remember those scuffle that ended in , "sorry " !,
So we could be together without a worry .

I remember the secret we shared ,
And laughingly teased each other about what we bared .

I remember the days you were there to guide me ,
For that l'd like to take the time to thank three .

ANKITA JETHY

Ankita Jethy is a graduate in mathematics from Ramadevi University. She is a voracious reader. But when it comes to writings, she writes those stuffs that reflects her inner voice. She strongly feels there are certain things that people should be aware of. So they find her writings very informative. Let's check out what she has to serve in our plates this time.

Getting Better At Feelings Instead Of Feeling Better

Feelings and emotions are all traits we share as humans. Many people use the term "feelings" and "emotions" as synonyms but they are not interchangeable. While they have similar elements but there is a marked difference between feelings and emotions. Feelings are both emotional experiences and physical sensations such as hunger or pain. Feelings are a conscious experience, although not every conscious experience, such as seeing or believing is feelings. On the other hand an emotion can only be felt through the emotional experiences it gives rise to, even though it might be discovered through it's associated thoughts, beliefs, desires and actions. Emotions are not conscious but instead manifest in the unconscious mind. Feelings change with development. Humans are born with a relatively small number of primary affects, which then combine with eachother and life's experiences to form our more complex emotional world. Emotions are critical part of human experiences. But sometimes our emotions get out of hand. Sometimes the sadness we feel isn't blues. Sometimes it is depression. Sometimes it is anxiety.

Depression and anxiety occurs often togather. Infact, they occur so often that people will mistake one for other. Depression blows. Anxiety isn't any fun either. Meanwhile there are some well intentioned friends and family who implore you to just "get over it" or advise you to " keep your head up" instead of addressing the issue.

Now let's expand our knowledge about depression. Depression is different from usual mood changes and short lived emotional reactions to challenges in everyday life. It is a common mental disorder involving persistent sadness or loss of interest or pleasure accompanied by several of the following symptoms: disturbed sleep or appetite, feelings of guilt or low self worth, feelings of tiredness, poor concentration, difficulties in making decisions, agitations or physical restlessness, talking or moving slowly than normal, hopelessness and suicidal thoughts or acts. When a person experiences these symptoms for at least two weeks and it's interfering with his daily life, it's called major depressive disorder. But if this symptoms go on for more than two years, then it is called persistence depressive disorder. Periods of depression can be long lasting or can come and go for different periods of time. When long lasting, it may become a serious health condition, when the affected person continues to suffer greatly and function poorly at work or at school and in the family and community. Depression can lead to suicide. However, it is very important to keep this in mind: DEPRESSION IS TREATABLE.

Let's understand what exactly happens in a depressed brain. Scientists have discovered that depression is a neurological condition and is caused by imbalance of certain chemicals within the brain. According to Monoamine hypothesis of depression theory, a lack of neurotransmitters like serotonin and dopamine two chemicals associated with feelings of pleasure and reward would lead to depression. Scientists have found that people with a particular genetic variation in the gene that codes for the serotonin receptor 5-HTT are more susceptible to depression after stressful life events when compared to the people who don't have that mutation. This mutation is thought to reduce the production of serotonin receptors in the brain leading to a decrease in serotonin signalling. There is also evidences from postmortem brains that people with depression have changes in the dopamine signalling in their brains. But scientists are no longer positive that depression is a direct result of a simple chemical imbalance. Some of the researches and treatments have been inconsistent with that idea. And the condition is really complex. So researchers are also exploring a lot of other possible explanations. Brain imaging studies have found that patients with depression generally have less gray matter in several different brain regions like cingulate cortex, hippocampus and amygdala. Gray matter mostly made up of neuronal cell bodies, dendrites, synapses and glia is the place where most neuronal signalling happens. So changes in gray matter volume can affect all kinds of things like emotions, memory and decision making. Basically depression shrinks the part of the brain that is important for controlling our emotions and making choices to take care of ourselves, making it hard for patients to recover from feelings of sadness.

On the other hand anxiety is a feeling of unease, such as worry or fear, that can be mild or severe. While occasional anxiety is an expected part of life. But an anxiety disorder involves more than temporary worry or fear. For a person with an anxiety disorder, the anxiety doesn't go away and can get worse over time. The symptoms can interfere with daily activities such as job, performance, school work and relationships.

Let's see how anxiety affects our brain. Just like how the occipital lobe handles vision and the temporal lobe processes sound, our emotional responses have their own brain regions. The lymbic system is a complex set of structures deep inside the brain that includes hippocampus, amygdala, hypothalamus and thalamus. This circuit is believed to handle most of our emotional processing, and the prefrontal cortex is responsible for integrating this emotional information into our decision making. Scientists think that anxiety disorder pops up when there is changes in the signalling of the lymbic system. The researches have found that patients with anxiety disorder have more activity than normal in the lymbic system and it is also seen that they have hyperactive amygdala which is the fear center of the brain.

Hence we conclude that it is not what happens to us that makes us depressed but how we respond to painful emotions. So treatment for depression and anxiety is to expand our emotional capacity. It is actually getting better at feelings instead of just focusing on feeling better. This is a skill that can be learned to increase our ability to feel joy by also getting better at feeling disappointment. So opening yourself up to pain makes sadness, grief and anxiety more comfortable.

Willingness to open up to all thoughts and feelings whether painful or pleasant takes us in the direction of building a meaningful life.

SONIT PATANAIK

Sonit Patanaik, a dreamer born on month of December, we can call him an achiever.. An achiever who never underestimate struggle of others, Either you sunk down in his ocean of thoughts or melt down through his words there is no in-between.. In his words:- जब ज़िन्दगी अपनी है, तो राह भी खुद चुन लो, खुद की सोच संग चलो, और तहजीब अपनी बना लो।।

Gratitude Apology Positvity

GAP - THIS IS THE GAP EVERYONE NEEDS TO HAVE IN THEIR LIFE.EVERYONE SHOULD BE GRATEFUL FOR WHAT THEY HAVE ,SHOULD HAVE APPLOGY IF THEY GO WRONG ANYWAY & MOST IMPORTANTLY ONE SHOULD STAY POSITIVE IN EVERY MOMENT OF THEIR LIFE.

It's obvious for every one of us to feel like looser at some sort of time & the main cause of this is our ignorance which makes us ungrateful of what we have in our life .One should not only pay gratitude to god for what he/she have but should also pay gratitude to everyone around them who are connected to them in anyway. The common thing in we all human being is making mistakes which we do sometimes knowingly & unknowingly ,but we all should exhibit the habit of apology.The mistakes in which we don't ask apology afterwords soon becomes blunder.

Life presents us neverending challenges and its very true that life is uncertain & sometimes its very unfair for some people but we can't stop the circumstances rightaway rather we should focus overcoming uncertain & unfair circumstances in rightway .So for this we need to stay positive & motivated through out our life which we can achieve mainly by spiritually by believing in god's decision & on ourselves. No matter how painful life becomes one should not lament & should have faith on god that tomorrow they will see a realm of true happiness.Depending upon our mindset or attitude,we can get the most out of the activities we are able to do & thereby by fully recharge our life force as a result we can accumulate immeasurable benefit. Youth is a truly wonderful thing but unfortunate is one who don't appreciate when they're young.Life passes by quickly before we know it that's why in our youth we should be as active as we possibly can,& should be humble towards everyone & should complete our roles towards our family & society.

-Life through my eyes...

दिल:-

इंसान सिर्फ दो बार अपने दिल को मेहसूस कर सकता है,
जब वो मरता है,
और जब उसका दिल किसी पे मरता है।

दिल की जरूरत:-

दिल की जरूरत,
मेहनत न मोहब्बत से पूरी होती है,
उससे तो बस सुकून चाहिए।।

कहानी:-

कहानी दो तरह की होती है,
हारे हुए की अपनी,
और जीते हुए की दूसरों की जुबानी होती है।।

चाहत:-

अब क्या गिला, क्या सिकवा,
और अगर हो भी तो किसको होगी इसकी आहट?
जब है ही नहीं किसीकी चाहत।।

ज़िन्दगी का सफर:-

क्या हुआ अगर रास्ते अलग हो गए,
सफर तो खत्म न हुई,
बस एक मोड़ है, नए रास्ते की ओऱ,
मुसाफ़िर तो हम ही होंगे,
पर सायद तुम्हारा हमसफर कोई और।।

उलझनः-

हम इतने समझे सुलझे नहीं थे,
वक़्त से परेशान थे जरूर पर अपनो से ख़फ़ा न थे,
भागना तो हम भी चाहते थे,
मगर कुछ एहसास छूटते न थे।।

दास्तान-ए-मोहब्बतः-

किसके बगैर जीना अगर मुमकिन न होता,
तो दास्तान-ए-मोहब्बत आज पन्नों पे न होता।।

ANKIT MISHRA

Ankit Mishra, whose pen would like to be called as Paras the Sorcerer's stone, is a law student by profession and a writer by passion. He is obsessed with urdu shayeris, a very effective medication for his insomnia. He only writes when his feelings screams out. He is one of those sensitive people who feels too much to express. So he records every bit of his emotions in a secret handmade diary. Devotion towards his one unrequited love is the essence of his poems. He is in a voyage of writing one perfect piece, made out of stardust.

The Autumn's Wind

The girl who drifted in my life like a single petal,
The one who changed every meaning of my life,
An experience I had never felt,
She's merciless, She adorable, she's rude, she's cute,
Like the colour in the rainbow she's everything,
The one to be adored and treasured,
She's like a breeze which brings happiness as it passes by,
soothes the hearts it touches,
I wish, I wish, I had felt it,
I dodged the breeze and moved on with the chaos in my mind,
She came again to show me the brightest star that shined.
She's the guiding star of my life,
I follow my heart and she resides in there,
I follow every bit of her,
I love every bit of her,
Today I shout it aloud,
Will it reach her?
I hope, it does.

Be By My Side

The day the night falls, the stars are at their peak,
Lighting the whole night, giving it the beauty we seek,
I will sit alone, just with your thought,
I will smile as my heart dies

I know you will be always by my side.

The day I burn inside, searching for the care,
I am ugly in deep inside, to come close no one dares,
I will seek just a smile, a ray of shine,
When everyone throws me aside,

I know you will be always by my side.

I don't want everyone to love me, but just a few,
I will be the morning, just be my morning dew,
Let's roll down the leaves, be the one with the love,
When no one's love is in sight,

I know you will always be by my side.

I will love you, for who you are,
I will touch you, for what you are,
I will never leave, for what we are,
Even if I leave you for a fool I am,
I know you will always be by my side.

Love me today, hate me tomorrow,
Laugh today, leave me tomorrow,
Hug me today, throw me tomorrow,
When god turns off all the lights,

I know you will be by my side.

Patronus

The darkness will drown the shadow,
You be my light,
Keep me alive,
Help me saty and breathe.

When breeze will hit the face,
I want you by my side,
I want to look into the eyes and just say beautiful they are.

Hold your hand walk down the river side,
Feel the warmth of your hand,
Your love for me,
I want to drown in the feelings with you.

Just be by my side,
I promise to hold you evertime,
Fight every battle with you,
Try to win you every time.

At the end we need to be together,
Trying exploring the roads of life,
Trying to find the adventures,
Keeping each other happy always.

I want to end my day,
Looking at you and just imagine,
How did we end up here,
I believe it is love, care, affection and every other feeling,
I just wish to tell you, how much I love you.

Jazbaat-

Kai dino baad ghr aa raha hu,
Sayad mai kisi khwab se bahar aa raha hu,
Uss ghar jaha kuch nhi tha,
Kya batau tere ankho me mere liye kya kya nhi tha.

Ek tasweer si basi hai tu dil me,
Ek sannate sa khamoshi me chaya hu,
Dil-e-jazbaat k iss samandar me,
Mai sayad tujhe wapas dhundne aaya hu.

Yaadon ki siyahi se ek kahani likhi thi,
Samajh na paya koi, uss jabani likhi thi,
Kuch ummeed jhalak rahi thi unn panno pe,
Sayad teri meri kahani likhi thi.

Kuch rahe hai jo kabhi taye nhi ki humne,
Kuch irrade hai jo adhure rah gaye humare,
Tum khwabo me mere bahut karib aa rahi ho,
Sayad tum mujse durr ja rahi ho.

VICKEY DAVID

Vickey David is an Indian English poet and short-story writer, writing profusely in e-journals and magazines. His poetry encompasses dominantly the themes of love, life, nature, aesthetics and so on. He uses different poetic forms like sonnet, couplet, free verse, haiku and others without following the conventional metrical structure.

Legs In Water

Once alone in a fine morning,
Sitting by the forest-centered pond,
Whose water fondles in the arms of breezes-
Gently creating small ripples.
I'm dangling my legs inside the water.

If close my eyes,
The same rippling sensation runs
Across and sooth all my nerves.
I forget my other body parts
Along with my self above legs.

Alive are my only two dangling legs
As if they were fish caught in the net of body-
Struggling, splashing in want of ease,
Albeit desirous to move into deepest water,
To feel the dark cool world,
To smell the rotten mud of the surface.

I am not what I came here.
Methinks legs are not dangling
But the green water of the pond is doing
Inside my conscious nervous system.
Or I am nothing but dangling legs
That breathe beneath the pond-water.
A sudden realization surfaces in me;
I merge into the existence of the pond,
And feel myself the calm water body.
Legs are dangling in the pond within me.

Make Me Free

Do not bottle me up! Make me free!
Your bridal bliss is suffocating me.

You beat me and rebuke me as much you can
Oh God! How innocent is my conjugal man.

You know I work, I earn but I hardly live
Is it home or a refugium I didn't ever conceive?

In your unfaithful arms do not me ensnare
O that I could show you my each bloody tear.

For a clamant need of love I am dying
Why don't you embosom me, leave me crying?

My robotic life has proved my sterile womanhood
Since I am away from the touch of your manhood.

This rectangular box of yours has a door to exit
This absurd xeric confinement I fail to elide it.

The ornaments on my body used to light
Those pretty things are no longer my delight.

In this manly flesh you're a devil in disguise
You've killed my womb in husband's guise.

Often you condemn me and love other
Make me free! I will never bother.

Standstill of Solitude

When unrequited thoughts subsided,
In the human desert of lonely sand.
In the great density of fallen serenity,
In my heart, I felt a standstill of solitude.

The vignettes of my life varying everyday,
Wayfaring through the winding ways,
Finding a sort of recluse inside or outside,
Then, I saw the darkest cave I'd made within.

As a sojourner, my moments were transient.
The lagoon of love stayed as if in limbo,
Unstirred, undisturbed, unperturbed eternally.
From its surface, were rising anxieties of mist.

Solitude hung like twilight against the glimmering sunset,
When a banished bucolic baboon rested on a tree,
Or when the eventide groves were agitated by birds,
Wasn't I one of them, flustered and befuddled for settling?

All sediments tremulous inside my soul,
Wanted to come to a standstill forever.
What was the colour of that solitude?
Alas! My inner brush knew not how to paint.

Autumn in My Heart

What shakes me from my deepest core?
Is it not the autumn in my heart of hearts
That compels me to shed off all those filthy
Thoughts emerged out of my overrationality?

Those thoughts like dead leaves decay more,
Perplexed for some originating from daily dirts
Waning song of the winter though seems healthy
Instead, the autumnal tone of my individuality.

No longer I've the wish to be a haply trodden leaf
Nor to be flown off by Shelley's wild West Wind,
Rather want to be left with my cankers within
So that I would be digested by this hungry earth.

This slow rumble flow of watery wind by the cliff
My unwanted thoughts are getting my body thinned
As if the anguished autumn is pinned with eternal sin
With my life implying the vainity of my mortal birth.

AZAD KUMAR

Azad kumar is a person having liberal thoughts and through his poem he tries to change the Rigid and Fundamental and more conservative society..which is living in old days where Religion plays a dominant role and he tries through his poem to eradicate some social evils and practices which exists till today in the Modern City Nation-state..

Shri Ram Ko Do Vishram

Thak gaye hain Shri Ram,Ab unhe aaram do..!
Treta yoga se abtak yudha hi kar rahe hain..Are Ab to unhe aaram do..!

Kyun unki achai ka majak banate ho(2)
Na samajh hain ye ye Bhagwan nahi samjh sakte aapki mahima ko,
Kshama kshama he Dev Dayamay ,aap humein kshama daan do..
Aapki yash kirti to sarvopari hai..phir kyun ye dhongi chillate hain..
Aapki Mahanta aur aapki Shrestha ko kyun ye nicha dikhate hain..

Aapko paane ki to ek hi upay hai apne saare abhiman aur ahankar ko tyag do.
. To kyun ye kooch log chillate hain aapke naam par jaan do..

Are jo sabke jivan data hain, jo sabke karm fal data hain,
Sarvopari ,sarvoday wahin parmatma hain, wahi vidhata hain..

Pashu ho ya pakshi ,Nar ho ya Narbhakshi
Sabke andar usi Hari ki aatma hain !
Sabke wahi janm data hain..
To kyun karte hain bhed he bhagwan,log manushya-manushya se hi..
Kyun ladte aaye hain ye Murkh..Aapke naam par sansar ke shubh aarambh se hi..

Kya yahi bacha hai dekhne ko,ki tune jo humein banaya hai..
Aaj har koi harpal, Dwesh, Raktpat,Dharmbhed ki Gandi Maansikta se sanaya hai..!!

Aree tune to sada sarvada apne bhakto ko apanaya hai..
Chahe wah kisi bhi dharm,ya kul ka hi kyun na ho!!

Aapne usae bhi Hridaya mein sthan diya hai,
Aapne usae bhi Gale se lagaya hai..
Magar aaj jis tarah se logon ke andar Mansikta ho aayi hai..

Yah Maryada purushottam Shri Ram ka Udaharan nahi hai..!!
Ye unki mahanta ka attahas hai,yah unki Jag hasai hai..

Acha hota He Prabhu Bhaktvatsal..Aap avtarit hi na hote..!
Na ye agyani aapak majak banate ,na koi kisi ke bairi hote..

Aapke treta Avatar ne humein bahut kooch sikhaya hai..
Maanavta hi parmo Dharm hai,yah aapne humein bataya hai..
Wah manushya to manushya hi nahi hai,
Jiske andar na karuna aur na hi maaya hai..

Wah vyakti Hridayaheen hai, kapti hai,swarthi hai,
jisne aapke naam ke aad par yrh aatank machaya hai..!

Jis tarah yah dharti anmol hai, jiska koi daam nahi..
Usi tarah uske rachayata shri Hari hain.una koi ek dham nahi..
Aaj aapke naam par yeah stambh gaadne chale hain..

Jinka khud ka koi wajood nahi..jeevanbhar dusro ko kasta diya hai..saare rakt dwesh aur abhishap se same huye !!

Aaj aapke naam par dhambh bharne chale hain..
Nahi chahta mai sach mein ki koi aapka Mandir banaye..
Insaniyat ko bhilkar wo shaitan ban jaaye..!!

Aaj jahan ek or bhukmari hai aur Garibi hai..
Kooch log jo hain dhan sampann..
Koshish mein hain aaj yeh dikhane ko tu unka karibi hai..
Aree nahi maanta mai kisi dharm ko jahan insaniyat dukhi hai..

Shri Ram bhi nahi chahenge us Mandir mein waas karna jahan Manavta biki hai..!!
Dena hi hai agar samaj ko naya rup to Shri Ram ke Aadarshon ko Maan lo..

Naa ki Mandir Mandir kehkar Gareebon ki jo bahushankhyak hain, Niraapradh hain ,
Bhole hain unki jaan lo..
Kitne bhole hain ye log ,chit mann se Jai shri Ram chillate hain..
Ye kooch Dharm paalak unhe unhe apne istemal mein laate hain..

Agar banana hi hai agar ek Bhavya Mandir..
To apni Antaraatma ko jagaiye..
Hum sab usi ke hi to Ansh hain.
.Bekar mein jaat dharm mein padkar apna Apna aur apni jaan mat Gawaiye..!!

Apni vikrit soch se samaj ko na Bhatkaayein..!!(2)

Aaiye Gandhi ji ke RamRajya Swapn ko satya kar jaayein..

VIVEKANANDA SAHOO

Vivekananda wants to express his emotions through his writings. He has seen a lot of UP's and downs in his life & he wants to share it with others. Let's see what he wrote -

दुनिया

दुनिया ने हमे गिराना चाहा और हम चलना सीख गए,
दुनिया ने हमे रुलाना चाहा और हम हँसना सीख गए,
अरे हम तो कभी मरना चाहते थे
, पर इस दुनिया से लड़ते लड़ते जीना सीख गए।

जख़्म

जो दुख नजर नहीं आते वो भी
उतने ही गेहरे होते है,
चेहरे पे मुस्कान लेके घूमने के बाद भी
कुछ जख़्म हमेसा हरे रहते है ।

सावालों का जवाब

कई बार पुराने सावालों के जवाब ढूंढते ढूंढते हम थक जाते है,
अतीत के किस्सों मै उलझ कर हम अपने मंजिल के राह से भटक जाते है।
तो बंद करो अपने पुराने सावालों से जबाब ढूंढना ,
तो बंद करो यु अपने जज्बातो से खेलना।
चाहे पुराने सावालों का जवाब मिले ना मिले ,
नया सावालों में जवाब हम खुद ही ढूंढ लेंगे।

तेरी यादों

अतीत के कई सवालों में उलझा हुआ हूँ
लेकिन अब जवाब ढूंढने की कोसिस नही करूँगा ,
तेरे चले जाने का गम आज भी है लेकिन
अब वजह ढूंढने की कोसिस नही करूँगा ,
बेसक सारी रात तेरी यादों में रोता जरूर हूँ लेकिन
अब तेरी लौटने की इंतेजार नही करूँगा ।

ANIL KUMAR BEHERA

Anil Kumar Behera is a senior student at the Visva Bharati University and currently taking up a master's degree in HINDI. As Hindi language student he has studied and trained to perform highly in different fields such as teaching, translating famous poems and essays, researching on this particular language .his dedication is what sets him apart from anybody else.He finished his primary education as salutatorian. Belonged to the top 10 students of his middle and high school class .Anil is also passionate about book reading and poem writing .He is also passi onate about short film making. He is excellent at videography. He is a well rounded individual who lives with passion, dedication, and grace.

Chocolate और Icecream

कौन बुलाएगा मुझे Icecream कहकर
जिसका पहला इश्क़ था मैं,
कौन गुस्सा होकर गाली देगा ओर
जिस गुस्सा से प्यार था मुझे ।

थी वह बड़ी घर की लड़की
मैं एक नीची लड़का,
उसकी lunch box में paneer
मेरी भूख की दवा पांता भात ।

बिना नाम जानते हुआ प्यार
कोई उसे कहता पागलपन,
दोनों को है दोनों से लगाव
पर वह प्यार था मौन ।

Chocolate कहकर बुलाता था
क्योंकि उसे पसंद है Dairymilk,
कैसे कहूँ उसे ; मालूम नहीं मुझे
लाकर दे दिया Chloromint ।

-×-

छोटी मुँह में बड़ी बात
कैसे करूँ इश्क का बयान,
थी वह अमीरी राजकुमारी
ये प्रेम पत्र बन जा मेरी जुबान ।

-×-

वह जो समझती थी राँझा मेरी कहानी की
उसे अपना दर्द सुनाकर लौट आया हूँ ,
जो मौत दिखाता है लोगों को अपनी औकात
मैं उस मौत को उसकी औकात दिखाकर लौट आया हूँ ।।

-×-

न जाने क्या कमी थी मेरे इश्क़ में कि
तुझे किसी और का होने पर मजबूर कर दिया ,
गज़ब है तेरी बेवफाई भी
न मैं तेरा हुआ न किसी और का होने दिया !!

-×-

अपनी उंगलियों से ज़ुल्फ़ें यूँ हटाया न कर
बेबसी लफ्ज़ें यूँ जताया न कर ,
पता नहीं ; किसी बुज़दिल को कब प्यार हो जाए तेरे से
ए नूर , तेरे चेहरे से यूँ घूंघट उठाया न कर ।

-×-

ए दिल , तु मोहब्बत की बात मत कर
मैं उसकी नफ़रत में भी प्यार देखा है ,
उसकी खुबसूरती भी भला बयां करूँ तो कैसे
जनाब,मैंने तो अमावस में चांद देखा है ।।

-×-

नजरों से तुम बातें बताया न करो
मोहब्बत हो किसीसे तो छिपाया न करो ,
हम तुम्हारे इसी अदाएँ पे दिल हार बैठे
यूँ थोड़ा चेहरे से जूल्फ़े हटाया न करो ।।

-×-

इश्क में तेरे
न मजनूँ , न शाहजहाँ बनूंगा ;
एक ही ख्वाईश है मेरी
तु रूह , मैं तेरी काया बनूंगा ।।

-×-

उम्र गुजरेगी इंतज़ार में क्या
नफ़रत मिलेगा अंत में क्या ,
बेअसर रही मेरी हर कोशिशें
मिलावट है यह इश्क में क्या ?
बोलते क्यों नहीं
सोच रहे हो जबाब क्या ?
क्या इजाज़त है , एक बात पूछूँ
क्यों हुआ बेइंतेहा मोहब्बत उससे
एक ही शख्स था इस जहां में क्या ?

-×-

औकात मेरी छोटी
पर सपने बहुत बड़े थे,
तब जेब मेरी भारी लगी
जब बगल में पिता जी खड़े थे ।

-×-

MADHUSMITA PADHI

Madhusmita Padhi from CET ,bbsr. She's a nerdy and otherwise cheerful girl. Sometimes sane, mostly drunk in poetry. She's an active member in college dramas & nukkad nataks, not to forget a flair in debates.

Brown Isn't for Girls

Yesterday,
I came home,
with bruised knees
shabby hands
and a sun kissed
brown body.
I sobbed a little,coz
my body ached with all
those treadles pushed.
On such a summer morn'
when I imagine to pedaL
the longest mile,
drench my undershirt
in the tiresome sweat,
And knock myself down
on rough white roads,
I'm stopped.
The patriarchal unknown tells me
It's not something
meant for girls'.
She teaches me,
that bruises,sunburns
and skin turning brown
are not for girls'.
Meanwhile, when I question
my conscience,
about where I went wrong,
My hands are fed with
Soaps and lotions,
to erase those Sun-Tans
that reflects my love

for the Sun,
which I adored,
Like that of
stones and jewelleries.
I'm then taught lessons
of skin tones defining beauty
where Fair,White, and Light
were the only chapters
that were talked of,
Brown and honey were
considered to be out of focus.
My body is treated
with heavy creams and fair waters
as if I've contracted
a disease that's a taboo.
They don't let
my brown body breathe
the outside air,
They don't let me smell coffee beans
Coz it's dark!
They don't let me pedal any more
Coz Brown isn't for girls'.

YUVRAJ SINGH

Yuvraj Singh is 20 years hailing from Debai bulandshar, uttarpradesh. Heis a student by profession he is a creative person who loves to write and is artistic and imaginative he loves to read novels he is is his parents Apple of the eye the ultimate aim of his life is to make everyone happy and he can go to any extent to do so he help and educate children's about importance of education in one's life he believes that we should start from where we are use what we have and do what we can.

Positive Vibes

Apne dard pe rona matt,
Rona aaye to, khudko khona matt
Bas ek daffa yeh sochlena
Shayad koi apse bhi jayda takleef mai ho
Sare gammo ko samait ke,
Khudki khushnaseebi ka sajda karna ki
Saansein dii h,
To khudko jeena bhi sikha hi dega .
Harrasment,abuse , family problem,
Financial problem, betrayals in love ,
Suffering,poor health aur na jaane kiya kiya ...
Bahut burri se burri problem hai
Or hogi lekin ek baar
Bas yeh sochna kiya
Pata koi ek insaan tumse
Bas ek problem extra hokke bhi ladd raha hai
To jb wph harr nahi mann raha
To tum kiyu give up nahi karna he
Yaad rakhna bhagwan ne roone ki kayii wajahyee di he ....
Usne to paida bhi hote hi rulla diya tha
Lekin haasna to hamare hath me he
Uski wajah matt dhundna
Warna thorda muskil hogaa.
Keep your positive vibes high.

MAA

It's just not about a particular day .
I swear, everyday i thank god for giving uh in my life .
The only person important in my life.
I want to give all happiness to uh .
Koshish karta hu aur aap choti si baat pe itna khush ho jati ho,
I really get emotional,
I love you maa you are everything to me ,
I have never ever consider any other person mattering to me .
It's only uh, my world, my everything .
Aur pata nahi q lekin har waqt darr lagta hai kahi apko kho na du .
I can bet on, no one can ever get a mother like mine.(nothing offensive).
She is my bestest buddy i share each and everything,
So damn comfortable bond,
Amazing understanding,
Non judging responses, lovely, cutest, bholi and my love ummmaaah
Love uhh ek bahut jayda keh diya aur bhi kehne ka man hai.
I can speak all day long fpr uhh.
Only person to whom i can surrender myself
Love and happiness is uhh maa.

SWAPNA TANMAYA JENA

Academically zoologist and by nature philanthropist. She believes reading about someone is the best way to know them. Person might not act much longer while defining its ownself in form of their writing. Thoughts give wings and when put into words that power is magical.

Divine Passion

There was a sound of bang on the ground
From the corner room of the compound

"Ouch!" Was a small whisper she made
As she stoodup again brushed her hands and looked afraid

"Let me check if anyone is coming" she said and peeped out of the room
With clear site around no one heard them she presumed

They looked at each other's serious face and broke into a small laughter
As if their secret was about to be slaughtered

"I don't think I can pull this off, it has been ages I last......" as Asha exasperated
Just in time Pallavi interrupted

"Could you please give your thoughts a break you are definitely going to win. We just need the drawing room space for the last practice. Shall I talk to him once?"
"Are you mad?" Asha spoke gripping Pallavi's arm "I am doing this only for your sake no one should know else we won't be allowed to walk forget about the dance"

It was a big day for them and they had it all planned out
As the family leave to attend a marriage, Pallavi has to stay back for exam and Asha to clear her doubt.

Saying goodbye to the family members, hurriedly they went to get ready as to reach the event at nine

Few minutes later as Asha walked out of the room in her
Odishi getup, Pallavi wouldn't held back her tears and
softly uttered
"Mom you look divine"

Sitting inside the taxi holding Pallavi's hand
Away from conservative in-laws Asha's soul was happy to
be in long lost dream land

Suddenly everything came to standstill
As the car got crashed with the divider and they lost all the
feel

As Pallavi opened her eyes next she saw her father
caressing her face
Looking at her plastered hand and the room surrounded she
knew it was a hospital space

All she could say was "How is Maa?", " I want to meet her"
As she entered the cabin seeing her mother lying all
wounded she felt shattered
She went near Asha and kissed her forhead
"I am so sorry I will make Dad understand. It was all my
plan, no one will shout at you" Pallavi muttered

Seeing tears rolling down her mother's cheek, of all that
Pallavi expected to hear
She got heartbroken at the words that buzzed her ear
" Pullu my legs are damaged the doctor said so does that
mean can't I dance anymore dear?"
More than the family confontration the grief of losing her
childhood passion forever was hard to bear.

JHILIK PATHAK

She is a teacher of biology in Tarapore school her name is Jhilik pathak .she is a good listener and a good writter .she teach in a easy why that we can understand all the consept easily .all the student like her way of taking and joking and she laugh all the time and make us also laughter .she is a teacher but for us she is a like our best friend .and she is pet lover . Thank you

My Rise And Shine Moments

After my birth I was always said to be lucky. As the day I was brought home my father along with 2000 other cable employees got a Rs.500 after not getting salary for 3 months. Yes I was born in the period of crisis where a whole company was dissolving leaving people in despair. Nobody has a clue what to do. I saw struggle. That moment made all the children of my age of the employees one thing that we need to be successful and prevent ourselves from these situations. Hence my grooming up was the same way done. I was always brought up to be extraordinary. I excelled and eventually the expectations increased. For the initial years I was very happy but later on the burden of being at par at everything started getting my nerves. I was too small to understand myself. My likes and dislikes and even younger to fight for my peace. I was a star they said. I justified my name they said. And that saying elated my parents with joy which made my day even though it was at the cost of my burden.

Finally I was expected to become a city topper during my boards. I was petrified of maths. And I remember working hard for it which eventually gain people's expectations over me again. While going inside the examination hall my teacher wrapped her arm around me and said we want 100. At that moment my ground shook. I was blank, I felt like a robot. I didn't know what to do there were waves of emotions hitting my empty mind. But I kept my calm. The triggering part was the results. I saw people upset. I got 94 but still couldn't make people happy. There was sadness, there was neglect there was disappointment. These emotions were beyond me to take. I felt helpless. I was drowned. I couldn't get up. I felt lifeless. I changed as a person

However the reality check with my lift up came when I out of school. Took a year gap. Went to Pune for studies and got what I want to do. My journey has been a lesson. I learn from me. And hence I work so that no children feel this way. I want a happy place for kids and work for them to speak out their mind ,emotions so that in real life they could be achievers of long term goals and not the short lived ones.

KUSHAL GANERIWAL

Aged 20 year, hails from Ratangarh, Rajasthan currently residing in a beautiful city Jamshedpur, Jharkhand. He is a student by profession but volunteering in a NGO since last 5 years. He has represented his school in a national level competition and won it as well.He was awarded in Delhi and get a chance to visit the Parliament house. Spreading smile around and being down to earth is his true identity. A tea-holic dream weaver who loves to play instruments and scribbles his random thoughts on paper. He is multi-talented, whether its writing, singing, delivering speeches or the burden of responsibilities, he has been proving himself from the first day. Street food , chai and traveling are his stress stealer. He completely believes in patience, because according to him, " Sometimes we are tired of waiting but still we hope for the best , because its our life and we can't compromise with worst".

चलेगा क्या

जो सांस बन कर तुम्हारे रूह में समा जाऊँ तो चलेगा क्या ,
जो तुम्हारी आँखों के रास्ते दिल में उतर जाऊँ तो चलेगा क्या ,
जो आए कभी कोई मुसीबत तो साथ निभाओगे क्या ,
सच सच बताओ मेरे दिल से दिल लगओगे क्या ।।

जो तेरी गोद को बना कर सिरहाना सारी रात गुजार दूँ तो चलेगा क्या ,
जो तेरी ज़ुल्फ़ों की खुशबू से मदहोश हो जाउँ तो चलेगा क्या,
जो तेरे लिबास की लज्जत मेरे रूह में बस जाए तो चलेगा क्या,
सच सच बताओ मेरे दिल से दिल लगओगे क्या ।।

जो देख कर तुझे मैं अपनी सुध-बुध खो दूँ तो चलेगा क्या ,
जो सुबह से शाम तेरी तस्वीर को दिवानो सा ताकता रहूँ तो चलेगा क्या,
जो तेरी दीवानगी में खो दूँ अपना वजूद तो चलेगा क्या,
सच सच बताओ मेरे दिल से दिल लगओगे क्या ।।

जो तेरे पायल की झंकार सुनते ही दिल मेरा दिवानो सा झूमने लगे तो चलेगा क्या,
जो तेरी चूड़ियों की खनक को मन हर पल सुनना चाहे तो चलेगा क्या,
जो तेरे आँखों की मधुशाला में दिल डूब जाए तो चलेगा क्या,
सच सच बताओ मेरे दिल से दिल लगओगे क्या ।।

नहीं आया

प्यार हम करते थे कितना क्यूँ जताना नहीं आया,
याद हम करते थे कितना ये बताना नहीं आया ।

हम तो रुसवाई दिखाते थे बड़े हिं आसानी से ,
क्या थे वो मेरे लिये ये भी दिखाना नहीं आया।

बिन कहे हिं जान लेते थे जो धड़कन मुसलसल हम ,
जान कर अब दर्द उनके भी मनाना नहीं आया ।

आज भी सब जानते हैं, हैं दिया तू मिरे दिल का ,
बुझ गया तो फिर दुबारा लौ जलाना नहीं आया ।

जबसे वो ओझल हुआ हैं ऐसा लगता कि जैसे अब ,
राह सारे हैं खतम पर क्यूँ ठिकाना नहीं आया ।

आसाँ कहाँ

तोड़ दूँ मैं बंदिशें पर तोड़ना आसाँ कहाँ ,
जान हैं वो,जान से मुँह मोड़ना आसाँ कहाँ ।।

लत अगर होती तो जाती छूट एक ज़िद से मगर,
ये मोहब्बत है इसे यूँ छोड़ना आसाँ कहाँ।।

इन बहारों में तेरी यादें सताती हैं बहुत ,
याद में जलने से दिल को रोकना आसाँ कहाँ ।।

है बुलाती उँगलियों को ये घनी जुल्फें तेरी,
जुल्फ में खोने से खुद को रोकना आसाँ कहाँ।।

आँख में तो अब उतर जाता कोई भी चेहरा,
पर तिरे उस चेहरे को भूलना आसाँ कहाँ।।

पिता

उंगली थाम कर जिसने चलना सिखाया ,
काँधे पर बैठा कर इस जहाँ को दिखाया ,
चोट लगने पर मुझे गले से लगाया ,
हर वक़्त मुझे माँ की डांट से बचाया ।।
सर उठाकर जिसने मुझे जीना सिखाया ,
संघर्ष की परिभाषा से रूबरू करवाया ,
हर मुसीबत से जिसने हम सबको बचाया ,
उस शख्स में मेरा ब्रह्माण्ड है समाया ।।

कुदरत

देख कर मौसम की बेरुखी दिल को अफसोस है ,
लगता है इस बेरूखी की वजह कोई ठोस है ।
दे रही है शायद कुदरत हमें किये की सजा ,
क्योंकि इंसान सताता इसे रोज है ।।

MOHIT CHATURVEDI

Mohit chaturvedi is a secretive person..he is born in November 22....he always have something new to say.. he appreciate the little things in life...Mohit have a dynamic personality...he is always alert and thinking person His personality is attractive and attention seeking... About his writers skills :-Every secret of a writer's soul, every experience of his life, every quality of his mind, is written large in his works." He is an abstract thinker..... he works untill his signatures turns in an autograph

एक दिन चला जाऊंगा

एक दिन चला जाऊंगा सबसे दूर में
होकर तन्हा अपनों से बेफिजूल में
फिर यादों में मुझसे मुलाकातें होगी
मैं ना रहूंगा पर मेरी ही बातें होगी
जब पुराने पन्नों को पल्टोगे तो नजर आऊंगा
जब टूट जाएंगे सपने तो कहीं चला जाऊंगा
मत खफा होना तुम दुनिया के लहजे से
सब कुछ मिल जाएगा तुम्हें दुख सहने से
एक दिन कहीं अजनबी बनकर मिलेंगे
बात तुमसे ही बीते वक्त की करेंगे
मुझे समझना और जिंदगी से लड़ना
तुम मेरी तरह इंसानों से मत उलझना
और कहीं टूट जाओ जंग लड़ते-लड़ते
तो संभाल लेना खुद को हंसते हंसते
वहां कुछ तुम्हारे अपने भी होंगे
सुनेंगे तुम्हें करीब से मगर साथ ना देंगे
जाग जाओ जब तुम सपनों से,हो जाओगे दूर तुम अपनों से
फिर मुस्कुराकर मुझे अलविदा कहना
मेरी तरह तुम इंसानों से मत उलझना

बादलों को कह दो बरसना छोड़ दें

बादलों को कह दो बरसना छोड़ दें ,
इन आँखों को कह दो तरसना छोड़ दे ।।
देखे थे कई सपने साथ तुम्हारे ,
तो अब इस दिल को भी कह दो कि धड़कना छोड़ दे ।।।
इस लम्हे को कह दो कि तू दो पल के लिए थम सा जा ।
इस चाँद को कह दो कि तू कहीं छुप जा।
इन आंखों ने किया था बेसब्री से इंतजार तुम्हारा,
तो इन पलकों को भी कह दो ना की टिमटिमाना छोड़ दे ।।
तुम्हें शायद अदाएं पसंद ना आई मेरी तो तुमने कुछ रुख सा मोड़ लिया ।।
एक बार कहते तो सही हमसे , की इन फूलों की तरह मुरझाना छोड़ दे ।

चुप चुप सा रहने लगा हूं

चुप चुप सा रहने लगा हूं
ना जाने किन ख्यालों में खोने लगा हूं
भूल गया हूं जीना इस जिंदगी को मैं
ना जाने कैसे खुद को संभालने लगा हूं
इस दर्दे दिल की सिफारिशें दफनाने लगा हूं
कुछ अपनों से दूर जाने लगा हूँ
फिर भी हारा नहीं हूं तुझसे ए जिंदगी
कुछ अपनों की वजह से लड़खड़ाने लगा हूं .

जिंदगी

निकला था मैं घर से
समझने इस जिंदगी को
लोग मिलते गए फासले बढ़ते गए
कुछ राहों में मिले लोग ऐसे भी
लगता था मौत तक साथ निभाएंगे
पर वक्त के साथ -साथ उन्होंने भी इस दिल की नुमाइशे ठुकरा दी

ONE LINERS

- कुछ बातें बताता हूँ , कुछ बातें छुपाता हूँ
  पर ए जिंदगी मैं तुझसे हमेशा हार जाता हूँ ।।

- चेहरे पर नकाब पहन कर, शब्दों के जाल बिछाते हैं।
  ये अपने ही है जनाब , जो अपनों को ही नीचा दिखाते हैं ।।

- पाया था मैंने भी उसे , अपना सब कुछ खो कर
  तोड़ दिया दिल मेरा और मार गई ठोकर

- गैरों से दगा कर बैठा मैं अपनों के लिए ,
  अब अपने ही अपने ना रहें ..

- दूर से देखोगे तो हँसता हुआ चेहरा ही दिखेगा,
  कभी पास आकर खैरियत तो पूछो

ANUBHA MINZ

Anubha Minz a shy and the most kind hearted and softspoken child who was presented to the earth with rain all over the steel city of India. A person who cares for others more than herself and is ready to sacrifice anything and everything for all her loved ones. She has been gifted with a very beautiful and the most cheerful smile which can vanish all the pain and suffering in one go. . She is a very sweet shy lady.

Pyaar To Bahut Hai Maa Bus Keh Nhi Pati Hun

Teri ungli pakad kar phir se chalna cahti hun
Maa pyaar to bht hai tumse
Bus keh nahi pati hun.

Jab kabhi aankhe nam huve
Maine humesha tujhe he paya
Raton ko neend na aaye
To jaag kar tune he sulaya.

Pyaar to bahut hai maa bus keh nhi pati hun
Meri har zidh ko
Pura kiya tune
Jab kabhi thes lagi
Hmesha thama hai tune

Pyaar to bht h maa bus keh nhi pati hun.

Mere kahe bagair
Mujhe samjh leti hai
Meri har musibat ko
Seh leti hai.

Pyaar bahut hai maa bus keh nhi pati hun.

Tapte mathe pe
Thandak ho tum
Andhere main jalta
Deepak ho tum

Pyaar bht hai maa bus keh nhi pati hun

Papa k dant se
Har bar bachaya
Jab bhi main udas thi
Pas tujhe he paya

Pyaar bht h maa bus keh nahi pati hun

Tawharo main khud k kapde na the
Mujhe designer suit dilaya
Apni har jaruraton ko mar kar
Mere khawabon ko hakikat banaya

Pyaar bahut hai maa bus keh nahi pati hun.

Rulane wale bahut mile
Sahara dene wali bus ek tu
Mujhe seene se lagane wali
Maa bus ek tu

Pyaar bht hai maa bus keh nahi pati hun

Kabhi pyaar se mujhe sehlati
Toh kabhi dant kar bulati
Duniya main sab ruth jate hai maa
Bus ek tu he kabhi na ruthti.

Pyaar bht h maa bus keh nahi pati hun

Sath jab koi na tha
Meri dost ban sath thi tm
Jeevan k har padaow m

Sikhchak ban sath thi tm

Pyaar to bht h maa bus keh nahi pati hun

Kitne khushnasib hai hum
Jo tum mere sath ho
Dukh main mere aashu bahati
Mere khushiyon main khush ho jati.

Pyaar to bahut hai maa Bus keh nahi pati hun

Tere bin main aadhuri ho
ek kore kagaj se suni suni hun
Sach maa,
pyaar bahut hai tujhse bus keh nahi pati hun

PRITAM MARANDI

Pritam Marandi was born and raised in Pakur, Jharkhand. He writes sweet, fun and romantic stories.He also writes poetry and short stories on trending and burning issues of the society. He can usually be found reading a book and that book is more likely to be a psychological suspense thriller stories and novels. He first began creating other world and characters during his secondary school. He loves travelling and exploring new places and getting different experience and knowledge from other people.

सफ़र ख्वाबों से हकीकत तक

यूँ कहने को तो सफ़र ही है यह जिंदगी,
चलते ही जाना है हमें मुसाफिरों की भाँति,
जब तक ना आए यहाँ अपना ठिकाना,
है यह सफ़र ख्वाबों से हकीकत तक का।

आए चाहे लाख मुश्किलें रास्ते में हमारे,
अटकाए चाहे रोड़े या लगाए लोग अड़चनें,
ठोकर खाकर भी है हमें आगे बढ़ते रहना,
है यह सफ़र ख्वाबों से हकीकत तक का।

अभी जो हैं अगर घुप्प अँधेरे तुम्हारे मार्ग में,
छँटेंगा अँधेरा निकलेगा सूरज होगा और सवेरा,
मंजिल पाएगा एक दिन तू हौसला बनाए रखना,
है यह सफ़र ख्वाबों से हकीकत तक का।

मत घबराना तू जिंदगी में मेहनत से राही,
अच्छे कर्म बदल देगी एक दिन तक़दीर तेरा,
बदलेगा मीठे पानी में माथे का नमकीन पसीना,
है यह सफ़र ख्वाबों से हकीकत तक का।

देख तू खुले आसमान की चिड़ियों को,
पँख फैला करती हैं मेहनत वे हर रोज,
तब ही जुटता है प्यारे घर उनके खाना,
है यह सफ़र ख्वाबों से हकीकत तक का।

सुख और दुःख हैं जीवन के स्थायी साथी,
बनाए रखना है जीवन भर संतुलन दोनों में,
कभी पड़ता है दुश्मन से भी हाथ मिलाना,
है यह सफ़र ख्वाबों से हकीकत तक का।

पीठ पीछे लोग सारे करते हैं बुराई,
पर तुझे नहीं छोड़ना है अपनी अच्छाई,
दिल बड़ा रख गलतियां उनके माफ कर देना,
है यह सफ़र ख्वाबों से हकीकत तक का।

आएँगे लोग कई जीवन में हमें गिराने,
खुद होंगे भले गिरे हुए लेकिन हमें सिखाने,
रास्ते हैं ऊबड़-खाबड़ फिर भी है चलते जाना,
है यह सफ़र ख्वाबों से हकीकत तक का।

सच्ची और पक्की दोस्ती रखो सबसे तुम प्यारे,
और रखो प्रेम बिना शर्त और निःस्वार्थ भाव से,
कुछ देने का मतलब नहीं होता है हमेशा पाना,
है यह सफ़र ख्वाबों से हकीकत तक का।

हूँ नहीं मैं गुरु तुम्हारा ना हो शिष्य तुम मेरे,
पर शायद दिखा सकता हूँ सत्य का मार्ग तुम्हें,
ज्ञान यही है जीवन का कि सदा दिल की सुनना,
है यह सफ़र ख्वाबों से हकीकत तक का।

अजनबी से हमसफ़र तक

ट्रेन का वक्त हो चला था। नयनतारा आखिरी मिनट पर स्टेशन पहुँची थी और आते ही अपनी सीट ढूँढने में लग गयी। उसके परिवार के सभी सदस्य उसे छोड़ने स्टेशन पहुँचे थे क्योंकि वह पहले कभी भी अपने परिवार और शहर को छोड़कर अकेली बाहर नहीं गई थी। जल्दी ही उसे अपनी सीट मिल गई। अभी उसे बैठे हुए कुछ ही वक्त हुआ होगा कि अचानक उसके सामने वाली सीट पर नवीन आ कर बैठ गया। वह दौड़कर आया था और अभी तक हाँफ रहा था। दिखने में लँबा-चौड़ा और मासूम चेहरा लेकिन रौबीले आवाज वाले नवीन को देखकर कोई भी उसे अनदेखा नहीं कर सकता था। लेकिन नयनतारा ने एक नजर उसे देखकर अपनी नजरें वापस खिड़की की तरफ घुमा ली। नयनतारा भी अपने नाम के अनुरूप सबके आँखों का तारा थी। सुंदर चेहरा, लंबे बाल और सुरीली आवाज उसके पूरे व्यक्तित्व को चार चाँद लगाती थी। उसे देखकर नवीन भी एक पल को ठहर गया था, लेकिन अगले ही पल उसे हकीकत का एहसास हो गया और वह सँभल गया। नयनतारा अपने शहर से बाहर कॉलेज की पढ़ाई के सिलसिले में पहली बार जा रही थी। अपनों से दूर जाने की वजह से वह थोड़ी उदास थी इसलिए सफर में आराम करने के ख्याल से उसने अपनी आँखें बँद कर ली। वहीं नवीन अपने राष्ट्रीय रक्षा अकादमी (NDA) परीक्षा के सिलसिले में दूसरे शहर जा रहा था। नयनतारा की उदासी नवीन को खटक तो रही थी, पर यूँ उसे उससे बात करना अच्छा नहीं लग रहा था। इसलिए उसने उसे तंग करना उचित नहीं समझा। इस उधेड़बुन में न जाने कब उसकी आँख लग गई और वह सो गया। अचानक जब अपने स्टेशन आने पर उसकी आँख खुली तो वह उतर चुकी थी। वह भी अनमने मन से उतरा और फ्रेश होकर अपने परीक्षा केंद्र की ओर निकल पड़ा। नवीन अब सिर्फ नवीन नहीं लेफ्टिनेंट नवीन था। भारतीय सैन्य अकादमी (IMA) में अपने पूरे ट्रेनिंग के दौरान उसने एक बार भी छुट्टी नहीं ली थी और सर्विस जाॅइन करने के बाद भी उसने कोई लंबी छुट्टी

नहीं ली थी। हालाँकि इस बात को काफी साल बीत गए थे लेकिन उसके मन में नयनतारा की एक हल्की याद जरूर थी। स्टेशन पहुँचते ही उसके परिवार वाले, दोस्त और रिश्तेदार भी स्टेशन पर उसके आने की प्रतीक्षा कर रहे थे। तभी उसकी दादी ने उसे पीछे से चिकोटी काटी "मैं इधर हूँ बच्चे! अब जल्दी बता क्या लाया तू मेरे लिए?"। "अरे दादी! अब पहले मुझे घर तो ले चलो" नवीन ने हंसते हुए जवाब दिया। घर आते ही सबकी फ़रमाइशें शुरू हो गई और नवीन ने अपने बैग से सभी के लिए एक-एक चीजें निकालते हुए सबकी फ़रमाइश पूरी करता गया। फिर कुछ देर बाद वह आराम करने अपने कमरे में चला गया। अगले दिन दोपहर को उसने अपने दोस्तों को शहर घुमाने को कहा तो वे तुरंत हाजिर हो गए। घूमते-घूमते उसकी नजरें एक दुकान पर ठहर गई। उसने गाड़ी रुकवाकर तुरंत सीधी दौड़ लगाई और अब वो नयनतारा के सामने खड़ा था। "अरे! आप यहाँ कैसे? पीछा तो नहीं कर रहे मेरा?" नयनतारा ने लगभग चौंकते हुए सवालों की झड़ी लगा दी। इन अप्रत्याशित सवालों से एक पल को नवीन भी सकपका गया लेकिन फिर उसने उसे सभी बातें बताते हुए उसका भ्रम दूर कर माहौल को सँभाल लिया। कुछ देर की बातचीत में ही वो दोनों ऐसे लग रहे थे जैसे बरसों के बिछड़े दोस्त हों। "हुजूर की इजाजत हो तो हम चलें" तभी नवीन के दोस्तों ने दोनों को हकीकत में ला पटका। नवीन का जाने का मन तो नहीं था लेकिन जल्द मिलने की बात कह कर उसने विदा ली। तभी नयनतारा की छोटी बहन नेहा ने उसे पीछे से बुलाया और कागज का एक टुकड़ा थमा कर भाग गई। अपने दोस्तों से लाख नजरें बचा कर भी वह उनकी नजरों में आ चुका था। "अच्छा जी! तो हमें घुमाने की बात करने वाले जनाब तो हमसे आगे निकल गए।" उसके दोस्तों ने उसे छेड़ते हुए कहा। उसने जल्दी से कागज में लिखे फोन नंबर को सेव किया और घर जल्दी पहुँचाने के लिए उनसे गुज़ारिश की। घर पहुँचते ही नवीन रात होने का इंतजार कर रहा था कि उसे अकेलापन मिले और वह उससे बात कर पाए। रात को जब सब खाना खाकर अपने कमरे में चले गए, नवीन तुरंत दो-तीन सीढ़ियाँ लाँघ कर छत पहुँचा।

"हेलो! जनाब ये जल्दबाजी किसलिए?" नयनतारा हरदम सवाल करने के मूड में रहती थी। "ये हसीन रात, ये जगमगाती रोशनी आज ये समाँ कुछ खोया-खोया सा है। हमें नींद आती नहीं है आजकल। तरस रहीं आँखें एक पल देखने के लिए आपको, आप जाग रही हैं या सो गईं?" यह सुनते ही नयनतारा खिलखिलाकर हँस पड़ी। ""शायर साहब आप तो कच्चे खिलाड़ी निकले। वैसे कोशिश बहुत अच्छी थी"। "शौक तो है लेकिन हाथ थोड़ा तँग है। वैसे आजमाने में कोई बुराई नहीं है।" नवीन ने जवाब दिया। इस बार दोनों हँस पड़े। बात करते-करते दोनों ने अपने बारे में एक-दूसरे को तसल्ली से बताया। नयनतारा और नवीन की ज्यादातर रातें अब एक दूसरे से बात करने में और उनका दिन एक दूसरे की यादों में खोने में बीतने लगी। एक दिन दोनों ने तय किया कि वह दोनों कल शाम को मिलेंगे। अब सुबह भी होने को थी। अनमने मन से दोनों ने फोन काटा और अगले दिन के इंतजार में सो गए। आज का दिन दोनों के लिए बेहद खास था। नवीन जल्दी से तैयार हो कर नयनतारा को उसकी कॉलोनी के बाहर पिक-अप करने पहुँच गया। नवीन चाह कर भी उसकी तारीफ़ किए बगैर न रह सका। रेस्तराँ पहुँचकर दोनों ने थोड़ी देर इधर-उधर की बातें की। नवीन ने रेस्तराँ में पहले जाकर पूरी तैयारी करवा रखी थी। कुछ देर की बातचीत के बाद नवीन ने अपने घुटने टेककर काफी रोमांटिक अंदाज़ में हाथ माँगते हुए कहा " मेरी प्यारी नयनतारा, मैं तुमसे बहुत प्यार करता हूँ। क्या तुम अपना पूरा जीवन मेरे साथ बिताना चाहोगी?" यह कहकर उसने उसके सामने अपना प्रेम प्रस्ताव रख दिया। साथ ही अपने दिल का सारा हाल बता दिया। यह सुनते ही नयनतारा की आँखें खुशी से चमक उठीं। वह भी नवीन से बेहद प्यार करती थी। उसने तुरंत सहमति में अपना हाथ आगे बढ़ा दिया। "हाँ मैं भी तुमसे बहुत प्यार करती हूँ, और जीवनभर तुम्हारा साथ निभाऊँगी लेफ्टिनेंट नवीन साहब"। नवीन ने उसके हाथों में रिंग डाली और रेस्तराँ में मौजूद सभी लोगों ने तालियाँ बजा कर दोनों को आने वाली खुशियों की बधाई दी। दोनों काफी खुश थे और अब तक का सारा इंतजार

और दूरियों का गम इस खुशी के सामने गायब हो गया था। एक दूसरे के हाथों में हाथ डाले दोनों काफी देर तक एक दूसरे को अपने दिल का हाल सुनाते रहे। सूरज डूब रहा था लेकिन उसकी फैलती लालिमा इस पल को और खूबसूरत बना रही थी। आज उनसे ज्यादा खुश शायद ही कोई और था। सच ही तो कहते हैं "बात चली है तो दूर तलक जाएगी"। अब वे अजनबी नहीं हमसफ़र बन चुके थे।

KAIBALYA PANDA

Pen holder

चाहे कितनी भी दर्द हो

चाहे कितनी भी दर्द हो छुपा लेना
अगर छल्के आँखों से आंसू
तो उसे अंदर दबा लेना
अगर कोई पूछे हाल तुम्हारा,
ठीक हूँ ये कह कर थोड़ा मुस्कुरा देना ,

हम हर किसी के घम मैं सामिल थे,
हमारी जरुरत मैं कोई आया नहीं।
टूटे हुए दिल बेचने चले थे,
लीकीन कोई भाऊ लगाया ही नहीं।

देखो दिल को आज क्या तसली मिल गया
की साला फिरसे कोई दिल से खेल गया
कब तक बेचे टूटे हुए दिल मोहब्बत के बाजार मैं ,
खुद की नादानी थी , खुद ही झेल गया।

देखो दिल को आज क्या तसली मिल गया

देखो दिल को आज क्या तसली मिल गया
की साला फिरसे कोई दिल से खेल गया
कब तक बेचे टूटे हुए दिल मोहब्बत के बाजार मैं ,
खुद की नादानी थी , खुद ही झेल गया।

देखो दिल को आज क्या तसली मिल गया
की साला फिरसे कोई दिल से खेल गया
कब तक बेचे टूटे हुए दिल मोहब्बत के बाजार मैं ,
खुद की नादानी थी , खुद ही झेल गया।

नहीं मालूम के किस कदर डूब रहे है
वफा से बढ़ कर बेवफा महबूब रहे है
थोड़ी झाँक कर देख लेती इस दिल् मैं
धढक् से ज्यादा तेरा रंग रूप रहे है।

जिंदगी

टूट चुका हूँ मैं
हर इंसान से रूठ चूका हूँ मैं
अब अपने हालत किसीसे नहीं कहे जाते
अब समझ जाना थक चुका हूँ मैं
दिल की सौदा कर गए
कुछ इस कादर उनसे
सुकून गिरवी है उनके पास
महोबत कर्ज लिया था जिनसे

क्यों कि उन्हें ये बात पसंद है

क्यों कि उन्हें ये बात पसंद है
इसीलिये हमारे उनसे एक पवित्र सम्बंध है
लाख गलतिया माफ़ करे, खाए आज ये सौगंध है
दिल भी अब धडकता है ये तेरी ही लफ्जों की पाबंध है
अब दूरी बी कैसी सही जाएगी तुझसे ये रहो की पदबंध है
क्यों कि उन्हें ये बात पसंद है

बदल दिए है हमने भी नाराज होने के तरीके।

बदल दिए है हमने भी नाराज होने के तरीके।
अब रूठने के वजह मुस्कुरा कर आगे बढ़ते है।

हर एक मुस्कराहट मुस्कान नहीं होती
नफरत हो या महोवत आसान नहीं होती
आंसूं, खुसी के गम् के होते है एक जैसे
ईन आसुओं की कोई पहचान नहीं होती

मिट्टी से बी यारी रख आये काफिर
यूँ तो आसमान मैं उड़ना सब को अछा लगता है
पर उस खुदा ने बी उस काबिल सिर्फ पंछी यों को बनाया है

ABHISHEK KUMHAR

A hardworking & struggling boy with a cool attitude having million dreams & an ocean of feelings inside.

Aaj Aayi Hai Yaad Firse Teri

Tujhe bhula diya tha,
Par dil k kisi kone me ab v tera naam hai.
Kaise bhulau tujhe,
uljhan me fasa hu,
Is pyar k Raste me manjil Meri dur hai.
Ab to lgta h Taqdeer me to tu nahi h meri,
Aaj aayi h yaad firse teri.
Meri Aasuon ki tujhe koi kadar nahi,
Teri rehem ki main mohtaaj nahi,
Fir v na Jane q aansu beh jati h meri,
Aaj aayi h yaad firse teri.
Milenge hum kvi kisi rah me,
ye yakin hai mujhe.
Us waqt na tu meri ho payegi or na me tera,
Dekh lena, ye baat satayegi tujhe.
Ehsas tujhe v hoga ek din ye mohabbat Kaisi thi meri,
Aaj aayi h yaad firse teri.
Fark bohot hai teri or meri duniya me,
Teri duniya fulo se saji hai,
or meri duniya angaro se bhari hai.
Sayad,, ye shi tha tera mera bichadna,
Avi to bohot kuch h mujhe zindegi se sikhna.
Chhodo jo hua wo to kismat ka likha tha,
Galti thi meri,, jo mujhe anjan logo ka pyar dikha tha.
Par aaj v wahi ijjat hai tere liye dil me meri,
Aaj aayi hai yaad firse teri.

PARWANA BIBI

I know someone I want to present you. A little moody and shy girl. She want to see people happy and she is so cute. Nd she is very talented and never give up any situation. Nd she is none other than parwana. Let's see what she has for us.

MAA

Mein hun dua teri,
Tu hai jannat meri.
Mein hun amanat teri,
Tujh se he to hai hifazat meri.
Mein hun aahat teri,
Tune sikhaya hai chalna mujhe pakad ke ungli meri.
Mein jahan bhi jaun tujh pe he aake ruke kadam yeh meri,
Tu he to hai manzil mere safar ki.
Saanse jab ruke teri,
Toh rooh bhi alag ho mujh se yeh meri.
Mein har ek lamha rahun sath tere,
Bas itni si khwahis hai dil mein mere.

Mere Humsafar

Tum nahi ho toh iss jahan mein,
Sab begane yahan ho gaye hain...
Dekh rahe ho kya tum meri bebasi ko wahan,
Dar dar fir rahi hun mein ban ke fakir yahan.....
Thhokrein mil rahi hai mujhe tum bin,
Ab mein humari sapno ko sach karun kaise aur kis din.......

Mehfil

Nahi chahate huye bhi ulajhte jaa rahe hain,
Iss mehfil mein jo tere aake thehere huye hain.
Yahan se nikalna namumkin sa ho gaya hai,
Lekin yahan jeena bhi duswar ho gaya hai.

Wo Lamha

Tere sehar se aaj jaa rahen hain,
Apni sari ummidein aur muskilein sath liye jaa rahein hain.
Dua bas itni si hai koi yaad na sataye hum ko,
Dil bhula paye tere sath bitaye woh pal ko.

Dilon Ki Dastaan

Bikhre pade hain armaan dilon ke,
Koi na jane kaise samatein halat yeh sab ke...
Lakhon dard yahan sab baithe hain chhupaye,
Fir bhi ban rahe hain ek dusre ke dardon ke sahare.....
Ajab si hai yeh dastan dilon ki,
Gujar jane do yeh lamha nafraton ki.......
Fir milenge sab ek he mehfil mein,
Jahan nahi gujare ga koi apni zindegi dard aur tadap mein

ANANYA NAYAK

A girl who believes in magic, miracles and fairy tales. She loves to read stories and listen rumors, as they make her life a bit spicy-er. And when she can't read or listen to the chaos, she fills the silence with her poems.

Forever And Never

Until you, forever was
always an achievable concept
I had seen the moon and stars
I had seen the sun and clouds
I thought eternity is here and now.

You promised me to love
For eternity and beyond
And may be you do, but
Staying together was out of option.
And when I left you never called me back.

That day I learnt , forever can be ocean and sand
Forever can be December January apart
Forever can be stretched into life time
And can be met in a skipped beat of heart.

Since then I'm not searching for forever of my own
I'm trying to accept that you will never give me enough
And I'll never trust anyone enough to chase it with him .
I'm trying to gather pieces of the forever you left behind.

While I'm gathering
The leaves from autumn,
The dusts of broken stars,
Stealing sands from the waves
And dreams from the night
I have come to realize that
Never is another end of the infinity loop .

Never is like forever ,

You spend a life time chasing both
Yet, they elude you in a blink of eye
As I have learnt to find forever
In the broken and lost things,
I'm also counting the Never spent in Futile restrictions .

As a person craving for forever
I know how much it must hurt
To hold on into the Never.
Leave it before it leaves you in shatter .
I'll try and live in between the fleeting moments
Stolen away from the clutches of promised forever and
broken Never.

SUBHASMITA MAHAPATRA

The writer would love to introduce herself as a saturated soul. She is a beginner and love to live in moments and to put them into her ink.

Will You??

Will you be considerate ?
of the grey repulsive holy ground.
That streaches from the palm of your hands.
To the ripples of my skin?
Will you ?
Read the possible paradox,
Of the stars shedding off the autumn tree.
settling beneath unmoving hinges of your creaking chair ?

Will you reside by your oath,
Of breaking every promise that conjures up the audacity of denying the absolute.
The absolute of the truth;
that the amalgamation of you and me into us is not rational ?
Will you see the blue unfoldings,
of the shy sea, or the crimson horizons,
of the setting sun ? Would you ?
or would you not?
see and remember how close you had me.
see and remember how far i went

Kuch Lamhon Ki Baat Hai.....

Kuch lamhon ki baat hai
Kuch lamhon ka hai fasla
Kuch munasib nhi ye shikayatein
Kuch mukhtalif hai ye raabta
Kuch dillagi hai
Kuch berukhi Kuch muntasir sa hai kaafila
Kuch tum dil se utre ho
Kuch gadbad sa he maamla
Kuch dheemi si phuwar he
Kuch mamnu he chaand ka dakhila
Kuch adaab ki shaayari me
Beadaab ban baitha he hausla
Kuch kirchiyan angan me ab bhi hai
Kuch mehfuz he ab bhi faisla.

If I......

If i show you,
how long i have been bleeding,
will it suffice,
to refrain you,
from stabbing me with your denial ?

If i sing to your predetermined chorus,
unhinging my flood gates to,
sweep all what i have rooted so dearly,
will it suffice ,
to prevent your,
disloyal departure ?

If i be the church,
conserving every sin,
you had the audacity to commit,
inside its wooden planks that creaks whenever
you walk in in order to offload another.
will it suffice,
to hold your hammer midair,
instead of its fluid motion shattering my heart ?

If i let you,

shift the creases of my bedsheet,
If i let you spill poems on my skin,
if i let you dream,
scream,
paint,
dance, ...

If i let you be,
Will it suffice,
to ignite a thought of coming back,
and using me some more ?

ASHISH MAHAPATRA

Aged 19 year, hails from Paradip currently residing in a beautiful city.He is a student by profession but so kind hearted and helps other in bad times. He has represented his school in as state level.He was awarded in as Rajya purashkar in Scout and guides camp. Spreading smile around and being down to earth is his true identity. A tea-holic dream weaver who loves to be friendly with others and scribbles his random thoughts on paper. He is multi-talented, whether its writing, singing, delivering speeches or the burden of responsibilities, he has been proving himself from the first day. Street food , chai and traveling are his stress stealer. He completely believes in the quotation "epitome of hope", because according to him, " Sometimes we are tired of waiting but still we hope for the best , because its our life and we can't compromise with worst

Joy Of Little Things

A pleasant morning 5am walks Or,
a warm coffee after a joyful task..
Some sweet memories that touched our heart Or,
a message from a friend far apart...
An afternoon meal that fills our heart Or,
a good song that makes us feel out of the world...
The smell of the rain that drenched our heart Or,
the late night Maggie that clump and bind us apart...
An evening friendly football match Or,
a movie that touched our heart..

TREACHEROUS

Still afraid to the faces that surrounds me...
May be millions of emotion pass through the mask they have weared...
May be they aren't true, just pretend to be the truthful ones...
May be their task is for the demolition of others...
Which makes them happy enough...
I just remembered that when I was a child...
I got scared by dark and the monsters...
But... When I grew up...
I just realized that these faces troubles and horrifies me more than that...

Come To Me

Come to me like moon in the darkest night...
Come to me like a sweet dream in sleep...
Come to me like the waves on seashore...
May be the night should be over...
May be the sleep should be disrupted...
May be the waves goes aback...
But the real fact that matters is.....
Is your presence....
Because the night is nothing without the moon....
The sleep is nothing without a dream....
And...
The sea is nothing without the waves in it......

BEING A BOY...

Being a boy is not that easy...
Storm inside the head but smile on the face...
Being a boy is not that easy...
From childhood onwards have given the responsibilities to take care of the family...
Being a boy is not that easy...
Have a bunch of expectations which can't be fulfilled...
Those expectations were the biggest nightmares....
Being a boy is not that easy...
Supposed to be strong but they often cry when got cheated or go through heartbreaks....
Being a boy is not that easy...
Face the world with a smile no matter even if they are fucked up inside...
Being a boy is not that easy...

SWATI UPADHYAY

SWATI UPADHYAY "There's a place between happiness & sadness on most days, you will find me there." A girl with the help of her worthful wings and words is shining in this cruel world from Dhanbad, Jharkhand. Her words are ' unsaid feelings ' of her ownself. She always quote two lines for her poems which are- "जिसे तुम हमारी शायरी की दास्ताँ समझ रहे हो,, वो दरअसल हमारी अनकही बातें और एहसास है।।

आओ कुछ बातें करते है

"आओ कुछ बातें करते है,
तुम सुनो और हम अपने दिल की बाते केहते है।"
जब देखा था उसे पहली बार
जब देखा था उसे पहली बार
धड़कने हो गयी थी बेक़रार
और जब देखा था उससे आखिरी बार
तो साँसे रुक सी गयी थी मेरे यार
"आओ कुछ बातें करते है,
तुम सुनो और हम अपने दिल की बाते केहते है।"
उनकी एक मुस्कुराहट
उनकी एक मुस्कराहट
को जीने की वज़ह मान चुके थे हम
मगर अब उनके बेहते अश्क़
मेरे जान के दुश्मन बन रहे थे अब
"आओ कुछ बातें करते है,
तुम सुनो और हम अपने दिल की बाते केहते है।"

उनकी मोहब्बत
उनकी मोहब्बत
खुदा की इनायत सी लगती थी मुझे
मगर अब उनकी नफ़रत
मेरे दुआओं की तौहीन सी लगती है मुझे
"आओ कुछ बातें करते है,
तुम सुनो और हम अपने दिल की बाते केहते है।"
कभी उनकी एक झलक के लिए

कभी उनकी एक झलक के लिए
खिल-खिलाती धुप में भी नंगे पाओ भागा लिया करते थे हम
पर अब उनका चेहरा
भीड़ में भी दिख जाए तो ग्रहण समझ छुप जाया करते है हम
"आओ कुछ बातें करते है,
तुम सुनो और हम अपने दिल की बाते केहते है।"
उनकी हलकी सी छुअन से
उनकी हलकी से छुअन से
जो रोम-रोम खिल उठ जाता था
आज वही बगल से गुज़र जाए
तो रोम-रोम छिल सा जाता है
"आओ कुछ बातें करते है,
तुम सुनो और हम अपने दिल की बाते केहते है।"
नाम सुन कर जिसका
नाम सुन कर जिसका
हमारे खुशी का कोई ठिकाना न रेह जाता था
आज एक अक्षर भी जुड़ जाए जो उनका
हमारे अश्कों की वजह सा बन जाता है
"आओ कुछ बातें करते है,
तुम सुनो और हम अपने दिल की बाते केहते है।"
अब खुश हूँ मैं,
हाँ ठीक सुना तुमनें, अब खुश हूँ मैं।
तुझसे दूर जो हूँ अब
तुझसे दूर जो हूँ अब
ज़्यादा तो नहीं मगर सुकून से हूँ अब!!!

रातें

रोज़ रातों में तेरी याद एक बार आजाती है;
रोज़ रातों में तेरी याद एक बार आजाती है;
फिर दिल को समझा लेती हूँ, और खुद को बेहला लेती हूँ;
की सो जा, वो भी सो गया होगा
फिर खुद ही को ये बात बता दिया करती हूँ की---
तू यहाँ उसकी याद में तड़प रही है,
तू यहाँ उसकी याद में तड़प रही है,
और वो वहाँ बाकियों के साथ ऐश कर रहा होगा ।।

SWATI BARIK

I do not remember my first bio

My Mother Ask Me....

My mother asks me why do I
Give my poems names
Like wheelchair, a crutch,
an inhaler
A one bedroom beating heart
Why can't i call them
something prettier, softer,
less sick and more
alive or simple literary devices that carry my sad
around when it gets bored inside
It's home, or when restlessness locks itself out of my
mind,
It doesn't happen often
But it happens.
What she means to ask
But is too afraid to is
Can you not put yourself on display
like that?
You're drawing the wrong crowd.
Most of the days i sneer at them,
The questions i mean.
Or the crowd (depends on what day it is)
A girl gone feral is a girl alone
But today is a question mark
Shaped freckle resting in the crook of my arm with the IV
needle
And time is throwing rocks at my window, so before the
tapping stops
Let me tell you that this poem right here, is a gas mask
A tiny piece of tech miracle
A small rebellion against death's tyranny,

This poem will make paper swans out of your discarded
suicide notes and teach them how to fly So that your
friends can find you on time,
This poem thinks you're beautiful
Even on the days you don't wash your hair or shower
because inside the blanket is a dark you feel safe in,
This poem will say i love you back
Exactly seventy three times and will not be afraid to hold
your hand in dimly lit parking lots, This poem will not
cancel plans,
This poems thinks love is coming,
Is just around the corner and is one call away.
This poem will dial the number.
This poem will help you
on the days medicine will fall short,
On the days you're the only person
In your one bedroom beating heart
And the walls start to close in on you
This poem will be there to paint the cabinets yellow,
it'll let the sunshine in,
This poem will kiss you behind the ear and rub that spot
on your back you can't quite reach when you're nauseous
This poem will love you, unconditionally.
Here
mom,
If it still doesn't sound pretty
Think of it like like this
This poem is just
Another reason to go on living
In a long list of reasons
For one more day
atleast.

AAYUSHI AGARWAL

Ayushi Agarwal a straight forward kiddish girl hailing from Cuttack Odisha who paints down when her heart is heavy and has a great affection towards art.

Caring loving sharing obedient and innocent are some of her attribute she hasbin gifted with the very beautiful and most fearful smile which can vanish all the pain and suffering at one go all she believes is creating real dreams

Frienship..!!

Frienship is something,
which can not be express, nor to impress..!!

It is life,
Which you can also do with your wife..!!

It can be with anyone,
If you love everyone..!!

Yes, in friendship life is full of joy,
But remember friend is not a toy..!!

With friends you can see the colour of clouds blue and yellow,
Without friends you cant even melow..!!

It is love, it is care.,
but yes it should be fair..!!

Do friendship with ur mom and your dad, do it with your brother who is ofcourse mad..!!

My dear do friendship with all because world is very small..!!

www.ingramcontent.com/pod-product-compliance
Lightning Source LLC
Chambersburg PA
CBHW050520240926
51846CB00003B/629
* 9 7 8 9 3 9 0 4 1 6 6 8 4 *